Love's Home Run

A Lilac Lake Book

Judith Keim

BOOKS BY JUDITH KEIM

THE HARTWELL WOMEN SERIES:

The Talking Tree – 1

Sweet Talk – 2

Straight Talk – 3

Baby Talk – 4

The Hartwell Women – Boxed Set

THE BEACH HOUSE HOTEL SERIES:

Breakfast at The Beach House Hotel – 1

Lunch at The Beach House Hotel – 2

Dinner at The Beach House Hotel – 3

Christmas at The Beach House Hotel – 4

Margaritas at The Beach House Hotel – 5

Dessert at The Beach House Hotel – 6

Coffee at The Beach House Hotel – 7

High Tea at The Beach House Hotel – 8

Nightcaps at The Beach House Hotel – 9

Bubbles at The Beach House Hotel – 10 (2025)

Canapes at The Beach House Hotel – 11 (2025)

THE FAT FRIDAYS GROUP:

Fat Fridays – 1

Sassy Saturdays – 2

Secret Sundays – 3

THE LILAC LAKE INN SERIES

Love by Design – 1

Love Between the Lines – 2

Love Under the Stars – 3

LILAC LAKE BOOKS

Love's Cure

Love's Home Run – (2025)

Love's Bloom – (2025)

Love's Harvest – (2025)

Love's Match – (2025)

SOUL SISTERS AT CEDAR MOUNTAIN LODGE:

Christmas Sisters – Anthology

Christmas Kisses

Christmas Castles

Christmas Stories – Soul Sisters Anthology

Christmas Joy

The Christmas Joy Boxed Set

OTHER BOOKS:

The ABCs of Living With a Dachshund

Winning BIG – a little love story for all ages

Holiday Hopes

The Winning Tickets

For more information: **www.judithkeim.com**

PRAISE FOR JUDITH KEIM'S NOVELS

THE BEACH HOUSE HOTEL SERIES – Books 1 – 8:

"Love the characters in this series. This series was my first introduction to Judith Keim. She is now one of my favorites. Looking forward to reading more of her books."

BREAKFAST AT THE BEACH HOUSE HOTEL – *"An easy, delightful read that offers romance, family relationships, and strong women learning to be stronger. Real life situations filter through the pages. Enjoy!"*

LUNCH AT THE BEACH HOUSE HOTEL – *"This series is such a joy to read. You feel you are actually living with them. Can't wait to read the latest one."*

DINNER AT THE BEACH HOUSE HOTEL – *"A Terrific Read! As usual, Judith Keim did it again. Enjoyed immensely. Continue writing such pleasantly reading books for all of us readers."*

CHRISTMAS AT THE BEACH HOUSE HOTEL – *"Not Just Another Christmas Novel. This is book number four in the series and my introduction to Judith Keim's writing. I wasn't disappointed. The characters are dimensional and engaging. The plot is well crafted and advances at a pleasing pace.*

MARGARITAS AT THE BEACH HOUSE HOTEL – *"Overall, Margaritas at the Beach House Hotel is another wonderful addition to the series. Judith Keim takes the reader on a journey told through the voices of these amazing characters we have all come to love through the years!*

DESSERT AT THE BEACH HOUSE HOTEL – *"It is a heartwarming and beautiful women's fiction as only Judith Keim can do with her wonderful characters, amazing location, and family and friends whose daily lives circle around Ann and Rhonda and The Beach House Hotel.*

COFFEE AT THE BEACH HOUSE HOTEL – *"Great story and characters! A hard to put down book. Lots of things happening, including a kidnapping of a young boy. The beach house hotel is a wonderful hotel run by two women who are best friends. Highly recommend this book.*

HIGH TEA AT THE BEACH HOUSE HOTEL – *"What a lovely story! The Beach House Hotel series is a always a great read. Each book in the series brings a new aspect to the saga of Ann and Rhonda."*

THE HARTWELL WOMEN SERIES – Books 1 – 4:

"This was an EXCELLENT series. When I discovered Judith Keim, I read all of her books back to back. I thoroughly enjoyed the women Keim has written about. They are believable and you want to just jump into their lives and be their friends! I can't wait for any upcoming books!"

"I fell into Judith Keim's Hartwell Women series and have read & enjoyed all of her books in every series. Each centers around a strong & interesting woman character and their family interaction. Good reads that leave you wanting more."

THE FAT FRIDAYS GROUP – Books 1 – 3:

"Excellent story line for each character, and an insightful representation of situations which deal with some of the contemporary issues women are faced with today."

THE SALTY KEY INN SERIES – Books 1 – 4:

FINDING ME – "The characters are endearing with the same struggles we all encounter. The setting makes me feel like I am a guest at The Salty Key Inn...relaxed, happy & light-hearted! The men are yummy and the women strong. You can't get better than that! Happy Reading!"

FINDING MY WAY- "Loved the family dynamics as well as uncertain emotions of dating and falling in love. Appreciated the morals and strength of parenting throughout. Just couldn't put this book down."

FINDING LOVE – "Judith Keim always puts substance into her books. This book was no different, I learned about PTSD, accepting oneself, there are always going to be problems but stick it out and make it work."

FINDING FAMILY – "Completing this series is like eating the last chip. Love Judith's writing and her female characters are always smart, strong, vulnerable to life and love experiences. This was a refreshing book. Bringing the heart and soul of the family to us."

THE CHANDLER HILL INN SERIES – Books 1 – 3:

GOING HOME – "I was completely immersed in this book, with the beautiful descriptive writing, and the author's way of bringing her characters to life. I felt like I was right inside her story."

COMING HOME – "Coming Home was such a wonderful story. The author has such a gift for getting the reader right to the heart of things."

HOME AT LAST – "In this wonderful conclusion, to a heartfelt and emotional trilogy set in Oregon's stunning wine country, Judith Keim has tied up the Chandler Hill series with the perfect bow."

SEASHELL COTTAGE BOOKS:

A CHRISTMAS STAR – "Love, laughter, sadness, great food, and hope for the future, all in one book. It doesn't get any better than this stunning read."

CHANGE OF HEART – "CHANGE OF HEART is the summer read we've all been waiting for. Judith Keim is a master at creating fascinating characters that are simply irresistible. Her stories leave you with a big smile on your face and a heart bursting with love."
~Kellie Coates Gilbert, author of the popular Sun Valley Series

A SUMMER OF SURPRISES – "Ms. Keim uses this book as an amazing platform to show that with hard emotional work, belief in yourself, and love, the scars of abuse can be conquered. It in no way preaches, it's a lovely story with a happy ending."

A ROAD TRIP TO REMEMBER – "The characters are so real that they jump off the page. Such a fun, HAPPY book at the perfect time. It will lift your spirits and even remind you of your own grandmother. Spirited and hopeful Aggie gets a second chance at love and she takes the steering wheel and drives straight for it."

THE BEACH BABES – "Another winner at the pen of Judith Keim. I love the characters and the book just flows. It feels as though you are at the beach with them and are a part of you.

THE DESERT SAGE INN SERIES – Books 1 – 4:

THE DESERT FLOWERS – ROSE – "The Desert Flowers - Rose, "In this first of a series, we see each woman come into her own and view new beginnings even as they must take this tearful journey as they slowly lose a dear friend.

THE DESERT FLOWERS – LILY – "_The second book in the Desert Flowers series is just as wonderful as the first. Judith Keim is a brilliant storyteller. Her characters are truly lovely and people that you want to be friends with as soon as you start reading. Judith Keim is not afraid to weave real-life conflict and loss into her stories._

THE DESERT FLOWERS – WILLOW – "_The feelings of love, joy, happiness, friendship, family, and the pain of loss are deeply felt by Willow Sanchez and her two cohorts Rose and Lily. The Desert Flowers met because of their deep feelings for Alec Thurston, a man who touched their lives in different ways._"

MISTLETOE AND HOLLY – "_As always, the author never ceases to amaze me. She's able to take characters and bring them to life in such a way that you think you're actually among family. It's a great holiday read. You won't be disappointed._"

THE SANDERLING COVE INN SERIES – Books 1 – 3:

WAVES OF HOPE – "_Such a wonderful story about several families in a beautiful location in Florida. A grandmother requests her three granddaughters to help her by running the family's inn for the summer. Other grandmothers in the area played a part in this plan to find happiness for their grandsons and granddaughters._"

SANDY WISHES – "_Three cousins needing a change and a few of the neighborhood boys from when they were young are back visiting their grandmothers. It is an adventure, a summer of discoveries, and embracing the person they are becoming._"

SALTY KISSES – "_I love this story, as well as the entire series because it's about family, friendship, and love. The meddling grandmothers have only the best intentions and want to see their grandchildren find love and happiness. What grandparent wouldn't want that?_"

THE LILAC LAKE INN SERIES – Books 1 – 3:

LOVE BY DESIGN –"*Genie Wittner is planning on selling her beloved Lilac Inn B&B, and keeping a cottage for her three granddaughters, Whitney, the movie star, Dani an architect, and Taylor a writer. A little mystery, a possible ghost, and romance all make this a great read and the start of a new series.*"

LOVE BETWEEN THE LINES – "*Taylor is one of 3 sisters who have inherited a cottage in Lilac Lake from their grandmother. She is an accomplished author who is having some issues getting inspired for her next book. Things only get worse when she receives an email from her new editor with a harsh critique of her last book. She's still fuming when Cooper shows up in town, determined to work together on getting the book ready.*"

LOVE UNDER THE STARS – "*Love Under the Stars is the third book in The Lilac Lake Inn Series by author Judith Keim. Judith beautifully weaves together the final story in this amazing series about the Gilford sisters and their grandmother, GG.*"

THE LILAC LAKE BOOKS

LOVE'S CURE – *Welcome back to Lilac Lake with a new spin-off series from author Judith Keim. For fans of the author, you will be reunited with previous characters, as well as being introduced to new ones. Even though this book can be read as a stand-alone, I highly recommend reading the Lilac Lake Inn series to get introduced to all of these amazing characters.*

Love's Home Run

A Lilac Lake Book

Judith Keim

Wild Quail Publishing

Love's Home Run is a work of fiction. Names, characters, places, public or private institutions, corporations, towns, and incidents are the product of the author's imagination or are used fictitiously. Any resemblance to actual events, locales, or persons, living or dead, is coincidental.

No part of *Love's Home Run* may be reproduced or transmitted in any form or by any electronic or mechanical means, including information storage and retrieval systems, without permission in writing from the author, except by a reviewer who may quote brief passages in a review. This book may not be resold or uploaded for distribution to others. For permissions, contact the author directly via electronic mail:

wildquail.pub@gmail.com
www.judithkeim.com

Wild Quail Publishing
PO Box 171332
Boise, ID 83717-1332

ISBN 978-1-962452-93-9

Dedication

This book is dedicated to M. Louise Williams,
my great-aunt, "Weezie,"
who introduced me to baseball as a kid
and taught me to love the game.

CHAPTER ONE

MELISSA HENDRICKSON REMOVED HER CHEF'S TOQUE and shook her hair out from the rubber band that had held it in place. Letting out a sigh of fatigue, she unbuttoned her coat and tossed it into the laundry basket in a room behind the kitchen. She had a satisfying, creative job working as a chef at Fins, her parents' restaurant, but she was frustrated by her lack of time with friends and her lack of a meaningful relationship. Many people, some from her old summer gang, were moving into town, and she wanted to be part of all they were doing. And though she hesitated to tell anyone else, she hoped to be subtle in convincing one newcomer to see her as wife material. If she only dared.

She was a popular social group member but was more comfortable with the guys than the women. She was a tall, trim, wiry woman who, growing up, had been a tomboy interested in sports and "guy" things. Her mother had always wanted her to be more like the charming Gilford girls and had continually pointed out all her faults. It left her feeling insecure about herself. She felt like two different people.

In the kitchen, she was strong, competent, and sure, orchestrating the work of the staff. And, after graduating from the Culinary Institute of America in Hyde Park, New York, she'd proved to have a brilliant gift when combining herbs, spices, and sauces to create spectacular entrees and desserts.

In a social setting, she tended to be quiet and a bit awkward when it came to dating. The men she knew loved having her as a friend who got their jokes and was a pal. It was both nice and annoying now that she was ready for something more in a relationship.

"Are you off to Jake's?" her mother asked, coming into the kitchen. "Better freshen up."

Melissa looked up at the wall clock. 10 PM. "I'll see if anyone is still there. If not, I'll go home. Thank goodness, it's my day off tomorrow."

She went into the bathroom and checked the mirror, making sure she was presentable. The face reflected there had pleasant features, brown hair that held a hint of red, and gray eyes that assessed her harshly.

Melissa grabbed her purse, anxious to leave.

She walked down Main Street, passing its numerous cute shops to Jake's, the neighborhood bar her friends in town used as a gathering place.

She loved living in the beautiful New Hampshire Lakes Region, in the scenic small town of Lilac Lake, where outdoor summer and winter activities were readily available.

By anyone's standards, Melissa was financially successful, with a job that brought her recognition and an excellent income. She'd just built a house in The Meadows, an upscale development created by Collister Construction at the far end of Lilac Lake and owned by two of her male friends, Aaron and Brad Collister. But she wanted the more important things in life—a husband and children, a family of her own. At thirty-three, she was beginning to wonder if that would ever happen.

As she stepped inside Jake's, she heard someone call her name and turned to see Ross Roberts wave at her. Smiling, she went to say hello to him and two of his buddies sitting at the table the locals called their own.

" 'Evening," said Melissa. "Is this all that's left of the gang?"

"We're it," said Ross. A famous former baseball player for

the New York Yankees, he was a pleasant man everyone liked. Though he couldn't play ball any longer because of a knee injury, he was still featured in television ads where his sandy-haired handsome looks, blue eyes, and boyish smile captured audiences.

"Come join us," said Mike Dawson, who once had been a rising tennis star. Now, he ran tennis clinics in Florida and was talking to Ross about opening a sports center in Lilac Lake where people could play tennis and/or participate in baseball clinics.

"Nice to see you again," said Ben Gooding, who used to play on the Yankees baseball team with Ross. With his stocky, sturdy body, Ben still looked the part of a catcher.

Melissa returned his smile and sat down. She was looking forward to a glass of red wine. Working at the restaurant, she limited alcoholic drinks to having one occasionally. Working with food and wine most of the time, she was careful not to have too much of either.

Ross raised his hand, and a waitress came right over to them. "My friend will have a glass of your finest pinot noir," he said, indicating Melissa.

She smiled her thanks. Ross lived next door to her at The Meadows, and she quickly stifled any romantic thoughts. Melissa knew Ross dated gorgeous women. She was much more comfortable keeping their relationship as friendly neighbors.

"What are you doing in town?" she asked Ben. "Here to make trouble for Ross and Mike?"

Ben laughed. "I'm thinking of investing in their sports complex. I love Lilac Lake, but I have my job in Washington, D.C., and don't plan to move."

She turned to the others. "Did Dirk show up?"

"He was here earlier with David Graham. They left a while

ago," said Ross. "How'd it go at the restaurant?"

"It was busy, as usual. But that's good. A profitable summer means being able to shut down for a couple of weeks in the winter. My parents love going to Florida and testing out new recipes."

"I imagine once you're into the food scene, it's hard to get out," said Mike. "Florida is a great place to discover new meal ideas with its diverse collection of cuisines."

"Yes. We must add new menu items each year to keep people coming back."

"Speaking of coming back," said Ross. "Sarah Miller, Bob and Edie Bullard's daughter, is moving here next week. I only met her once, but she seemed nice. It's unfortunate her husband died, leaving her with twin girls."

"It was such a shame. Sarah is lovely. I'm sure her parents, like mine, love the idea of having their daughter close," said Melissa.

"Isn't it hard to work for your parents?" asked Mike.

Melissa thought about it. "Yes and no. Working together is easier than handling other personal interactions with them." She chuckled. "Mothers and daughters. That's the tough part at times."

"I have only brothers, so I wouldn't know," said Ross.

"How many?" Melissa asked him. It was the first time he'd mentioned them.

"Three older brothers, all working in the New York City area in successful careers. I was the little bro who wanted to play ball all the time. At least, that's what they tell me. They were surprised when I informed them I intended to play professional ball when I got older."

Mike grinned at Ross. "You're a natural."

"My high school played Ross's once. I knew then that he'd make it," said Ben, nudging Ross playfully.

JoEllen Daniels came into Jake's and walked right over to them. "Hi, guys. How's it going?" she asked, smiling at the men ignoring her.

Melissa kept quiet. Everyone in her circle knew JoEllen, Brad Collister's ex-sister-in-law, had thought she could manipulate Brad into marrying her after his wife's death. Now that Brad was happily married to Dani Gilford, JoEllen had her eye on any man she could get to pay attention to her.

"We're just sitting here chatting with Melissa," Ross said pointedly.

"Oh, yes, hi, Melissa," said JoEllen, not perturbed by Ross's comment. "I've got tickets to see one of my favorite bands, 'Neverland,' this weekend. Anyone want to go with me?"

The three men glanced at one another and shook their heads.

"Guess not," said Mike. "Thanks, anyway."

"Maybe another time," said Ben.

Ross remained quiet.

"Oh, okay. I'll just find someone else." JoEllen flounced off as the waitress headed their way.

"Anyone want another drink? They're on me," said Ross.

"Thanks, but one is fine for me," Melissa said.

"Mike and I are going to Stan's to check it out," said Ben.

Ross turned to her. "Hey, neighbor, want to give me a lift home? Ben is borrowing my car, and I need a ride."

"Sure," said Melissa. "You're welcome to come with me."

"Thanks," said Ben. "I have a meeting in Portsmouth tomorrow morning. I'll return the car in the afternoon before I fly back to D.C."

The group broke up, and Melissa and Ross walked back to Fins to pick up Melissa's car.

"JoEllen has a nasty habit of ignoring the women in a group in her pursuit of men," said Melissa.

Ross grimaced. "I try to stay away from her. In the past, she's made a lot of moves to try and get my attention. She makes me uncomfortable."

"I understand," said Melissa. "But what does someone do to get a man's attention?"

"Who are you talking about? Dirk?" asked Ross, giving her a steady look.

Melissa sighed. "I like him a lot and want to get to know him better. But I can't just go up to him and blurt it out."

"No, you can't."

"Will you put in a good word for me now and then?"

"Do you mean like a Cyrano de Bergerac thing?" he asked, his eyes widening."

She laughed. "Lord, no. It's just that I can't seem to do it on my own. And the last thing I want to do is act like JoEllen."

Ross nodded. "I understand your problem. Okay, if that's all you want, I'll try to help."

Placing a hand on his arm, she smiled at Ross. "Thank you. You're the best, like the brother I wished I had."

While growing up, she had wanted a sibling who could help counter her mother's criticism about her appearance and manner.

They got into her car and had a silent ride home.

She pulled into his driveway to let him out and turned to him. "I owe you. How about coming to dinner at my house tomorrow? It's my day off, and I'll fix you something special."

"An offer I can't refuse," he said, grinning. He unbuckled his seat belt and got out of the car. "Thanks, Melissa," he said, giving her a little salute.

She watched him go, pleased by their friendship. He was a very nice guy.

At home, Melissa went through her emails and regular mail before preparing a cup of her favorite nighttime tea. Then she took the tea and a book to the master bedroom on the first floor. She loved her house and enjoyed using this quiet time to settle down from a hectic day. Cooking for customers who expected the best wasn't for the weak. You had to be strong and in control, with split-second timing to get everything prepared and delivered to everyone at their tables simultaneously. Melissa enjoyed watching Gordon Ramsay exposing people to the rigors of the kitchen on television. The professional kitchen scene wasn't quite like that, but one had to have common sense and excellent timing to make it work.

She got ready for bed in one of her usual pajama tops and opened the book. Gazing down at the words of the romance novel she was reading, her thoughts filled with the image of Dirk McArthur, the new dentist in town. Was a relationship with him hopeless?

CHAPTER TWO

MELISSA AWOKE AND SAW THE BUTTERY SUNSHINE shining through the blinds on her bedroom windows. She let out a grateful sigh. It was a lovely summer day to relax and enjoy her time off. She remembered her invitation to Ross for dinner and tried to think of something easy to make. Today, she was going to work outside in her vegetable and herb garden. She might even go down to the common waterfront the development had built and take her canoe out on the water. It was awkward paddling alone but not impossible, and something about being on the lake was so peaceful she didn't care about the work.

She got up and padded down the hall to the kitchen to fix herself a cup of coffee. She opened the sliding glass door to let in some fresh morning air through the screened-in porch and let out a deep, satisfying sigh.

Melissa fixed her coffee and carried it through the porch to the wooden deck facing south, making sunny mornings pleasant. Sitting in an Adirondack chair, she lifted her face to the sky. With her eyes closed, she breathed in the fresh lake air and basked in the sun like a lazy cat.

Noises next door drew her attention, and she opened her eyes to see Ross out on his deck with a dark-haired woman. A cardinal sang in a pine tree at her yard's end, and when the two turned to the sound of it, they noticed her. They both waved. Melissa realized the woman was Taylor Gilford Walker and waved back.

It was interesting living next door to someone famous like

Ross. She'd seen other neighbors approach him with paper and pen, asking for autographs. Well-known people came to the restaurant, but though they were greeted warmly, they purposely weren't fussed over. However, her mother, who acted as hostess, liked being able to ask about other lives without appearing too nosy.

Melissa took a sip of her coffee, her thoughts becoming darker. While her father adored her, her mother made her feel like she never met her standards.

Growing up, she'd envied the Gilford girls. It all seemed so silly now. She'd since become good friends with the three of them and loved being part of a congenial group whose members shared memories of the past. New people were added to the mix, making the group even better. From the moment she'd first met Dirk, she'd felt a spark of interest.

Dirk could make it seem like he was interested in what anyone was saying and had an easy, almost impish smile—important attributes for a dentist. Attractive, he was of average to above-average height with auburn hair and green eyes. She liked that he worked steady hours. It helped with her off-beat schedule to know someone would always be there for them if they ever got together and had pets and/or children.

She chided herself for those thoughts. How could she be thinking of such things when Dirk had never called or asked her out? As far as she knew, he hadn't asked anyone out, but still …

When she got up, she noticed Ross and Taylor had left his deck.

She went inside, fixed a piece of sourdough toast with peanut butter, and headed to her room to change.

In the shower, she let the warm water sluice over her and wondered what it would feel like to have Dirk's hands caress her body. She washed her hair and, after hand-drying it, shook it in place. Her hair was thick and straight, easy to maintain. Though it was dark brown, the hint of auburn gave it a different, pretty look. She let it hang to dry further while she dressed in shorts and a T-shirt. Then she pulled her hair up in a ponytail.

She rubbed suntan lotion on her face, arms, and legs, slid her feet into L.L. Bean boat shoes, and headed outside.

Her vegetable garden was larger than she would've planted for herself, but her father had helped her prepare and plant it. They both liked the idea of farm-to-table food and thought it would be a true test of what she could create. The Collister Family Farm Stand provided them with many extra goods during the summer months, but it was fun to think some of the food they served came from her garden.

Now, seeing the weeds, she wondered if they'd been overly ambitious. She gamely pulled out her gardening tools from the garage and got to work pulling invasive weeds and cultivating the soil. She was hot and sweaty in no time.

She'd just finished half the garden when Ross appeared.

"That's quite a project," he said as she struggled to stand. "Hey, listen, I've been thinking. You don't need to invite me to dinner tonight. I'm just doing you a favor, no strings attached."

"I'd relish the company," said Melissa. She hesitated. "Unless you just don't want to."

"No, no. I didn't want you to feel obligated. That's all," said Ross. "Any plans for the rest of the day?"

Melissa shrugged. "I thought I'd take a canoe ride on the lake. It's so peaceful."

"Want company?"

Surprised, Melissa said, "Sure. It's a little awkward paddling by myself, but I've done it."

"I'm waiting for Ben to return my car before I do some

errands. Paddling around the lake would be a great way to spend some time."

"Well, then, let's go now, and I can cool off," said Melissa.

She put her tools away, locked the back door, and joined Ross out front. Together, they walked down to the newly constructed marina area for the residents of The Meadows. Storage racks for canoes sat away from a dock that had places to tie up small fishing boats. A clubhouse held comfortable couches and chairs, a wall-mounted television, a mini-kitchen, and a fireplace.

Several canoes were pulled up on the shore of the lake, lined up like colorful crayons in a box.

"Which one is yours?" asked Ross.

"The light-blue one," she said, walking over to it. "I'm glad you're here to help me put it in the water." She went inside the clubhouse to get her paddles and lifejackets from the storage room. Each owner had a special cubby to keep equipment like this. So far, no one had abused the easy access.

Once they got the canoe in the water, Melissa climbed in, and Ross pushed them off.

Out on the water, Melissa paddled from the bow in smooth, even strokes as they quietly made their way along the shore. The real estate with lake frontage was carefully controlled. With land values so high, no ramshackle cottages were built here and there. Residents took care of their property and abided by the rule of no motorboats on the lake except for small fishing boats with quiet trolling motors.

Melissa glanced up at the blue sky and sighed in appreciation. Even though it was the busiest time at Fins, summer was her favorite season. Once more, she thought of finding ways to give herself more time away from cooking at the restaurant. She was beginning to feel trapped by her work.

"Look! A Great Blue Heron," said Ross in a hushed voice.

She turned, smiled, and gave him a thumbs-up. They stopped paddling and watched the bird on stilt-like legs combing the water for fish among grasses at the water's edge. In one swift movement, the bird dove its head into the water and came up holding a wiggling fish in its beak.

"That reminds me, what are we having for dinner?" teased Ross.

She laughed. "I haven't decided. Any orders?"

"If you want to keep it simple, I grill a mean steak."

"Terrific. I'll put together the rest of the meal but leave the grilling to you. I've got some delicious-looking New York strip steaks in the freezer. I'll get them out when we get back." She liked the fact that he was willing to help.

It took a while, but they paddled down to the far end of the lake where the Lilac Lake Inn and the Gilford girls' Lilac Lake Cottage sat overlooking the lake.

Melissa strained to see what was happening at the cottage and saw Taylor sitting on a chair outside with a computer in her lap.

"Hello!" Melissa called.

Taylor looked up and waved, set her computer down, and walked down to the lake's edge. "What are you two doing down here?"

"Getting some exercise," said Melissa.

"I'm taking a break until Ben gets back with my car," Ross said. "And helping a neighbor out with her canoe."

"What good neighbors you are," said Taylor, giving them a teasing smile.

"It's nothing, really," said Ross.

Taylor studied them. "Okay, whatever it is, I hope it works. I have to get back to work. Thanks again, Ross, for allowing me to interview you for my book. I may have to come back for more information as my plot develops, but I've made careful notes about our talk this morning."

"Glad to do it. Ask any time," said Ross.

"See you later. Are you two going to be at Jake's tonight?" Taylor asked.

Melissa and Ross exchanged glances and nodded simultaneously.

"Meet us there," said Melissa. She wanted to take advantage of her day off. "The more the merrier."

"I'll tell Cooper and ask my sisters to try and meet you," said Taylor.

"Thanks," said Melissa. "And ask others, too." She didn't dare mention Dirk's name.

"Yeah, maybe Dirk," said Ross helpfully.

He helped Melissa turn the canoe around, and they took off again. She didn't intend to discuss it with Ross, but maybe having Dirk see her with Ross might make him think of her as someone he'd like to get to know better. Anything was worth a try.

By the time they were back at the neighborhood marina, Melissa's arms were aching, but she didn't mention it. Ross's knees might be in bad shape, but there was nothing wrong with the rest of his body. He didn't seem the least bit tired.

After storing her paddles and life jackets, Melissa walked with Ross to their houses.

At the end of her driveway, she turned to Ross. "Thanks for going out on the lake with me. See you later. Come at six. We'll have drinks and an early dinner."

"It was pleasant. I'm glad you're not a big talker like some women I know."

"Sometimes it's pleasant to let the lake do the talking."

He smiled. "I'll try to remember to bring that up when I'm with Dirk."

CHAPTER THREE

WHEN THE DOORBELL RANG THAT EVENING, MELISSA was busy making twice-baked potatoes with a mushroom and cream mixture. She raced to the door, pleased to see Ross was on time. It didn't matter much in this case, but sometimes she cooked a meal for others, and timing was critical. When she opened the door, she saw he'd put on a golf shirt and a pair of khaki shorts, perfect for a summer night.

He smiled and held up a bottle of red wine. "My favorite. For tonight."

"Thanks," Melissa said and checked the Chandler Hill Inn label. "You have good taste. Let me decant the wine right away, so it'll be perfect with dinner."

Ross followed her into the kitchen and stopped to look around. "You can tell a chef owns this kitchen. Mine is sparse compared to this."

"I'm thrilled I was able to save enough money to build this house and design the kitchen. It's fabulous to be out of the tiny house on my parents' property and to have a place of my own. I love every day that I live here."

Ross studied her. "That's a great way to see things. I like my house too."

Melissa decanted the wine and handed him a plate of homemade mini-cheese-and-bacon quiches. "Thought we could have these while we wait to cook our dinner."

"Ah, bacon. A way to a man's heart."

Melissa poured the red wine into two glasses and handed him one. "Let's sit on the porch. If we stay here long enough, we might be able to see a deer. In the evening, a couple of them sometimes like to graze along the edge of the woods."

"We're lucky, aren't we?" said Ross, sitting in a chair and looking out at the landscape.

She sat on the couch. "We certainly are. I know you grew up in New Jersey and have three older brothers. What was that like? Though I desperately wanted some, I never had siblings."

"Being the youngest of four boys could be tough. No one wanted me to tag along, but when my mother assigned one of them to keep an eye on me, they didn't dare refuse. Especially after she got sick with cancer. Now, my father is dying from a different cancer, and I try to make it to New Jersey as often as I can to visit him."

"I'm sorry to hear about your parents. It's heartwarming that you try to visit home often," Melissa commented.

"I was only nine when my mother died. My dad used to help coach my baseball team and spent a lot of time with me, working to hone my skills. I owe a lot to him for helping me become a professional baseball player, among other things. What he didn't do to keep me in line in other ways, my brothers did."

"Are you still close to them?" she asked.

"Yes. They have families, some teenagers, and one of my nieces, my oldest brother's daughter, is driving now. They're good men, and we stay in touch. One of my sisters-in-law is always trying to fix me up, but I haven't found the right woman yet."

"You will," said Melissa, smiling at him. He was so darn cute she was sure some glamorous woman, more his type, would come along and snatch him up. Her thoughts turned to Dirk. She'd been told he was another guy waiting for the right woman. She hoped he could get to know her and see they shared many common interests. They both liked sports, the theater, and even classical music—something she hadn't found in another man. Dirk told her that Bach, Chopin, Debussy, and other composers had created compositions that made soothing background music while he worked on teeth, especially with kids.

"Do you want a family one day?" she asked Ross, thinking of Dirk and having a family.

"I'd like three or four. I will be very open about it when I'm dating."

"Music to some women's ears," said Melissa.

"We'll see," said Ross, taking one of the tiny quiches and popping it into his mouth. "M-m-m, these are delicious."

"Help yourself to more. I keep some frozen in the freezer for last-minute treats," she said, checking her watch. "Let's get the grill started. While you cook the steak, I'm going to make a green salad with tomatoes from Collister's farm and Maytag blue cheese that I ordered online. Instead of a mushroom sauce for the steak, I made a mushroom and cream potato dish I think you'll like."

"I'm sure I will. Let's see about that steak. I use special seasonings on it."

"Take a look in my cupboard. I promise you'll find what you want there," said Melissa.

Melissa lit the grill, and they walked into the kitchen.

Ross opened the cupboard she'd indicated and let out a long whistle. "You're right. It looks as if there's every spice in the world inside."

Melissa chuckled. "Every time I see something new, I can't resist."

After seasoning the meat, Ross carried it on a platter outside.

While he cooked the steaks, Melissa prepared the

ingredients for a salad and set the carafe of red wine on the dining room table. The dining room was open to the kitchen. Melissa liked to use the more formal space for dining because that signified it was a meal to take seriously.

Ross served the meat while she plated the potatoes and tossed the salad.

They carried their meals to the dining area and sat at the glass-top table opposite one another.

Ross looked around the room. "This is attractive."

"Thanks. The contemporary look is quite different from what I knew growing up, so it's a welcome change."

They ate slowly, chatting with one another about their childhoods and college. Though it might seem recent to some, Melissa and Ross agreed those days seemed ages ago.

After eating, they carried their dishes into the kitchen, and while Melissa loaded them into the dishwasher, Ross took care of the grill.

"Thanks for doing that," Melissa told him. "You're such an easy guest. We'll have to do this often. I love sharing a meal with someone."

"Yeah, me too. I'm not a real cook, but I can supply you with excellent wine to go with the food."

"That would be worth a couple of meals," said Melissa.

"Deal," he said and bumped her fist with his.

"Shall we go to Jake's? I'm anxious to see who shows up," Melissa said, checking her watch.

Ross winked at her. "If you're in luck, Dirk will be there."

When Melissa and Ross walked into Jake's, she saw Dirk sitting at the locals' table and let out a sigh of relief. This was the best way for Dirk to get to know her without any pressure. She, Misty, and Sarah, who was now a widow, were the only unattached women in the group.

Sitting by Brooks Beckham, one of the owners of Beckham Lumber, Dirk looked up at her and smiled.

She beamed at him and sat down beside him. "Where is everyone?"

"Cooper texted me that he and Taylor were on their way," said Dirk.

"Brad and Dani should be here anytime," said Brooks. "We delivered lumber to The Meadows site late this afternoon, which might've delayed them."

JoEllen Daniels entered the bar, saw them, and hurried over. "Great! The gang's here." She took a seat next to Brooks.

Melissa glanced at Ross sitting across from her and rolled her eyes. He winked at her.

Melissa turned to Dirk. "How's your week going? Are you busy?"

"Yes, I've had an interesting group of patients. Doing different procedures with them keeps me happy."

"I was surprised when you told me you like classical music," said Melissa. "My grandmother on my mother's side loved it and shared that appreciation with me."

"That's my story, too. It was my paternal grandmother who loved all classical music, even operas. She used to go to the Metropolitan Opera back in the day. I didn't like classical music at first, but I find it soothes people while I work on their teeth."

She chuckled. "I hope your patients like it too."

"Better than listening to the drill," he said, laughing with her.

Taylor, Dani, and Whitney arrived one after the other with their spouses, followed by Crystal and Emmet. The gathering turned into a party with a lot of joking between them. Melissa didn't know how the topic turned to food, but Ross suddenly said to Dirk, "You ought to see Melissa's kitchen. She has an entire cupboard filled with spices and seasonings."

"How do you know?" Dani teased Ross.

"Melissa and I are neighbors and friends. I did a favor for her, and she fixed me dinner," Ross said.

Crystal nudged Emmett. "That's sort of like us, huh? Be careful, you two. You might end up engaged like us."

Melissa shot Ross a look for help.

"No, no. As I said, Melissa and I are neighbors and friends. That's all," said Ross. "That's why I suggested Dirk take a look at her kitchen ... uh, you know, just as something new to do."

"I'm a good cook, too," said JoEllen, smiling at Dirk.

"Yeah, what do you make?" Dani challenged her. The words were said harshly, but no one who knew what a pain JoEllen had been to Dani and Brad could blame her.

"I make delicious brownies," said JoEllen, lifting her nose and facing Dani.

"Out of a box, no doubt," Dani muttered.

Whitney gave her sister a warning look and said sweetly, "Brownies are a favorite."

"Yes, I know," JoEllen said and glared at Dani.

"What's going on with you?" Cooper asked Ross, and while the men talked baseball statistics, Melissa turned to Taylor. "You mentioned interviewing Ross. Does your new book have to do with baseball?"

"Yes, it's a romance between a baseball player and a female sports announcer. It should be fun, but I want to make sure everything is correct. Ross has generously given me time to talk over certain points."

"He's a nice man," Melissa said.

"I think he likes you a lot, Melissa," Taylor said quietly.

"I'm interested in someone else," whispered Melissa.

Taylor studied her and indicated Dirk with a nod. "Is he the one?"

Melissa glanced at Dirk and couldn't stop a smile from spreading. Life with him would be steady, comfortable, and entrenched in Lilac Lake.

He caught her looking at him and returned her smile, sending a frisson of happiness through her.

Ross noticed, and a look of satisfaction crossed his face.

Their conversation moved to a fundraising baseball game Ross and Mike were setting up to gain support for a tennis and baseball training center in town.

"The town selectmen are all for the center, especially if we pay most of the construction cost. But we'll still need community financial support to pull it off."

"You mean for a tax break, things like that?" asked Dirk.

"Yes. For the game, I think I can get two of my old teammates to head the opposition team, which will consist of them and our high school baseball team. Town officials, noted community members, Mike, and I will play them for fun," said Ross.

"Tickets to the game will be sold for the cause, though children under ten will get in free," added Mike.

"With the blessing of the selectmen, Mike and I have already bought the land," added Ross. "Later, we'll hold a gala at the Lilac Lake Inn. My PR person is working on that with them now."

Impressed, Melissa clapped with the others. "What fun. And a worthy cause, too."

"This will be a wonderful addition to the town," said Brad. "Collister Construction plans to put in a bid to build it."

"I love how the town supports local businesses," said Dani, turning to Ross.

He held up his hand. "It won't be up to me alone to decide."

"Of course not," said Brad. "It must be open and fair. But we intend to outbid everyone else."

Melissa listened to the conversation and was happy to be part of the group. Growing up in Lilac Lake had felt confining to a child who didn't quite fit in. Today, as an adult with different experiences behind her, she was a real part of the group—something she treasured.

On the ride back to The Meadows together, Melissa stared out the car window while Ross drove. Her thoughts were spinning. Dirk had been pleasant to everyone and had been part of the group discussing the future of the tennis and baseball project, but he still seemed reserved toward her. How was she going to get the chance to know him better?

"Why the silence?" Ross asked.

"I can't figure out how to get Dirk's attention," said Melissa.

"I gave you the perfect opportunity," said Ross. "Ask him to dinner. He lives alone; he'll be happy to have someone cook for him."

"JoEllen is willing to make him brownies. I can do better than that. I'll ask him tomorrow." She faced him. "You are a dear friend, Ross. It means a lot to me."

"It's a satisfying situation for both of us. As neighbors, we can be there for one another." He pulled up to the front of her house. "Thanks again for dinner. It was delicious."

"I thought so, too. Nothing is stopping us from doing it again."

Ross leaned over and gave her a quick kiss on the cheek. "See you tomorrow."

"I'll be working in the afternoon, but maybe I'll catch up with you in the morning. I usually jog around the neighborhood before I have my coffee. It's amazing what wildlife you see at that time of day."

"I usually stay up late, but I may try getting up early in the morning and going to bed earlier too."

Melissa got out of the car and headed for her front door. She unlocked it and turned to wave at Ross, who'd politely waited for her to get inside.

She entered her house, paused in the hallway, and leaned against the door. Dirk had looked so handsome at Jake's—adorable, really. She'd do as Ross suggested and invite him to dinner.

CHAPTER FOUR

MELISSA AWOKE TO GRAY SKIES, STRETCHED, AND LAY back against her pillows. She'd slept restlessly, thinking of the best way to approach Dirk to ask him to dinner.

A sudden idea hit her. She sat up and quickly got ready for her day, dressed, and headed to the Lilac Lake Café. She'd heard Crystal tease Dirk about how prompt he was to get his morning coffee before going to work. She'd mentioned 7:30 A.M. Jake's might be the gathering spot at night, but Crystal's café was where many of the townspeople got their start for the day.

Pulling out of her driveway, she waved to Ross, who was jogging in shorts and sneakers and stretching in front of his house.

Afraid she might miss her chance to meet Dirk, she went on her way.

When Melissa walked into the café, she saw Dirk sitting at the counter and walked over to him.

"Mind if I take a seat here?" she asked him.

He turned and smiled. "Not at all. Where's Ross?"

Melissa could feel the blood drain from her face. "What?"

"You're together now, aren't you?"

"No, he's my neighbor." She cleared her throat. "I'm here to invite you to dinner at my house. Tomorrow is a slower day of the week at the restaurant, and I thought it would be a way for us to get to know one another better."

"Thanks. I'm not much of a cook, and any free meal I can get is much appreciated," he said.

It wasn't quite the response she was looking for, but she gave him a thumbs up. "Okay, then. Come to my house at 6:30 tomorrow. If the weather is pleasant, we'll have drinks on the deck before we eat."

"Excellent." He checked his watch. "I've got to go. See you then."

As he walked away, Melissa sighed and watched him leave. She'd need more help from Ross if she wanted a better response.

Taylor walked into the café carrying her laptop. She waved to Melissa and came over. "I'm getting a corner table. Want to join me?"

"Sure. I was just wondering if I should leave, but I'm happy to stay," Melissa said.

"What's up with you?" Taylor asked, looking puzzled.

"I came to ask Dirk to dinner. I figured I could catch him here," she said, following Taylor to a corner table that had a reserved sign on it.

Taylor removed the sign and sat down. "With Cooper working at the cottage, I sometimes find it easier to write here. I know it sounds crazy, but I can block out the noise here."

Misty, Crystal's sister, came over to them. "Good morning. May I take your order?" She gazed at Melissa. "I saw you talking to Dirk and didn't want to interrupt you earlier."

Melissa smiled but realized she'd made a big mistake by coming to the café. Before the end of the day, everyone in town would know she was talking to Dirk, and many would know she'd invited him to dinner.

Taylor ordered coffee and an oatmeal muffin, and Melissa decided to do the same.

"So, how'd it go with Dirk? Taylor asked her.

"Okay, I guess. He says he likes any homecooked meal he can get." Melissa frowned. "It doesn't sound great, does it?"

"I've noticed Dirk is shy. I'm not saying he's difficult, not at all. But I imagine it'll take work to make him feel comfortable about dating," said Taylor.

"I think you're right. But I like him. I'm not the most outgoing person, so I'll give him all the time he needs."

"What about you and Ross?" asked Taylor.

Melissa let out a long sigh. "I don't know why everyone keeps asking me that. We're friends. I like him, but I don't love him. I'm not the usual type of woman he dates—high fashion models, glamorous actresses, and the like. I wouldn't be a good fit for him. I think we both agree on that."

"Oh, I see," said Taylor. "I'm such a romantic that I've imagined possibilities there, not reality."

"I'm interested in Dirk as someone I could build a future with. I can imagine a very peaceful and happy life with him."

Taylor made a face. "I just want you to be happy, Melissa. We've been friends since early summer days." She hugged Melissa quickly and turned as Misty brought their orders to the table.

They ate breakfast together in companionable silence, though Melissa's mind raced, wondering if she should wear her new sexy top for dinner with Dirk. Maybe he needed a little encouragement in that direction.

When Melissa returned to her house, she decided to walk through the neighborhood. It wasn't as effective as jogging, but she still felt full of her breakfast. Crystal had sent over some hot cinnamon scones, and she hadn't been able to resist.

She put on sneakers and decided to see what new construction was taking place. She and Ross were in two of the first houses to be built, but others were under construction in the far reaches of the development. She'd heard the governor and his wife were building on a double lot in the woods.

Primary paved roads had been put in throughout the development, though Dani had assured her they would install a smooth top coating to the road once they had finished most of the houses.

Melissa walked past two houses that were similar to but not like hers. She liked that all the houses had different exterior designs. She knew the houses shared many of the same amenities inside them, but with Dani's architectural help, a buyer could easily change the basic design.

She moved past some open lots until she reached two houses under construction at the far end. One on a larger plot of land was obviously for the governor and his wife. She didn't know who'd bought the other one. Aaron had talked of building here; maybe it was his.

She walked down to the waterfront, contemplating taking her canoe for a solo spin.

When she arrived, Dani and Brad were standing on the dock and gazing around. Dani had a notebook in her hand.

Melissa joined them. "Planning something new?"

Dani held up her notebook. "Jotting down a few ideas to build some small cottages near the water. It's just in the thinking stage now. What are you up to?"

"Enjoying a morning walk. I didn't take my usual jog this morning, and I needed to work off some scone and muffin calories from Crystal's café."

Dani chuckled. "Me, too. We're through here. I'll walk you back to your house on my way to the office."

"Deal," said Melissa, pleased.

"I'll meet you at the office later," Brad said to Dani and then kissed her.

Observing them, a pang of envy hit Melissa in the solar

plexus. She caught her breath and turned away, giving the lovers some privacy.

Moments later, Dani came up behind her. "Ready?"

Melissa turned to her with a grin. "Are you?"

Dani laughed. "We've been working hard, and Brad and I need every moment alone we can get."

"You two are great together," said Melissa, hoping she and Dirk could be like that one day. She'd heard he was very good with his patients—competent and gentle, with a warm way about him. So perfect.

Melissa and Dani chatted easily about the development as they walked together. As they approached her house, Ross looked up from his front yard, waved, and headed toward them.

"You two are just the people I want to talk to," Ross said, smiling at them. "At Jake's, Mike and I talked about the fundraiser baseball game we're setting up, and now we've decided we need women on both teams. You both are perfect. Will you join us?"

Melissa glanced at Dani.

"Sure," said Dani.

"Okay, but I haven't played baseball in a long time," said Melissa.

"You'll have to help me," Dani said to Ross. "I'm usually okay at sports, but this is something new for me."

Ross smiled at them. "I'll train you and anyone else who wants practice sessions."

"It better be in the early morning when it's cooler, and I haven't worked all day," said Dani.

"Yes, that's a convenient time to do it before I head to work," Melissa agreed.

"Okay. We can do it then. When do you want to start?"

"Tomorrow?" Dani said, giving Melissa a questioning look.

"Okay, tomorrow," Melissa said. "That'll give me time to rest to prepare dinner for Dirk."

"So, it worked?" Ross asked her.

"He's coming, just like you said he would," said Melissa.

Ross clapped his hands for attention. "Okay, then, I'll see the two of you at the high school athletic field at seven tomorrow morning. Thanks. We'll make a useful time of it." He waved goodbye and left.

Dani looked at her and grinned. "What have we got ourselves into?"

Melissa chuckled. "I'm not sure, but we're about to find out."

When the alarm went off the next morning, Melissa groaned and turned it off. She was a morning person, but the thought of putting herself on display at the baseball field made her want to reconsider her offer. But Dani hadn't hesitated. If Dani could do it, so could she.

She got out of bed and dressed for the practice session. Dani was right about one thing. It would be the coolest time of day. Still, she dressed in shorts and a halter top, grabbed a baseball hat, a towel, and a water bottle, and then took off.

When Melissa reached the high school athletic field, Ross was already there, talking to a group of people, including Dirk. Surprised to see him, Melissa nervously adjusted her top, which exposed her belly. Then, chiding herself for feeling nervous, she went to join them.

" 'Morning," said Ross cheerfully. "We've got a full team of nine. I've brought extra baseball gloves, and Dani has some from the members of their building crew who aren't playing."

Melissa accepted the leather baseball mitt he handed her.

"Now, let's get started," said Ross. "For now, we'll just throw the ball back and forth. Later, Mike and I will bat a few balls to you to see what positions work best for you."

Melissa glanced over at Dani, who was talking to Misty. It looked like the three of them would be the only females on one of the teams. Dani and Misty both looked hot in their outfits. Melissa tugged on her baseball cap, wishing she could disappear.

"Pick a teammate and spread apart so we can watch you play catch," said Mike. "Dani, you and Melissa play together. I'll take Misty."

The guys easily chose someone to toss the ball to, and they all practiced. Mike and Ross helped with a few hints about picking up a ground ball, cupping the ball in the glove, and other usual maneuvers.

Melissa remembered some coaching hints from when she played softball in high school and discovered she was enjoying herself as she caught some balls from Dani. Both Dani and Misty seemed comfortable with what they were doing.

"Okay, now head to the outfield so Ross and I can bat some balls to you. They may be fly balls or grounders, so be prepared."

She heard the sound of a bat and looked up as a fly ball flew toward her. Automatically, she reached up and caught it.

"Great job," called Ross.

"You're good," said Dirk, standing next to her.

She laughed, pleased she'd performed well.

At the end of the practice session, Mike told them they were looking good but needed to come back tomorrow for more practice. "We have only a few days to get ready. Tyrus Jackson and Bo Bonner have put together a superb team with our high school players. We have to represent the town well against them."

Melissa caught up with Dirk as he was leaving the field. "I'm happy you're coming to dinner tonight."

He smiled at her. "Yeah, me too. I'm looking forward to it."

"The baseball game should be fun," said Melissa. "And it's for an excellent cause."

"I didn't know you were such an athlete," said Dirk.

"My parents always pushed me to play sports to make new friends," said Melissa, hiding that her shyness had sometimes made it difficult for her to socialize with her peers. She'd also had to face bullying from another girl in high school, which made things worse.

"Well, it's easy to see why it would be no problem for you to get chosen for a team," said Dirk. "Talk to you later." He waved to Cooper and took off running after him.

Dani walked up to her. "What was that all about?"

"I've invited Dirk for dinner. We were just confirming it."

"Maybe you're asking the wrong guy. Ross does seem interested in you," Dani said.

"We're just friends. That's how he wants it, and I've told him I'm interested in Dirk."

"You told him that?" Dani asked, her eyebrows shooting up on her face.

"Yes, that's what I meant about being friends. We can talk to each other about a lot of things."

Dani studied her with a puzzled frown. "Okay, I guess."

CHAPTER FIVE

AFTER SPENDING THE AFTERNOON COOKING AND PREPPING for dinner service at the restaurant, Melissa went home to prepare for her meal with Dirk.

She'd brought a beautiful piece of cod from the restaurant that she intended to broil with a lemony butter sauce and breadcrumbs. She'd quickly steam green beans from her garden and garnish them with butter and almonds. Seasoned rice would complete the main course. Simple and easy.

As she moved around her kitchen, she turned on Chopin piano concertos heard through the sound system she'd had installed in her house. The music helped her concentrate on the meal, stop conjuring up images of Dirk, and wonder what it might feel like to make love with him. Ross had told her to be herself, but he didn't know how awkward she sometimes felt.

She'd had boyfriends before, but none that made her feel truly accepted for herself. Since she'd been back in town, she'd made male friends, but none interested her until Dirk. He was someone she could imagine a future with. Ross and his friends were successful men accustomed to a more glamorous life and gorgeous women. None of those words described her.

Dirk was attractive in his own way and was a sweet person, someone who might be able to accept her sometimes awkward ways.

When Dirk arrived at her door, Melissa had convinced herself to relax and enjoy the evening.

Smiling, Melissa waved him inside.

He stood in the hallway momentarily and then said, "Chopin's Nocturne in E Flat Major. One of my favorites."

She smiled with satisfaction. "I thought you might like it. Come on in. It's a lovely evening. We can sit out on the porch for drinks and appetizers. I hope you're hungry. I think I got carried away with the shrimp cocktail. You aren't allergic, are you?"

He chuckled and shook his head. "As long as it's legitimately food, I'm all in. I don't count insects and bugs as real food."

"Have you tasted things like that?" Melissa asked.

"My family took a trip to China, and we experienced some pretty weird stuff," he said. "My father works for the government."

"How interesting," said Melissa, leading him into the kitchen. "What'll you have to drink? I have both red and white wine and beer, of course."

"Thanks. I'll take a beer. So refreshing on a warm evening."

She handed him a cold Heineken from the refrigerator and poured herself a sauvignon blanc.

She handed him a plate of cooked shrimp topped with lemon slices and a side container of cocktail sauce for dipping. She carried small plates and napkins and led him to the screened-in porch.

"This is nice," said Dirk. "My rental is perfect for now, but eventually, I want to have a house of my own."

"You can't do better than building with Collister Construction," Melissa said. "I have no complaints and many compliments about their work."

"It's so cool that many "townies" have returned to Lilac Lake to live. It says a lot about the town and the area."

"Yes, it does. At one time, I would never have thought I'd want to live and raise a family here. But I think it's a wonderful place to do just that." She hoped she hadn't been too outspoken.

"So, you want a large family?" Dirk asked.

"Yes. I was an only child and desperately wanted a sibling or two. I would never want a child of mine to be a 'lonely only.'"

Dirk studied her. "Interesting. Many of the women I've met aren't sure about having kids. Not a lot of them, anyway. Even my sister tells me she doesn't think she wants kids, that they're a commitment she doesn't want to consider."

"Sarah Bullard Miller, an old friend of mine, is a widow and is back home with 4-year-old twin girls. I see how adorable they are and think about a family of my own."

"It's nice to know not all women think like my sister," said Dirk. He picked up a couple of pieces of shrimp from the bowl of ice onto which she'd placed them. "How did you become interested in becoming a chef?"

"My father is a chef, and I grew up thinking and talking about food. When I was young, he worked for a restaurant in Boston, and when I was eleven, he and my mother bought Fins. I grew up knowing I'd be there to help them. It was a vision we all shared, and I admit, it gave me a purpose in life."

"I did the same thing with my career. My uncle, Rich, was someone I looked up to, especially when my father was unavailable because of work. I saw how happy he was living in Lilac Lake, enjoying sports in the area, and I knew I wanted a life like his. It is something better than the pressure cooker lifestyle my parents have always had."

"Rich Robinson has always been a part of Lilac Lake," she said, grinning. "Not that I wanted to go to the dentist that often. But he made it as comfortable as possible."

"I like the idea of helping people," said Dirk. "The hours are regular, much more than other medical services."

"So, you're looking forward to many years here?" she asked.

He nodded. "Yeah, as soon as I started working with my uncle, it seemed right."

"Good. We need you," said Melissa, beaming at him. He was perfect for her.

It satisfied Melissa's ego to see how enthusiastic Dirk was about her food. Like any chef, she enjoyed watching someone smack their lips and rave about her cooking. Wasn't that what it was all about?

"Let's enjoy the rest of the evening on the porch. It's cooled off and is peaceful. Can I fix you coffee, get you a beer or water?"

"Water would be great," said Dirk. "That was such a delicious meal; I don't want to disturb my tastebuds too much."

Melissa laughed. "Okay, water it is. Go ahead and get settled, and I'll bring it out to you."

Dirk left, and Melissa went into the powder room to rinse her mouth and ensure nothing was caught in her teeth. It had been a wonderful time so far. She hoped the evening would continue with kisses and wanted to be ready.

Satisfied she was fine, she carried their water out to the porch.

Dirk was sitting on the wicker couch. He looked up at her, smiled, and patted the cushion next to him. "Have a seat."

She lowered herself onto the couch and handed him his water. "Here's to an enjoyable evening!" she said, raising her glass in a salute.

He clicked his glass against it. "It's been great. Delicious dinner." He took a sip of water and gazed out at the woods behind her house. "I understand you still have a lot of wildlife visiting the neighborhood occasionally."

"Yes, though my favorites are the little brown bunnies. With the tall fence I've put around my garden, they can't get in, which makes them even cuter."

Dirk laughed, then, becoming serious, set his water glass down on a nearby table and turned to her.

"Thanks for a nice time. I enjoyed the food and conversation and the music, of course." He was giving her a look that sent tingles through her. His gaze went from her eyes to her mouth, and he reached for her.

She went into his arms and lifted her face in anticipation.

His lips met hers, and his kiss was warm and comfortable.

She gave an inward sigh and kissed him back.

He responded, and they continued kissing, learning the touch and taste of one another.

When they pulled apart, Melissa couldn't hold back a smile of satisfaction.

"I'd better go." Dirk sat up and checked his watch. "I didn't realize it was so late."

Melissa got to her feet. "Okay. Thanks for a great evening." She realized she was sounding like the guest, not the hostess. "I mean, thanks for coming. I hope we can do this again."

"Me, too," said Dirk, heading for her front door.

She followed, feeling confused and let down. The evening had held such promise. Maybe he didn't like her as much as she'd thought.

Over the next couple of days, Melissa didn't hear from Dirk. At first, she told herself he was too busy to call. But before long, she scolded herself for thinking he'd ever been interested in her.

She continued going to the baseball practices, hoping to see him there, but he'd mysteriously disappeared. Ross hadn't asked her about the date, and Melissa was too embarrassed to talk to him about it.

When the time came for the fundraising baseball game, Melissa was jittery with pent-up emotions over having to see Dirk again. When she said hello to him, he smiled and responded as if they hadn't ever kissed, making her wonder about him.

Determined not to let it ruin her day, she lined up with the others as Ross and Mike told each team member where they'd be playing in the outfield.

Melissa was glad to be placed in right field. Hopefully, not many balls would come her way. Ross was taking center field, and Mike was pitching. Melissa was relieved Dirk would cover third base away from her. He made her feel so unsettled, so insecure.

From her place on the field, Melissa gazed at the bleachers, noting how crowded they were. Hopefully, seeing all these people positively indicated support for the tennis and baseball center.

Ross's baseball-playing friends, Tyrus Jackson and Bo Bonner, were easy-going guys in their late thirties and had been stars in their day. The high school baseball team members were thrilled to be guided by them and were excited to play with them. Her team of locals seemed more relaxed about the game. She didn't know if that was good or bad; she just knew she would try her best, no matter what it took.

The first inning was full of laughter and no runs.

Between innings, Mike pulled their team together. "Okay, we need to step it up. They've got some heavy hitters coming up. Everyone, be alert."

She trotted to the outfield and stood ready. When the batter hit the ball with a resounding smack of bat against ball, Melissa watched, as if in a dream, as the ball flew toward her.

She lifted her glove and, keeping an eye on the ball, she ran to get it.

Wham!

Melissa ran into Ross with a thud that took her breath away. They fell in a heap, with Melissa sprawled on top. Shocked at how fast everything happened, she gazed down into Ross's face, hoping he was alright.

He gazed up at her, his blue eyes sending a silent message of interest in her as more than a friend. Her pulse sprinted. Melissa felt the world around them slipping away as they stared at one another. She looked up to find Dirk running toward them.

"Hey! Is everyone okay? Melissa, are you hurt?" He helped her to her feet and then offered a hand to Ross.

"No, don't help me." Ross grimaced. "It's my left knee. I twisted it. It's bad."

Mike stood by. "Can you make it back to the bench?"

Ross shook his head. "I need a few minutes, and then you'll have to give me a hand. I don't think I can make it there on my own." He looked up at Melissa. "Did you catch it?"

Melissa held up her baseball glove and stared at the ball tucked inside. "Wow! I did! I caught the ball."

"Fantastic!" said Brad Collister. He stepped forward from the players crowding around them, took the ball from her, and held it up for the other team to see. "Tyrus Jackson, you're out!"

"Great job," said Ross, gazing up at her with a look of satisfaction.

She studied him. He was wearing shorts, and she could see his knee was swelling already.

She knelt beside him. "I'm so sorry. Are you going to be all right?"

"I think I'd better watch the rest of the game from the

sidelines," he said, grimacing.

Tears sprang to her eyes. "I didn't mean to hurt you." She moved out of the way so Mike and Brad could help him to his feet.

Ross made it to the bench using their support and hopping on his healthy leg.

Emmett, who'd been watching from the bleachers, examined the leg. "I think a specialist should look at it. In the meantime, let's get some ice packs on it."

They made room on the dugout bench for Ross to stretch out his leg, and Emmett placed an ice pack on both sides of the knee and offered him a pain pill.

"Do you want me to sit with you?" Melissa asked, wringing her hands.

"No, you're good at this. We need our team to win," said Ross.

"I'll stay with him," said Crystal.

Melissa did as Ross asked and went back onto the field. She had to help the team win for Ross.

When she wasn't worried about catching a ball, she thought about how Ross gazed up at her. No man had ever looked at her quite that way. If it were anyone else, she might have thought it was lust. But she knew it couldn't be that. Ross had had many opportunities to change their relationship but had never tried.

She glanced at Dirk at third base. It was sweet how he'd run over to see if she was okay. Taylor had called him shy, and his concern made her happy.

CHAPTER SIX

ROSS STEADFASTLY REFUSED TO GO TO THE E.R. SO HE could cheer his team to victory. After the game was over, Emmett convinced Ross to have his knee checked out. Mike and the other professional players offered to take him to the hospital, but Melissa insisted on doing it herself.

"I'm the one who caused the accident," she told them. "I won't rest until Ross gets proper medical treatment."

Ross held up his hand. "No E.R. visit. I've called my sports medicine doctor, and he's referred me to a surgeon at Mass General in Boston, who will see me right away. Thanks for your offers, guys, but it's important for you to stay here and do your part to promote the center."

"Okay, then I'm driving you to Boston," Melissa told him. "The surgeon will see you this evening?"

"Yes. If they must operate, it'll be done as soon as possible. Remember, I've been through this routine before."

"Okay. Why don't I pack an overnight bag and help you pack one for yourself?" said Melissa.

"Do you really want to do this?" Ross asked.

"Yes. This will make me feel a whole lot better about being the cause of this injury."

Ross placed a hand on her shoulder. "It was an accident."

"I know, but I still feel bad," said Melissa. "Besides, my SUV is large enough to give you plenty of space to stretch out either in the front or on the back seat."

"I'll ride with you to Ross's house to make sure he has everything he needs and to see that he's as comfortable as possible in your car on the ride to the hospital," said Emmett, standing by.

"Thanks. I appreciate that," said Melissa. "You can give me instructions on handling his injury."

Dirk approached. "I'm sorry this happened, Ross. I guess this means you won't be going to the special event this evening, Melissa. I'll miss you. Are you going to be all right traveling home by yourself?"

"Yes, thanks. I can stay in Boston for as long as it takes. I've got culinary friends who live there who'll give me a place to stay if it becomes necessary."

Melissa left the crowd and went to her SUV.

She drove her vehicle as close as possible to Ross in the dugout, then got out and studied the logistics of getting him inside. Emmett helped her rearrange the seating in her car so Ross could either stretch out across the back seat or sit in the reclining front passenger seat.

Mark and Tyrus helped get Ross into the car. Melissa watched his face closely and knew from the pained expression that he was hurting. Guilt stabbed her.

Ross opted to stretch his leg out across the back seat. Emmett got into the passenger seat, and Melissa took off for home.

"I'll park at Ross's house and run across to my house to pack," she said as they headed for The Meadows.

As she drove, Emmett talked to Ross. "There comes a time when it's easiest to take care of the situation once and for all. This knee has been a problem for some time. No doubt your doctor is right, and arthritis has set in, and what was mended may now need replacement. Without specific knowledge of your situation, I agree that what your doctor told you makes sense."

Ross let out a long sigh of resignation. "I've had one knee

replacement done, and I guess the time has come for the other. I should never have gone for that motorcycle ride years ago."

"It's not my favorite form of transportation for anyone. I've seen too many accidents with them," said Emmett. "Okay, give me a list of what to get for you, and I'll go into your house and pack up what I can."

"The master suite is on the first floor. Help me inside, and I'll get my stuff together."

"I'll help you, too," said Melissa. "One on each side of you."

Ross looked at her. "Okay. Thanks."

Melissa pulled into Ross's driveway and stood by while Emmett got Ross out of the car onto the driveway's pavement. Then she came close, and Ross wrapped one arm around her shoulder and the other around Emmett's, and they slowly made their way inside his house and into his master bedroom.

Sweating from the effort, Ross collapsed into an overstuffed chair and told her what he wanted and where it was.

While Melissa worked to get his toiletries together, she observed the double spa tub, the extra-large shower, and the cute shelf holding some plants and candles next to the spa. White towels offset the pale-gray tile flooring and lighter gray walls with a few sunset orange accents that matched the bedroom's gray, white, and burnt-orange theme.

She remembered Whitney had helped him decorate his house and silently applauded her.

"Ready?" Emmett said to her.

Melissa put the last of Ross's toiletries in his leather Dopp kit and returned to the bedroom.

"I think I've got everything you wanted. If not, I'll see that you have them," she said.

"Thanks," said Ross. "Let's get on the road."

"I'll drop you off on the way," Melissa told Emmett.

"Thanks. I promised Crystal we'd go to the dinner event tonight. I'm going to ask for donations in Ross's name. That ought to bring in some extra money."

"It's not necessary to use my name," said Ross.

Emmett clapped him on the back. "You're a hero to people in town. If that helps with fundraising, I say let's go for it."

Ross frowned but didn't protest.

After dropping Emmett off at his house, Melissa programmed the destination into the car's GPS unit and took off for Mass General.

She kept an eye on Ross in the backseat and saw that, after a few minutes on the road, he'd fallen asleep. She put on some soft classical music and settled down for the two-hour drive. She knew enough about Boston to feel comfortable. She'd travel south on I-93, get onto Route 3 in Boston, then onto Charles Street, and turn left onto Fruit Street. She just hoped traffic would be okay.

Listening to the music, knowing Ross was safely tucked away in her car, Melissa drew a deep breath, recalling the incident. Everything had happened so fast. She was running, and the next thing she knew, she was lying on top of Ross and feeling as if she couldn't catch her breath. It didn't help that Ross gave her a look of ... something. Then, in a flash, it was gone, and pain spread across his face, erasing any softness it had held.

She'd just reached the outskirts of Boston when she heard Ross stir and whisper, "Son of a bitch, that hurts."

Concentrating on the traffic around her, she kept quiet as tension inside the car grew. They were almost there.

She found the Emergency Room entrance and parked outside the door.

"Stay here. I'll get someone to help us," she said to Ross. She got out of the car and hurried inside.

Moments later, she returned with a staff member who got Ross into a wheelchair.

"I'll park somewhere and return," she told Ross.

He acknowledged her with a wave and was wheeled inside.

When she entered the Emergency Room, she checked in at the desk and told the woman she was there with Ross.

"Yes, Dr. Rusko is with him now," she said. "You can wait here. Someone will let Mr. Roberts know you're here."

Melissa sat in the waiting area, nervously flexing her fingers. A short while later, a stocky bald man of average height wearing horn-rimmed glasses approached her. "Melissa Hendrickson? Are you with Ross Roberts?"

She stood and clasped her hands. "Yes. Is he okay?"

"Hello. I'm Dr. Rusko. Ross told me it was okay to give you his medical information. He's in a lot of pain, and his knee is in bad shape. We're going to keep him here so we can run several tests. And because the joint is so badly damaged, we'll operate as soon as possible. My colleague, his sports medicine doctor, has requested we not wait. It's a matter of the sooner, the better."

"May I see him?" Melissa asked, feeling sick to think of her part in his injury.

"We've given him some pain medication, so he may be a bit groggy," he said. "Follow me."

Dr. Rusko led her to an examination cubicle and stepped away. "I'll give you two some privacy."

Ross looked up at her. "Guess I'm going to become even more bionic. Thanks for bringing me here. Dr. Rusko seems excellent." His eyelids fluttered.

"I'm so sorry this happened," said Melissa. "I'll stay in Boston until after your surgery."

He gazed at her and closed his eyes. "It's not your fault, Melissa."

"Oh, but ..." She stopped when he realized he'd fallen asleep.

Before she left the hospital, she called Annette "Nettie" Mancini, her friend from culinary school. Nettie worked and lived in the North End of Boston. Melissa had promised to visit her one day soon, but not under these circumstances.

Since it was a Saturday night, Melissa knew not to expect Nettie to be home and left a message telling her about her predicament. Satisfied she'd done her best to reach out, Melissa went outside to her car. On the way, she was pleasantly surprised when Nettie called.

"Hi, Melissa. I got your message. I'm working as usual, but I'd love to see you. We've got room for you to stay for as long as you need. It's about time we caught up. It's been too long."

"Thanks. It'll be nice to see you. When will you be at your condo?"

"Not until eleven or so. Jason will be home even later. But I keep a key inside a planter outside my door. The planter is specially made with a spot for a key inside, not under it. You'll see for yourself. And the code to get into the building is 4624."

"No animals to know about?" Melissa asked. "I know you wanted a dog."

"No, not yet. When we move to the 'burbs, I'll try for one. The city is too inconvenient for pets."

Melissa smiled at the way Nettie, as usual, seemed to have things planned out. They'd always gotten along well. It was a shame that, with their busy schedules, they hadn't seen more of one another. Annette was engaged now to Jason Rockwell, who was part-owner of the restaurant where they both worked. They were a good match. Nettie was busy making wedding plans for the following June. Melissa had already agreed to be a bridesmaid.

The North End was conveniently close to Mass General Hospital, and the condo Nettie and Jason shared was on Cooper Street with parking nearby. It couldn't be better. Melissa liked Jason and was used to Nettie's half-hearted housekeeping. They'd shared a room at culinary school.

Melissa parked the car. Shaking her head at the cost of the overnight fee, she realized how simple life was in Lilac Lake. She walked down the street to the brick apartment building, passed the entry point, and took the elevator to the fourth floor. She found the key in the planter in the hallway and opened the door. She'd always liked the condo. Barely over 1,000 square feet, the space was well laid out with two bedrooms and two small baths. The kitchen had undergone an upgrade before Nettie and Jason bought it. Since then, they repainted and decorated each room with inexpensive but creative art done by local artists.

She put her overnight bag in the den/office/guest room and decided to take a walk. The North End was European in flavor. Contemporary buildings sat side by side with historic brick buildings. Cobblestones and bricks covered some of the ground surfaces and walkways. And always, the shops and restaurants beckoned. Now, in the early evening, people strolled the streets lured no doubt by the wonderful aromas floating from places like Mama Maria's. In one small area, a person could choose any Italian cuisine they wanted. Hanover Street, Salem Street, and North Street were just three of the streets loaded with Italian restaurants and bakeries, enough to satisfy anyone.

Melissa realized how hungry she was and stopped at a casual restaurant serving homemade pasta and seafood. She placed a to-go order, and when it was ready, she headed back to the condo, stopping at a bakery on the way for a chocolate cannoli for dessert. She'd worry about calories later.

Feeling content with her walk, Melissa entered the condo and plated her dinner. Aware her parents were working at the restaurant, Melissa called her mother to update her on Ross. Her mother was the heart and soul of the restaurant, greeting people and making them feel welcome.

Her mother, predictably, said she'd call a few people at the fundraising event so they could share the news.

"Thanks, Mom. I'm still trying to get over the fact that all this has happened. After I eat dinner, I'll return to the hospital to see what I can do to help Ross. He was pretty out of it when I last saw him. Hopefully, he'll be a little more awake."

"You're alright staying with Nettie?" her mother asked.

"Yes. She said I was welcome for as long as I wanted. Both Nettie and Jason are working at the restaurant now. Depending on how long I'm here, I may return home for more clothes if necessary. I'll let you know about work as soon as I can."

"No worries. That's why we have Geoffrey and you acting as chefs. The time will come, I hope, when you work less and less after you marry and start a family of your own."

"Mom," Melissa groaned. "Don't go there."

"I know, darling. I'm sorry. I just can't help wondering when that's going to happen."

"I've got to go now. Thanks for your help." Melissa ended the call and emitted a long sigh. She knew her mother wanted the best for her, but talk like that always made her feel like a failure.

CHAPTER SEVEN

AFTER EATING PART OF HER PASTA AND SHRIMP DISH with a lemony sauce and Caesar salad, Melissa stored the remainder in the refrigerator. She'd eat the cannoli later after visiting Ross. She'd need a sweet treat by then. It had been an emotional day.

She got her things settled in the den and, knowing how it worked, pulled out the couch to make it into a bed. Then, she added sheets and a blanket so it would be ready for her without bothering Nettie to help. It was the least she could do for a last-minute stay.

Glancing around to make sure she wasn't being too intrusive, Melissa picked up her purse and headed to the parking garage to get her car. She'd paid an overnight fee so she could come and go.

Walking along the street, she was amused when an apartment window opened, and a woman stuck her head out and hollered, "Anthony! Time to come home." Down the block, she could see a group of boys on skateboards. Anthony, no doubt, was one of them.

When she walked into Ross's room, he looked up and smiled, sending heat through her. She told herself her reaction was merely because he was more alert.

"I'm happy to see you more aware. How are you doing?" she asked, standing by him. His injured knee was supported by a series of pillows on either side, helping to keep his leg straight and immobile.

His lips curved again, and she was reminded of seeing him on television with the same crooked smile. He really was adorable.

"Is there anything I can do to help you? Does your family know about this?" she asked.

"No, they don't know, and I don't want to bother them. I'll call when the surgery is complete, and we have all the facts."

"Dr. Rusko said they'd be doing a lot of tests. Have you had any?"

"I'm scheduled for an MRI later this evening. They have my records from New York to do some comparisons."

"Have they helped with your pain?" she asked Ross.

"I'm feeling foggy, but the pain is something I can handle. Have a seat. I like your company."

She pulled a chair closer and sat down. "I intend to do everything I can to help you. There's no need to get a nurse. Once you're home, I'll see you have meals and everything you need."

"Aw, thanks. I know why you're saying that, but you don't have to do this. The accident was just that, an accident. I can hire someone to come in and help."

"No, I wouldn't feel right about that," said Melissa. "You've promised to be my friend, and I'll reciprocate. Subject closed."

He grinned. "I like it when you go all tough woman."

She chuckled. "I mean what I say."

"I like that too," he said. "Okay, deal. You come to my house to help following surgery and give up the idea of feeling guilty about the accident."

"Deal," she quickly said, eager to resolve the issue. "Now, have you had anything to eat?"

He shrugged. "They don't want me to have more than liquids because they'll operate as soon as they're ready. I suspect first thing in the morning."

"Okay. What are some of your favorite foods? I can bring some to you after the surgery, and then when you get home, I'll take care of it."

"Thanks," Ross said, studying her. "You are a nice person, Melissa. I'm glad we're friends."

"Me, too," she said quietly, realizing how much it meant to her.

"You're a decent ball player, you know?" Ross said. "I can't believe you held onto that ball. Our team won by one run. That run belongs to you."

Feeling her cheeks grow hot, she waved away the compliment. "We were a team. Everyone tried their best."

"True," said Ross. He shifted in his bed and let out a soft groan.

She jumped to her feet.

He waved her back down. "I'm okay. I'd just as soon get the show on the road and get this surgery over with."

"How about something to distract you? Should I change channels on the TV?"

At his nod, she clicked through several channels until she came to a country music show."

"There, that's it," said Ross. "I'm a fan of country western music."

Melissa gazed at him wide-eyed. "How about classical music?"

He shook his head. "It's not my thing."

After Ross showed signs of falling asleep, Melissa rose. "I'm going to leave. I'll check in with the hospital tomorrow morning." She took hold of his hand. "If they decide to operate before I see you again, I've asked them to call me. I wish you the best. I like your doctor, and I'm sure it'll turn out fine."

He squeezed her hand. "Thanks, Melissa, for being here. It

means a lot." He tugged on her hand to bring her closer.

She leaned down and kissed him on the cheek. When she stood, Ross's eyes were closed.

Melissa was leafing through one of Nettie's cookbooks when Nettie walked into her condo.

"Melissa! Such a pleasure to see you! I'm sorry it's under less-than-perfect conditions, but I'm happy you're here."

Melissa felt like a giant as she hugged Nettie, who was five feet four inches tall compared to her five feet nine inches.

Nettie stepped back and gave Melissa an approving look. "You look lovely as usual, even though I know you won't agree with me. Seriously, there's something different about you. Is it a man?"

Melissa couldn't stop a huge smile from spreading across her face. "I've met someone I'm excited about, someone I could see myself with in the future. He's a new dentist in town. Very caring. He even likes classical music."

"Well, well. Let's pour a glass of wine, and you can tell me all about him," said Nettie. Goodness radiated from her as she beamed at Melissa. She made up for her short, curvy stature by seeming larger than most people around her with her natural energy and excitement about life. She usually wore her curly black hair tucked into a Red Sox baseball cap whose visor almost met her big blue eyes. She'd taken her cap off tonight, and her curls bounced as she walked into the kitchen to get their wine.

Melissa followed eagerly. Nettie always made her feel good about herself, and she couldn't wait to tell her about Dirk and learn more about her friend's upcoming wedding.

"I'm settled in the den and have already made up the bed, so you don't have to worry about it," said Melissa.

"I knew you'd make yourself at home. Tell me more about

your neighbor and the accident."

Nettie poured them each a glass from the bottle of red wine that Melissa had picked up on her walk. She handed a glass to Melissa and raised hers. "Here's to friends. We may not see each other that often, but I know I can always count on you to be there for me."

"True," said Melissa. "And you for me. That's what friends do for one another." She thought of her friendship with Ross. Theirs was shaping up that way.

They walked into the living room and sat down facing each other on the couch. "Okay, spill, girlfriend," said Nettie, sipping her wine. She held up the glass and inspected it. "Nice legs on this one, and the taste is fruity and lovely. Thank you."

"You're welcome. It's one of my favorites. A Chandler Hill Inn pinot noir."

"I must remember to tell Jason about it," said Nettie. "We're always looking for something special."

"How is Jason?" Melissa asked. She'd always thought he was perfect for Nettie. He offset Nettie's darker looks with his sandy hair, hazel eyes, and height. A native of New Hampshire who'd attended the Hotel and Hospitality Management program at UNH, he was ambitious and hardworking at the small restaurant he partly owned.

"Jason is great, but I wish I could encourage him to slow down. Getting him away from the restaurant for our honeymoon will be hard. That's why I chose Tahiti. He won't be able to hop on a plane and return to Boston whenever he thinks of something. That, and the sexy little nothings I've bought, will, I hope, keep him busy."

Melissa laughed with her. Jason adored Nettie. She couldn't imagine him not enjoying their honeymoon trip. "You know I'll come to work at the restaurant while you're gone if you need me."

"Thanks, hon, but by the time we leave, his brother will have graduated from Cornell and should be able to handle the restaurant, while my sister will handle the kitchen. It turns out she's as talented a cook as the rest of the family."

"And the rest of your families?" asked Melissa.

"Still living in the Boston suburbs and loving it," said Nettie.

'You're lucky to have so much family around you. I guess that's why I'm so happy to have long-time friends return to Lilac Lake. They're like family, in a way."

"That makes you lucky, too. Right?"

Melissa looked at Nettie's bright expression and agreed.

They were still chatting when Jason walked through the door. "Hi, Melissa. Nice to see you."

Melissa stood, wobbling a bit after sharing the bottle of wine with Nettie. "You look great. I'm excited about the wedding plans. It's going to be lovely."

Jason kissed her hello on the cheek and went over to Nettie. "Anything more I should know about?" he teased before he kissed her.

"Nothing new," said Nettie, smiling.

"Let's keep it that way," he said, tweaking her nose affectionately. "Now, let me get a beer, and I'll unwind with you two."

Observing the easy way they conversed and the sweet way they interacted, Melissa wondered if that's how she and Dirk would be once they got to know one another

.

CHAPTER EIGHT

THE NEXT MORNING, MELISSA ROSE QUIETLY, DRESSED, and left the condo, allowing Nettie and Jason a chance to sleep in. Working night shifts at the restaurant was exhausting, and she knew they appreciated every opportunity they had to sleep in. She tried Ross's phone, and when he didn't answer, she decided to go ahead and go to the hospital to see what was happening.

She checked in at the information desk, asked for Ross's room number, and discovered he'd been moved to a surgical floor. She took the elevator and went to his room to find it empty. Concerned, she checked at the nurse's station and was told he was in the recovery room and would be sent to his room within an hour or so.

She thanked them and told them she'd be in the cafeteria.

"Are you a friend of his?" a pretty nurse asked, appraising her.

She forced a smile, though she was suddenly struck by how it must look—a famous baseball star with someone like her. "Yes," she answered. "He's a neighbor."

"Lucky girl," said another nurse. "He's a hottie."

As she turned to leave, Melissa couldn't think of what to say.

Sitting in the cafeteria, Melissa looked up Ross's biography online. She studied photos of Ross, his father, and his brothers, all handsome men. After he was awake and able to talk, she'd suggest again that he call his family. Even though he'd told her they were busy, she thought they'd want to know.

She ate a healthy breakfast, uncertain when she'd get the chance to eat again, and hung out in the cafeteria until she thought Ross would be back in his room.

When she entered the floor where Ross's room was, one of the nurses waved her over. "Is your name Melissa?"

Melissa nodded.

The nurse gave her a friendly smile. "Ross is asking for you. I said you were here and would be up to see him soon. He seemed relieved when I told him. He's awake and lucid. Better go in and see him."

"Thanks," said Melissa.

She walked to Ross's private room, tapped lightly on the door, and stepped inside.

"Hello," she said, studying him lying in bed with tubes and monitors in and on his body. She observed his bare chest and noticed the light hairs across it. She'd read up on procedures and watched as the continuous passive motion machine caused Ross's leg to straighten and bend repeatedly.

Melissa went over to him and took hold of the hand that didn't have a tube attached to it. "How are you? Are you relieved it's over?"

"Yeah, I am. I guess it was time to stop trying to repair the knee and get new parts. I'm glad to see you. Where did you stay?"

"I'm a guest of a friend in the North End. She's a dear friend from culinary school and told me I could stay as long as I wanted. What can I do for you?"

"How about helping me drink some water? They're supposed to be bringing me breakfast soon. Orange juice, scrambled eggs, and toast."

"Let me get you something to drink, and then I'll check to see where your food is," she said. She poured water into a glass from the insulated pitcher on his bedside table, and, holding the straw between two fingers, she lifted it to his lips. He gazed up at her as he sipped, his features softened.

She felt a little thrill go through her at the look he gave her. When he was through drinking, she set the cup down. "I'll go see where breakfast is."

Still feeling a sense of warmth from the look of appreciation he'd given her, she headed to the nurse's station. The elevator opened, and a food cart rumbled onto the floor. "Are you going to deliver to Room 417?" She asked the man wheeling the cart.

He checked the list attached to the side of the cart. "Yes. I've got it here."

"Good. He's waiting for breakfast after surgery."

She returned to Ross's room and said, "Food is on the way."

"Thanks. I'm starving."

She stepped aside as the man with the cart knocked on the door. "Ready for breakfast?"

Ross gave him a thumbs-up.

Melissa helped put the tray table in place and the meal on it. "It smells good," she said, giving Ross an encouraging smile.

He picked up a fork, poked at the scrambled egg, took a bite, and then picked up a piece of buttered toast. "Maybe I'm not as hungry as I thought."

"Here, I'll add a little salt to the egg. Maybe it'll taste better then." She looked at the food and wondered if she could bring in a homemade meal for him. "Tomorrow, I'll bring you breakfast."

He looked up at her and grinned. "Would you do that for me?"

"Sure," she said. "You know how important food is to me. I want the best for you."

"Thanks for being here for me." He leaned back against his pillow and closed his eyes.

While he was napping, Melissa returned to Nettie's condo for a break, grateful that her place wasn't far and she had another day of parking.

Nettie was alone in the kitchen when Melissa returned to the condo.

"Morning!" Nettie said cheerfully. "Jason has already gone to the restaurant, but I don't have to work until later. I'm happy you came back. I wanted to spend some time with you."

"Me, too. You wanted to show me some pictures of brides' gowns. Do you want to look at them now?"

"Yes," said Nettie. She clapped her hands and jumped up from her chair. "Grab a cup of coffee and a piece of toast, and I'll bring the magazines to you. I'm dying to hear what you think."

Chuckling at Nettie's usual enthusiasm, Melissa fixed herself a cup of coffee, spread strawberry jam on top of Italian bread toast, and took a bite, relishing the flavor.

Nettie reappeared lugging several magazines. She spread them out on the table. "I'll show you my favorite so far, but I want you to look at several others for comparison."

Melissa finished her toast and coffee and sat beside Nettie, who showed her a picture of a V-neck lacy gown with capped sleeves and a full skirt.

"What do you think?" asked Nettie.

"I want to see all the ones you like before making a decision," said Melissa. She loved the excitement on Nettie's face but couldn't help wondering if the day would ever come when she'd be looking for her own wedding gown.

After looking through the other six magazines, Melissa knew she didn't love the dress Nettie had chosen for herself. She didn't know what to say.

"Okay," said Nettie. "I want the truth. I get the distinct impression that you don't like my choice. Fess up, girl."

"Okay, I will. Nettie, you're a beautiful woman, so I don't understand why you're leaning toward full-skirted, lacy choices that I don't think suit you as well as some others."

Nettie nodded thoughtfully. "Thanks. I don't have a tall, lean body like yours, and with my job, I won't be thinner for the wedding. I see what you mean, though. I need to go with simpler designs."

Melissa let out a breath of relief. "Yes. You don't need to hide behind some big, fancy gown. Choose one that shows your body. Jason loves you as you are."

Nettie threw her arms around Melissa. "Thank God, you're being honest with me. That's exactly what I've been trying to do. Hide."

Melissa gave Nettie a squeeze and smiled at her. "You're beautiful, Nettie. Let's look for something different. I saw a dress earlier that I think would look lovely on you."

They went through the magazines more slowly, discussing different dresses.

"Found it!" said Melissa. She showed Nettie a simple, A-line, short-sleeve dress with a V-neck, whose skirt fit at the hips and fell softly to the floor in lovely, silken folds.

Nettie studied it and turned to Melissa with tears in her eyes. "It's perfect. I see what you mean about letting it be simple. I'm so glad I asked for your opinion. When your time comes, I hope you'll ask me for mine, though I must tell you that you'll look fabulous no matter what you choose."

"Don't hold your breath about helping me. At this point, I'm trying to get Dirk McArthur interested in me. I have a feeling it's going to take time. But it'll be worth it. On paper, he seems perfect."

"Melissa," said Nettie. "It's more than about looking good on paper. The chemistry has to be there."

Melissa waved away Nettie's concern. "Oh, I know. But it's a smart place to start."

Nettie looked up at the kitchen clock. "I had no idea it was so late. I've got to head to the restaurant. Make yourself at home here. I'll try to get back early. Sunday nights are slow."

"Okay. See you then," said Melissa. "I'll go back to the hospital and see how Ross is doing. I feel bad seeing him in bed with monitors and his knee a mess."

"You're doing everything you can for him."

As they said goodbye, Melissa hoped Nettie was right. It was the least she could do after the accident.

CHAPTER NINE

ROSS WAS ON HIS PHONE WHEN MELISSA WALKED INTO his hospital room. She stopped and waved at him, then turned away to give him some privacy.

"Melissa, come here. My father wants to talk to you," said Ross.

She walked over to him and accepted the phone he handed her. "Hello?"

"You're the woman who lives next door to Ross?" he said. "I want to thank you for your help. But I need to know if he needs family around, you'll call me."

"Yes, sir. I'm Melissa Hendrickson. I've promised to help him all I can. I'm the person who ran into him."

"So, you're a ball player?" he asked, teasing gently before chuckling.

"I caught the ball. That's all I'm saying," she said, enjoying his joke.

"It sounds as if you'll be good medicine for him. I can't come to Boston to see him. But I'll keep in touch with you to make sure he's all right. Is that okay?"

"Yes, that's fine," Melissa said. "It was nice talking to you." She gave him her number and then handed the phone back to Ross.

"See? I told you I'll be fine," Ross said into the phone. "I've got helpful neighbors. I'll be in touch. I promise."

Ross ended the call and turned to Melissa. "Thanks for reassuring my father. His concern is appreciated, but he's not able to come. He wouldn't be much of a nurse anyway. That was always left up to my mom. And with four boys, she had a lot to handle."

"Have you eaten since I've been gone?" she asked him.

"No, but now I am hungry."

"Let me see if I can rustle up a snack for you," said Melissa. She left him and went to the nurse's station. A nurse handed her menus from the hospital's cafés and cafeterias.

She borrowed them and took them back to Ross's room. "I haven't had lunch. I thought I'd get some for both of us. What sounds tasty to you?"

"It may sound crazy, but I want a hamburger with ketchup and nothing else," he said. "And a chocolate milkshake."

"That's easy," said Melissa. "I'll go get it for you now. Anything else?"

He smiled at her. "Thanks. That'll be great."

They both turned as Mike arrived. He waved at her and said to Ross, "Hey, buddy. How're you doing?"

"I'm not ready to go jogging yet, but the doctor told me that once this heals, I'll be better than ever. No more constant pain. I wonder where I'd be if I'd never ridden that motorcycle."

"Happy news. The people of Lilac Lake have spoken clearly with their donations. We'll end up co-owning the center with the town and using some of the land we bought for an outdoor park, just as we envisioned."

"Great to hear," said Ross.

"I'm going to pick up some things from the cafeteria," said Melissa. "Can I get you anything to eat, Mike?"

"No, thanks. I grabbed a bite before coming here."

She left the men talking. She liked the idea of a sports center aligned with an outdoor park. It would work well for everyone.

Melissa returned to the room to find Mike and Ross deep

Love's Home Run

in conversation. When they saw her, they stopped.

"Sorry to interrupt. Are you ready for lunch, Ross?"

"And how. I'm feeling better than I was this morning. I've dealt with pain before, and overall, this isn't too bad with the drugs they give you. I hope to get off this motion machine and be on my feet tonight."

Melissa handed him the hamburger and milkshake he'd wanted, made sure he had napkins, and sat in the chair Mike offered her so she could eat the chicken salad she'd ordered for herself.

"I'm going to hang around until tomorrow," said Mike. "And then I can drive Ross back to his house if he gets out of the hospital as he's hoping. That will give you a break, Melissa."

"Oh, but ..."

Ross held up his hand to stop her. "Let Mike do that for me. I'll need you in the weeks ahead to come to help me at the house. I won't be able to get back and forth from my house to the sports rehab center in Concord, and I'll need you or someone else to drive me."

Deflated, Melissa sighed. "Okay. That makes sense. I'll drive you if you make morning appointments at the rehab center. And what days I can't do it, I'll find a substitute."

"Wow, thanks. That's a huge relief. It should be a matter of six weeks or so before I'm able to drive. We'll take it day by day because I don't want to be a burden to you or anyone else." He smiled at her. "You're the best."

"I'll be your substitute driver," said Mike.

"Crystal texted me that she'd take care of meals for the first week or so," said Ross.

"It seems as if, between all of us, you won't need to worry about a thing. That's what neighbors are for." She smiled at him though her emotions were in a whirl. She was disappointed that he didn't seem to need her, yet she knew it was better this way. She was finding herself drawn to him, which was a bad idea.

After she finished her salad, she rose. "Guess I'll go back to Nettie's condo and get ready to go home. My parents will be pleased I'm coming back to work. But, Ross, I want you to know I'm sincere about helping you in any way I can."

"Thanks," said Ross. "I know that, and I appreciate all you've done for me." He beckoned her to come closer, and then he squeezed her hand and gazed up at her with a look of tenderness that weakened her knees.

Fighting for composure, she looked away. When she faced him again, his expression was neutral.

Mike stood and walked her to the door. "We'll be home tomorrow or the next day. I'll let you know."

"Thanks. I'll have the house ready." She held up the keys to Ross's house. "I'll keep these for a while."

"Yes. You should just keep them."

"Okay," she said. It made sense. She was his next-door neighbor.

On the way home, Melissa mulled over her time with Ross. There was a definite connection between them for a few brief moments. But, in reality, their relationship was more like brother and sister than anything else. She reminded herself that she and Dirk had more in common, which was important to any future relationship with him. She knew she made it seem like it was all about being logical. But the one time she'd thought she had a future with another student at culinary school, her heart had been wounded as deeply as if it had been burned by one of the kitchen stove's open flames. While she'd been dating him, he'd been sleeping with someone else.

Pushing the past away, Melissa called her mother to tell her she'd be in to cook tomorrow and was pleased by her reaction. "Thanks. It makes such a difference to have you in the kitchen. How's Ross doing?"

Melissa gave her an update and said, "I've agreed to take him to rehabilitation when it's time. He'll set up morning appointments, so it won't disturb my work schedule."

"I know you feel guilty about the accident, but you have responsibilities here too."

"Of course. But I'm happy to drive him. As I said, I won't come to the restaurant tonight. I have to take care of some things. Then I'll be on my regular schedule tomorrow."

"That's fine, dear. See you tomorrow."

After she got settled back at her home, she decided to go over to Ross's house to see what needed to be done to make it comfortable for him.

Melissa felt awkward unlocking his door and stepping inside, but she wanted to make sure he'd have everything he needed when Mike brought him home, hopefully the next day.

She stood in the front hallway and gazed around. Even with Whitney's help decorating his home, it felt like a bachelor's pad. She walked into the open living area and noted the lack of photographs and other finishing touches that turned a house into a home. Feeling as if she was snooping, she checked the other rooms on the main floor. A guest suite sat at one end of the house, away from the master suite. A third bedroom sat next to it and held unpacked cardboard boxes.

She went into the kitchen, automatically rinsed the dishes in the sink, and put them in the dishwasher. She opened the refrigerator and sighed at the lack of nourishing food. She'd go to the grocery store and shop at Collister's Farm Stand to take care of that problem. Making a note of what groceries to buy, she shook her head. No wonder Ross had told her that

Dirk would appreciate a homecooked meal. So would he.

After completing her grocery list, Melissa walked into the master suite on the first floor in a wing of its own. This is where Ross would recover.

She stood a moment, inhaling his spicy aftershave, the one she thought was so sexy. The bed was unmade. She hesitated and then went ahead and made it up, imagining Ross sleeping there. Unsettled, she checked the master bath, picked up the terry robe he'd left on the floor, and straightened up.

Not wanting to linger, she left and went to the grocery store. She was selecting orange juice when Dani walked up to her. "Hi, Melissa! What are you doing here? Is Ross home?"

Melissa turned to her. "No, but he's hoping to come home tomorrow. If not, then the following day. Mike is staying with Ross and will bring him back to Lilac Lake."

"Oh, that makes sense with your job and all," said Dani. "How's he doing?"

"He was pretty out of it this morning but seemed to be doing well this afternoon. I've already made plans to drive him to the sports rehab center in Concord when it's time, and he told me Crystal will take care of his meals for a while."

Dani smiled. "That's what I love about this town. Everyone is willing to help. Please let me know if you need me to take Ross to rehab."

"Thanks. I will." Melissa quickly gathered the things on her list, added ice cream for a treat, and checked out.

She returned to Ross's house, stored the food she'd bought, and left to go to the Collister's farm stand for fresh fruit and vegetables. The owners, Mary Lou and Joe Collister, were well-liked in the community. A stop at their farm market was as much about catching up with them and others in the area as it was about buying fresh fruit, vegetables, and other things foodies like her loved.

###

As soon as Melissa had parked her car and entered the red barn used for the farm stand, Mary Lou hurried over to her. A heavy-set woman with pretty hazel eyes and brown hair, Mary Lou was the type of woman you wanted to hug. She was always pleasant and was an eager listener. Her pet pig, Pansy, was never too far away.

"How's Ross?" Mary Lou asked. "Joe and I were in the stands when it happened, and I swear I heard a bone crack. It was terrible."

As she thought of that moment, a shiver traveled through Melissa. She thought she'd heard that sound too. "Ross is recovering from knee replacement surgery. He's hoping to be home in a day or two."

"It was such a shame that his motorcycle accident some years ago ended his baseball career. Now this." Mary Lou sighed. "He's such a personable man too. I'm happy he's staying in Lilac Lake, and he and Mike are building a sports center."

"Me, too," said Melissa. "Mike is with Ross now and will bring him home. I'll be taking care of trips to the rehab center, and Crystal is taking care of his meals for a while."

"You young women have it all worked out. Let me give you some early Honeycrisp apples to take to him."

"That would be lovely. I was going to buy some for him, but I know he'll love your gift. However, I need to stock up on produce for him, and I thought I'd pick up some of your frozen dinners for him and me."

"Splendid. Let me pick some out for you."

By the time Melissa was ready to leave, she had plenty of everything the farm stand had to offer.

"You come back now," said Mary Lou, hugging her. "More apples will be arriving along with fresh apple cider."

"Thanks. I'll let my parents know about the apples, and they'll place an order for the restaurant, along with the usual."

She was finishing putting away food in Ross's kitchen when her cell rang. *Dirk*.

"Hello, Dirk," she said, chiding herself for her sudden shyness.

"Hi, Melissa. I'm calling to see how you are. I know the accident on the baseball field has upset you. Are you still in Boston?"

"No, I came home this afternoon. Mike is staying with Ross and will bring him home in the next day or two. He's had his left knee replaced."

"I thought that might be the case after I heard about his motorcycle accident years ago. I guess he's been suffering with both knees since then. I hope he heals quickly."

"Me, too. What's going on with you?" Melissa asked and then waited breathlessly to find out why he'd called.

"I'm busy as usual," he said. "In addition to the usual maintenance and upkeep with patients' teeth, I'm now setting up an orthodontics clinic as part of the practice my uncle and I are sharing. I studied orthodontics, and I'm anxious to get started. So many kids here need braces."

"It's wonderful that you'll have that practice right in town. You'll be super busy."

"Not too busy to ask you out. I know it's last minute, but are you up for dinner tonight? I hear that Chica's has fabulous Mexican food."

Melissa heard the hopefulness in his voice and felt a shiver of excitement travel up her spine. "Their food is delicious. What time are you talking about?"

"I was thinking seven-thirty. Does that work for you?"

"Yes. This is a day off for me, so I can do it. It will be fun."

"Okay. I'll pick you up then."

Melissa ended the call and danced around Ross's kitchen. Having Dirk call her was perfect. She'd been waiting for a sign from him, and this was as positive as it could get.

CHAPTER TEN

AFTER PUTTING GROCERIES AWAY AT ROSS'S HOUSE AND her own, Melissa took a glass of iced tea out to her deck and sat in the sun, letting its warmth weave through her, melting away some of the day's tension. Just this morning, she'd awakened in Nettie's condo worried about Ross. Her emotions had been as confusing as her fatigue. She took a sip of tea, stretched her long legs out in front of her chair, and lifted her face to the sky.

The sound of birds chirping and calling to one another in the woods lining the backyard was as comfortable as a quilt in winter. She felt her limbs relax.

Sometime later, Melissa blinked in the sunlight and shook herself awake. She checked her watch. She still had plenty of time to get ready for Dirk and needed every minute because she intended to look her best. This was their first real date.

Following a soak in the tub, Melissa stood in front of her mirror, giving herself a steady look. Her grey eyes, sometimes stormy, now reflected excitement, adding a hint of green to them. Her rich brown hair held natural highlights of red, and hanging straight to her shoulders, it gleamed in the light from the mirror.

She added another swipe of coral color to her lips and turned away. She'd opted to wear a short denim skirt and an orange top lined with lace and now had doubts about her choice. She heard the sound of Dirk's car, gazed out the window, saw his blue jeep, and realized it was too late to make any wardrobe changes.

She greeted him at the door and relaxed when he said, "Wow! You look nice!"

Telling herself to enjoy the evening, she followed Dirk to his car and climbed into the passenger seat as he stood by.

"Thanks for agreeing to go out at the last minute. Some days, that's how it goes for me. I get so embroiled with my work that time slips away."

"I don't mind doing things without a lot of planning. My work consumes so much of my day that being flexible like this is the only way I get free time."

Dirk turned to her. "I like that."

Melissa returned his smile, silently chalking up another reason a relationship with him might work. "I love Mexican food, and Chica's is the best in our area. They've won some state awards, too."

"That's what I've heard. I can't wait to taste it," said Dirk.

Melissa gazed out the car window as Dirk headed south to a small commercial area outside of town. She noticed the colored lanterns lighting the parking perimeter at Chica's even before Dirk pulled into a parking space. The lanterns were part of the décor used inside and out to give the restaurant a festive feel. Seeing them always made her smile.

Dirk helped her out of the car and into the restaurant. The aroma of tomato, cilantro, and various spices swirled around them.

Mama Montoya greeted them, wearing a red-tiered skirt and a white blouse embroidered with colorful flowers, vines, and greenery. Her black hair had streaks of gray, but her face was unlined, and her dark-brown eyes warmed with friendliness.

"Melissa! So happy to see you!" Mama cried, hugging Melissa. She turned to Dirk. "And who is this handsome man?"

"This is Dirk McArthur, the new dentist in town," Melissa responded and turned to him.

"Mama Montoya is why so many of us in Lilac Lake love Mexican food. Her recipes are the real deal."

"Oh, yes. We use my mother's recipes and her mother's, too," said Mama Montoya. "All natural. From one chef to another, we appreciate that. Right, Melissa?"

"Absolutely." Melissa waved as a pretty, dark-haired young woman approached them.

"Hi, Melissa. I've fixed you a special table over by the window." She glanced at Dirk and said, "It's very romantic there."

Mama Montoya laughed. "My granddaughter, Pilar, is always talking about romance. But go and enjoy yourselves."

Dirk and Melissa exchanged shy glances and followed Pilar to the table.

"I think the occasion calls for a drink. What would you like?" Dirk asked her after they were seated.

"Chica's makes the best margaritas by adding a touch of orange juice. That's perfect for me."

"I'm going to stick to beer," Dirk said.

Pilar wrote down their order and said, "I'll be right back with your drinks." Melissa looked around the restaurant. It was crowded even for a weeknight. Tables were covered in red tablecloths, offsetting the bright turquoise-painted walls. The floor was terra cotta tile offset by the wooden tables and chairs. Mexican music played softly on the sound system, and each table held a large round flickering candle. Melissa sighed with appreciation.

Their drinks came, and after toasting one another, Melissa set down her glass. "Are you getting settled in Lilac Lake? You said things were chaotic at work, but do you like living here in this small town?"

"I really do. Growing up in the D.C. area, I was worried I'd find things too slow and too settled here. But I've seen how healthy it is to change pace, get outside, and enjoy sports. I don't want to get too insular, which is why I want to continue to enjoy traveling. My family went to China once, and I found it fascinating, notwithstanding the politics. Have you done much traveling?"

"Not too much," she said. "Not with my parents owning a restaurant. But when I was a child, they made sure we went to Disney World and visited Washington, D. C., and the west coast. But all our trips were in our country."

"There's so much to see in this world. I think you'd really like France and Italy for their food. You should go sometime."

"That's an enticing goal," she responded, wishing he'd said 'we' should go sometime. She reminded herself to slow down. This was only their first date.

A waitress in costume brought tortilla chips and salsa to their table. "Pilar says she's making you a special plate of tasting food. She hopes that will be okay with you but wants you, Melissa, to sample some of her new dishes."

"That would be delightful," said Melissa.

"Agreed," said Dirk.

The waitress left, and Dirk joked, "It pays to go to a restaurant with a chef. Did you always know that's what you wanted to be?"

"Pretty much," Melissa said. "I spent a lot of time in the restaurant's kitchen as a child. Back then, my father did most of the cooking. Since the restaurant is now enlarged and has a bigger staff, he no longer does as much of it."

"I have to admit I'm not much of a cook. That's why it was so nice to be invited to your house."

"Ross said you'd appreciate it," said Melissa without thinking.

"Ross? What's with you and him?" asked Dirk.

"He's a neighbor. A friend," said Melissa. "You could say he's like the brother I never had." Even as she spoke, she wondered if she was being honest. She didn't think a brother would look at her the way Ross had when he was dopey with medicine.

"He seems like a terrific guy. But then, everyone in your group seems likable. That's one of the reasons I enjoy Lilac Lake."

"Tell me more about your family. We've all met your sister, Diana."

Dirk grimaced. "I know she didn't make a favorable impression, but she's a nice kid sister. My father works for the government, and we've always lived in the Washington, D. C. area, mostly in Virginia. My mother has been a big organizer for a charity that deals with inner-city children. So, while they were doing important work, they weren't home often, making Diana and me close. Being able to be home with family is one reason small-town living is important to me."

"Do you want a big family?" Melissa asked, intrigued.

"At least two children, but I'm not ready for that. There's too much to see and do right here before I intend to settle down."

"Yes. Lilac Lake offers lots of things. Sports, hunting, canoeing, skiing. You'll be very busy," said Melissa, trying to show her support.

"And work, too," he said. "I'm going to be very busy with that."

They were still talking about life in Lilac Lake when Pilar delivered their meal. "In addition to accompaniments of beans and cilantro rice, your plates hold a chicken enchilada with a true molé sauce, a grilled lobster taco with serrano salsa verde and cilantro, and a duck carnitas quesadilla with a cheese blend, served with pasilla sauce and guacamole." She smiled. "There will be plenty for you to take home, but I wanted you to enjoy some different tastes. Especially the lobster taco."

"Boy! Does this look delicious!" said Dirk, giving Pilar a beaming smile.

Melissa couldn't help but smile, too.

"Enjoy!" said Pilar. "And, Melissa, I want your honest opinion."

"Presentation and aromas are A+," Melissa said, giving her a thumbs up.

After Pilar left, Melissa and Dirk were silent as they dug into their food. After a few bites, she murmured, "M-m-m."

"I know, right?" said Dirk. "Delicious. The taco is outstanding."

"I'm enjoying the enchilada. Did you know molé sauce is made with chocolate? It's so delicious."

"I'll try it now."

Melissa watched him enjoying his food and filled with satisfaction. "You know, it makes any chef happy to see someone enjoying their food."

"No worries there," said Dirk, taking another forkful.

At the end of their meal, Melissa and Dirk both asked for take-home boxes.

"Well?" said Pilar, coming over to them. "What's the verdict?"

"A total win," said Melissa. "I will tell my mother to tell visitors about you. Our restaurants are very different, but if they like one, people will likely like the other. This isn't typical American/Mexican food; this is truly a gourmet meal."

"Thanks," said Pilar. "That's what I try to tell my parents. They should be advertising the restaurant differently."

"Wonderful food," said Dirk, pulling out his wallet.

Pilar held up her hand to stop him. "No, no. This is on me. Thanks for helping me."

As she walked away, Dirk placed a thirty-dollar tip on the table. "For our waitress."

"Thanks," said Melissa. "Tipping is really important to servers, and you were very generous."

He grinned. "I'm a nice guy."

Her lips curved. "You certainly are."

CHAPTER ELEVEN

ON THE WAY BACK TO HER HOUSE, MELISSA FELT HER nerves tingling. She hoped Dirk might want to stay a while, but she didn't know how to ask without sounding awkward. But she was dying to see what chemistry they had. They were both reserved, so it might take time to be comfortable with one another alone.

Dirk drove onto the driveway to her house and stopped the car.

"Would you like to come inside?" she asked, feeling her fingers growing cold. *What if he said no?*

"Thanks. I would," he answered somewhat formally, and she realized he was as nervous as she.

She led him inside and then turned to him. "Want a cup of coffee? Water?"

"Water sounds great. Thanks," he said.

"Why don't you go out to the porch, and I'll bring it to you," she said. "Make yourself comfortable."

As Dirk headed outside, Melissa hurried into the powder room to check her appearance and then went into the kitchen to get them each a glass of ice water.

Melissa carried their water to the porch and was pleased that Dirk had chosen to sit on the couch rather than in one of the chairs.

He looked up and smiled at her.

She sat beside him, and they playfully clinked their glasses together.

After sipping his water, Dirk set down his glass and turned

to her. "I hope you enjoyed the evening as much as I did."

"Oh, yes." She placed her glass on the coffee table and faced him. "It was fun. And such delicious food."

"Exactly. Though I'm not a cook, you could call me a foodie because I love to try different things."

"That's so important. Being free to try something new is important to me." She laughed. "But I'm not sure I could eat everything you did with your family in China."

He chuckled. "For political reasons, it was important. We didn't want to lose face in front of our hosts." He wrapped an arm around her and pulled her close.

She nestled against his chest and felt the beat of his heart.

When he tilted her face up to his, her pulse raced. This was what she wanted. And when his lips met hers, she let out a soft groan of pleasure.

His lips were soft but sure.

When they pulled apart, he smiled at her. "I want to get to know you better, Melissa. I hope this will be the beginning."

Her heartbeat thudded in her ears. "Me, too."

When he kissed her again, she responded.

And his kisses deepened.

She thought how wonderful it felt to be in his arms when he suddenly sat up.

"I'm sorry, Melissa. I'd better go. I just remembered I have an early appointment tomorrow, and I didn't realize how late it was."

Caught off guard, Melissa got to her feet and straightened her clothes. Uncertain about what was happening, she said politely, "I'll walk you out."

At the front door, he gave her a quick kiss on the cheek. "Thanks. See you soon."

Melissa closed the door and leaned against it, breathing hard as disappointment pounded through her, and her emotions took a nosedive. Dirk had left so abruptly. Had she done something wrong?

The next morning, Ross called to tell her he'd be home that afternoon. "Thought I'd better warn you because they let me leave when I promised I'd have help at home and getting to the sports rehab center. I hope that doesn't put you in an awkward situation."

"Of course not. It makes me feel useful to be needed," Melissa said. "I've restocked the refrigerator, and the house is straightened, ready for you."

"Melissa, you didn't have to do that," said Ross.

"That's what neighbors do," she responded.

"Thanks. I'm grateful you live next door. I'll see you later."

"You will," she said, content to have an excuse not to worry about Dirk.

Filled with purpose, Melissa made a couple of her quick and easy dishes to take over to Ross's house. He could use or freeze them for when Crystal couldn't provide a meal.

As she worked in the kitchen, she thought about her friendship with Ross. It was so natural. Maybe because there was no pretense between them, they both knew where they stood. That's the same openness she'd hoped to develop with Dirk, with the idea of moving forward together. They seemed such a perfect match ... at least on paper.

Melissa was placing the last of her casseroles in Ross's refrigerator when she heard a car pull into his driveway. She went outside to greet them.

Mike ran around the back of his car and opened the door for Ross. He helped Ross to his feet, and they turned to face Melissa.

"Welcome home," she said, coming over to them. "I've put a blanket and pillows on the couch in the living room if you want to rest there. And I've got casseroles in the refrigerator. Come inside, and we'll get you settled."

"Thank you. Seems as if you've got it all set," said Ross, struggling to get upright.

Mike handed him the portable walker, and Ross used it to balance himself until he got a little steadier.

Observing him, Melissa smiled. Ross seemed to be showing off. Mike caught her eye and winked at her.

Inside, Ross and Mike made their way to the couch.

As Ross sat down, Melissa hurried to put pillows behind him.

Ross looked up at her and smiled. "Ah, that feels good. Thanks, neighbor."

She felt her cheeks flush but tried to ignore it. "You're welcome. Do you want me to put a chicken casserole in the oven for you? Crystal will bring you a meal later on."

"I'm ready. How about you, Ross?" said Mike.

"Sure. Hospital food isn't at all the same as something of yours."

Melissa saw that Ross was tired and turned to Mike. "I'll set the timer for the casserole, and when the buzzer rings, you can serve it. It's made fresh, so it shouldn't take longer than thirty minutes. In the meantime, I have lemonade, water, and some sodas in the refrigerator. I also made cookies that are ready to eat anytime."

Mike placed a hand on her shoulder. "Thanks. I'm ready to move into the neighborhood, so you'll be this nice to me."

Melissa laughed. "The more the merrier. Let me know if I can do anything else. And, Ross, let me know when you're due to go to rehab. I've scheduled my time, so I can take you any morning."

Ross gave her a little wave, and she left, feeling happy about all she'd done for him. She'd never forget the sound of the two of them hitting the ground with a jarring thud.

When she returned to her house, she showered and changed for her shift at the restaurant. Cooking for others and giving them pleasure with excellent food was an important part of who she was.

At the restaurant, her mother smiled. "How did it go with Ross?"

"He's home. He's using a walker to steady himself. I have a feeling he will recover quickly because he's in great physical condition."

Her mother lifted her eyebrows and studied her.

Melissa pushed away her mother's hopeful look with a wave of her hand. "Mother, it's not like that. Besides, most men in my social group are in shape, including Dirk."

"How was your evening with Dirk?" her mother asked.

Though she was concerned and uncertain, Melissa forced a smile. "Nice."

"He's a likable man," said her mother with approval. "Everyone who's been to the dentist lately has told me how professional he is, how gentle."

"He's going to open an orthodontics practice at the office. That's what he studied," Melissa said, hoping for more approval.

Her mother smiled. "With our growing population, something like that is needed." Her mother checked her watch. "You'd better head into the kitchen. I have to get busy here."

As she worked, Melissa found her rhythm chopping ingredients for a fresh fish chowder and couldn't help thinking about the Mexican meal she'd shared with Dirk. She could tell Mama Montoya liked him, and it made her happy. She'd dated someone a couple of years ago who Mama hadn't been impressed with. She'd let Melissa know in subtle ways. It stung at the time, but he'd turned out to be a player who would've ruined her life if Melisa hadn't ended the relationship. Because, once again, she'd shown how naïve she was about men.

That night, after an early evening at the restaurant, Melissa headed to Jake's to see who in her gang might be there.

She was pleased to see Misty, Crystal, and Emmett with Mike and Dirk.

"Ah, I'm happy to see you're still here," she said, sitting at the community table.

"We got off to a late start," Crystal said. "I can't stay long, but Mike has been telling us about Ross's recovery. It will be several weeks until he's left on his own."

"Yes, but knowing Ross, he'll recover quickly," said Mike. "He's a very determined, independent guy. But thanks to Melissa, he will be well taken care of." He winked at her.

Melissa smiled. "I hope so." She turned as a waitress appeared and ordered a glass of merlot.

After the waitress left, Melissa told Misty, "It's nice to see you. I hear you'll become a teacher in one of our local schools."

"Yes, at the elementary school. I can't wait. Of course, I might still be working part-time at the café."

"That'll keep you busy for sure," said Melissa. She liked Crystal's little sister and remembered how Crystal had raised her in the past days when their mother couldn't. "Anything else exciting going on?"

"I'm talking to Mike about a refreshment stand at the baseball field he and Ross are building," said Crystal. "I'm thinking it could be run by high school students, giving them a chance to learn how to provide food to a group. I'd hire someone to help them get started and give them a list of the food they need to order."

"Interesting idea. It would give the kids training and a chance to earn some money. Kudos to you, Crystal. You're always doing something for the community. Adding the kids' baked goods to the Summer Faire baking contest was genius. We need to get more teenagers interested in the hospitality business, even if the work is sometimes exhausting."

"That's why I'm hoping to help Crystal. To give her more time to herself and Emmett," said Misty, smiling at her sister.

"I wish I had a younger sister to help me," said Melissa.

"How about a brother?" teased Mike.

Melissa, Crystal, and Misty looked at one another and laughed.

"Brothers, I'm sure, are special, but women need sisters, even if they're just sisters of the heart," said Crystal, more serious now.

Looking at her female friends sitting with her, Melissa thought how true it was. She glanced at Dirk and smiled.

While she talked to Emmett, Dirk rose. "I'll see you guys later. I have to go."

Melissa waited for him to say something to her, but he turned and walked away. Embarrassed, she sat silently, wondering what was going on.

CHAPTER TWELVE

THE NEXT MORNING, MELISSA DID HER NEIGHBORLY duty and crossed her lawn to Ross's house. He'd put on a brave face yesterday, but she could well imagine the pain he must be in. A hot breakfast might make a difference.

When she knocked on the door, Mike answered it. "Good morning! Come on in."

Melissa smiled. "I thought a healthy, hot breakfast might be welcome."

"A definite yes from me," he responded. "Let me go find Ross. He's just getting up."

He left her and quickly returned. "Ross is all for it. He says it sounds great."

"Give me a few minutes, and I'll whip up bacon, eggs, and English muffins. Ross needs to eat well following surgery."

Melissa went to the kitchen, comfortable with where everything was, got coffee going, and started to cook bacon.

She was mixing seasonings into a bowl of eggs when Ross appeared, making his way slowly to the kitchen table with his walker. "Something smells good."

"Nothing like bacon to win a man's stomach," she said.

He chuckled. "I thought the saying was 'cooking is the way to win a man's heart.'"

She laughed, too. "Test it out. Then we'll talk about it." She handed him a strip of crisp, cooked bacon.

He ate it and then patted his stomach. "I liked it. Thanks."

Melissa continued cooking the meal, pleased she could do this for them.

After serving them each a plate of food, she helped herself to an English muffin and joined them at the table with a mug of coffee.

"When do you start rehab?" she asked Ross.

"I have someone coming to the house to do some exercises for the next four days. Then, as long as you're still willing, I'll need you to start taking me to the Physical Therapy Center outside of Concord."

"That's a definite yes," said Melissa.

"Good," said Mike, "because I'm leaving for Florida later this afternoon. I have to check in on my tennis clinic. I'm running a tennis camp there for the next four weeks."

"No worries. I've already scheduled my mornings to do this," said Melissa. "Now, I'm going to go home and work in the garden before heading into the restaurant."

She got up from her seat, bussed the dirty plates and silverware to the sink, and turned to Mike. "Will you load the dishwasher?"

"Sure," he said. "I'm used to 'batching' it and keeping my condo clean."

She smiled with approval, gave him a little salute, and left. "See you tomorrow. Crystal is fixing your dinner. Right, Ross?"

"Yes, Ma'am. My dinners are taken care of for the next week or so."

"I love our little town and the people in it," said Melissa. "Safe trip home, Mike."

A few days later, Melissa stood in the kitchen of her parents' restaurant, wondering what her life might have been like if she hadn't grown up in the restaurant business. There were days when she loved working in the kitchen, and her soul was filled with satisfaction because she could do something she loved. And then, like today, she felt restless. Were all her days going to be spent cooking in this kitchen? Wasn't there more to life? She'd tried to have more free time for other things, but inevitably, she ended up back here.

"Hey, are you alright?" her father asked her.

She looked at him and smiled. He was a man of medium height, with gray hair and enough of a tummy to look the role in his chef's uniform of black-checked pants and white jacket. His brown eyes were all-seeing and filled with the soft love she knew he had for her.

"I'm wondering if I can get another day off each week. I'm missing out on so many interesting things all my friends are doing."

His gray-eyed gaze, like hers, rested on her. "I know how busy we've been. Summer is the most important season for us. But we'll work it out as long as you're not asking for Thursday through Sunday off. You already have Monday off. Want to make it a two-day rest and take off Tuesdays too?"

"That's a help, I suppose," Melissa answered unenthusiastically. "Mom has already agreed to let me take off after the kitchen closes Saturday night. Normally, I'd help with the clean-up, but if I can leave at ten, it gives me some time with my friends who might still be at Jake's."

Her father clapped a hand on her shoulder. "I appreciate your help, Melissa. After years of cooking together, we know what one another will do before it happens. That's a big deal in a commercial kitchen."

"I know how much you appreciate me, Dad. But everyone else in town seems to be pairing up, and I don't want to miss my chance to create a family of my own."

Her father clapped a hand to his mouth. "I had no idea. You've always been so determined to be your own woman, do things your way, and be on your own."

"Please, Dad, don't say anything to Mom about my reasons for wanting time off. She'll have a wedding planned before I even get a chance to date. Maybe it's my hormones talking, but I don't want to miss out on having a life outside of Fins."

He wrapped his arms around her. "My darling girl, I'll cooperate however I can, but I can't give you up in the kitchen on Friday or Saturday nights. Do you understand?"

Melissa nodded, knowing it was the truth. "Maybe next winter, we can do something about my schedule."

"Maybe we can interview for a sous-chef to add to the mix." Her father patted her on the back. "You're right. Let's not say too much to your mother, or she'll worry about you and the business."

"Thanks, Dad." Feeling better, Melissa went to put on her jacket. Dirk was acting as if they hadn't dated. Was she wasting her time hoping they had a chance of building a relationship?

The next morning, Melissa drove next door to Ross's house. This was the first day of his recovery at the rehabilitation center in Concord. As precious as time was to her, she was happy to chauffeur him there. Being with him and sharing companionship was easy.

It was satisfying being able to talk to Ross about anything. Even Dirk. She still didn't know what was going on with him. Dirk had said he'd call, but he hadn't.

"How are you feeling overall?" she asked Ross as he greeted her at the door. "You seem much more agile."

"I've had other injuries before and have learned just to keep going, keep my mind off it," he said. "I don't have the pressure to get back into a game. The physical requirements and expectations for playing a professional sport can be difficult."

She helped him to her car and stood aside as he carefully lifted his leg into the passenger side.

She shut the door, went around the car, and slid behind the wheel.

As she drove, she said to Ross, "You told me you always wanted to play baseball. I knew from a young age I wanted to cook with my father. So, I understand your willingness to do whatever it takes to make sure you have a speedy recovery."

"Do you ever get tired of your job? My injuries forced me out of baseball, but I still miss it."

"Funny you should ask that," said Melissa. "I talked to my dad recently to see if I could have another day off because I'm missing out socially. He said yes, but I'm not sure what it would take to make me quit completely. It's always been part of my life, even as a young child."

"I get it," said Ross. "It's hard to strike a balance when you are successful at your job."

Though the trip wouldn't take long, Melissa enjoyed being out in the countryside. She loved seeing the stacked-stone walls and trees lining many of the back-country roads leading to the highway.

Concord, the capitol of New Hampshire, was home to the State House, a gold-domed building completed in 1819. Melissa never tired of seeing it and being in the attractive New England town. It was home to many historic sites and was famous for their carriage making—Concord Coaches. It was this sort of history that drew people to the city. Melissa was no exception. After living in small-town Lilac Lake, it was a treat to go there occasionally.

Melissa pulled up in front of a red brick building that housed the physical rehabilitation center and two other medical offices. She got out of the car and went around to Ross's side to help him inside.

"You don't need to do this," said Ross, but Melissa noticed he held onto her arm as he walked up the ramp to get inside.

At the door, she said, "I'll wait outside in the car. I've got a book series going."

"Come on inside and wait. You'll be more comfortable there," said Ross with a note of concern.

She walked into the office with him to please him and noticed a comfortable waiting area.

The receptionist checking him in smiled up at Ross. "It's quite an honor to have you here. Margo can't wait to work with you."

A young woman with long blond hair woven into two braids walked over to greet him. Wearing jeans and a sleeveless top, she appeared to be at the height of physical conditioning. "Hi, Ross. I'm Margo, your new torturer."

He grinned at the challenge. "We'll see about that. Meet my neighbor, Melissa Hendrickson. She's kind enough to drive me here for my appointments. She's a talented chef, so if you come to Lilac Lake, be sure to eat at Fins."

"I've eaten there, and the food was delicious," said Margo.

"Hi, Margo, and thanks for the promotion, Ross," said Melissa, feeling her cheeks burn. She wished she could be more sophisticated and handle compliments better, but she wasn't used to them.

After Ross and Margo headed out back, Melissa sat and opened her eReader. While she read, she could hear Ross's efforts echoing in the workout room as he pushed through the pain of getting full use of his leg again. This surgery was simpler than the ones he'd endured before, the ones following his motorcycle accident, and she realized how hard he'd worked to walk naturally again with pins in his leg.

She felt fortunate to have someone like Ross as a friend. He was kind, hard-working, and determined. In some ways, they were alike. Her thoughts flew to Dirk. What had happened to make him back away?

CHAPTER THIRTEEN

LATER, WHEN ROSS STEPPED INTO THE WAITING ROOM, he had a towel wrapped around his neck, and his face was still flushed from the exercise.

"How was it?" she asked him, turning off her reader, sliding it into her bag, and standing.

"Like Margo warned, torture. But it's all good. The few weeks following surgery and what you do to get back into shape determine what a full recovery will look like."

They went outside, and as Melissa helped him into the car, he turned to her. "Can you do me a big favor?"

"Sure, what is it?"

"I know how important healthy food is. And I've had a lot of food delivered to my house. But what I want right now is a drive-through hamburger and fries. I don't care which restaurant it is. Can we do that?"

Melissa laughed. "What makes you think I don't enjoy a double-double burger now and then? Though I must admit, no one makes better fries than Fins."

"The treat's on me," said Ross, pulling his legs into the car.

She closed his door and climbed into the car, already hungry.

Later, Ross turned to her as they sat in her car eating their lunch. "You're such a good sport, Melissa. Thanks for doing this."

"No problem. In return, I need to ask you something. My

first date with Dirk went well. Or so I thought. But he hasn't called to set up a second date."

A look of surprise crossed Ross's face. "Haven't you heard? Dirk's uncle has some sort of health issue and can't work. Dirk has been covering for him while getting his orthodontist practice going. No one has seen or heard from him in days. I guess he's working like crazy to keep everything going smoothly."

"I must have missed the news. No one at Jake's has mentioned it, but then, I haven't been to Jake's in a while. Sometimes, I feel so left out."

"I get how you must feel, but believe me, his not calling has nothing to do with you. Just circumstances. The only reason I know is that I had to cancel my appointment with him."

"Oh, good. I thought it had something to do with me," said Melissa, feeling her stress ease.

Ross studied her. "You've been holding out on me. You never mentioned you were a state champion for the high school softball team. What's up with that?"

Melissa shrugged. "It seems silly compared to your career."

"You underestimate yourself, Melissa. I bet the boys in high school were crazy about you."

"A couple," Melissa admitted. "But it never went anywhere. High school is tough for some of us. It certainly didn't help me. I was the tall tomboy with no fashion sense at all."

"Well, things have and can change," said Ross. He crumbled up the paper bag that had held their lunch. "If you drive by the bin, I can pitch this inside."

"Deal," said Melissa, relieved their conversation had ended.

At home, Melissa texted a message to Dirk. *"Sorry to hear about your uncle. Anything I can do?"*

About an hour later, she received a reply. *"Working hard. Will call when I can. Thanks."*

Feeling much better, Melissa headed to work.

It was a slow Wednesday night, so Melissa encouraged her father to take the evening off. He worked as hard or even harder than she, and as August was nearing the mid-point, fatigue was setting in for all of them at the restaurant.

As Melissa cooked and kept the kitchen organized, she didn't have time to think about her personal life. Being the head chef was like being a conductor of an orchestra. It was her job to shout the orders to the staff and to make sure food was being cooked to time the arrival at the pass together. Each person at a table had to receive their meal at the same time. The hot items had to be hot, and the cold ones had to be cold. Tasting occasionally to make sure the blend of seasonings and flavors was right was also part of her job. It was tricky cooking fish. If not carefully watched, it could quickly go from raw to overdone.

When the evening rush was over, Melissa was ready to step outside for a breath of fresh air. Standing by the kitchen door, she saw storm clouds rolling in. If the forecasters were right, they were due for some thunderstorms, which would, hopefully, clear out some of the humidity. She patted her forehead with her handkerchief, loving the cooler air outside the kitchen.

Staring up at the roiling sky, she hurried to get everything cleaned up. No matter how messy the kitchen might become, every night, it was cleaned until spotless. Keeping a kitchen in order was part of being a good chef.

Inside, the staff had begun the process. "Thanks, everyone," she said, picking up a spatula to scrape off the residue from the grate of the indoor grill.

With everyone as anxious as she to beat the storm home, they made quick work of it. By the time they were done, her mother was closing the door on the last customer.

"I'll help vacuum in the morning," said Melissa to her. "Why don't you go home? There's a storm coming. They said it could be a wicked one."

"Thanks, sweetheart. I think I will," her mother said.

Melissa walked out of the restaurant with her, checked the sky, and dashed to her car, hoping to make it home in time.

In the middle of the night, Melissa's cell phone chimed. She stirred in bed, annoyed. *Who would be calling her at such an early hour?* She grabbed her cell. "Hello."

"It's Dad. You had better get to town as quickly as you can. Fins is on fire."

CHAPTER FOURTEEN

WITH SHAKING HANDS AND A SENSE OF HORROR, MELISSA managed to get dressed and hurried to her car.

Backing out of the driveway, she saw how peaceful her neighborhood looked, and, for a wishful moment, she could almost imagine her father had made a bizarre crank call.

But as she tore down the road toward the center of town, she heard sirens coming from neighboring villages and knew it was all too real.

That sense of reality didn't compare to seeing her family's restaurant going up in flames. Her stomach wrenched, and she struggled to hold in its contents.

She parked her car as close as possible, got out, and looked for her parents.

They were standing in the street with a crowd of supporters watching the flames. Melissa's heart began to beat so fast she thought she might faint or throw up. She rushed over to them. "Oh, my God!"

"The fire department is here, but it's not looking good," said her father. His grim expression told its own story. "I suspect we're in for a total loss."

"What happened?" she asked.

White-faced, her father shook his head. "We don't know. Some think the fire started in the attic and that lightning may have struck the building. But most restaurant fires start in the kitchen. The fire department will investigate."

"All our life's work gone," her mother said as tears ran down her cheeks.

Unaware of her tears, Melissa hugged her and watched as the firemen worked to save nearby buildings. Thankfully, Fins was a free-standing structure, but the fire was so hot it was peeling paint off the exterior walls of a nearby insurance company's building.

Numb, Melissa was momentarily unaware that Crystal and Whitney were holding her up between them.

"I'm so sorry," murmured Whitney. "I know what this restaurant has meant to you, your family, and the entire town."

"They'll find a cause for it, I'm sure," said Crystal, whose café was far enough away not to be harmed.

Melissa stared at what was fast becoming the remnants of her family's livelihood. The building seemed to be collapsing into itself.

"A couple of minor explosions had occurred when the fire erupted in the kitchen," said her father. "We're just grateful no one was in the building."

The thought of that happening made Melissa feel even sicker. She looked up as Ross hobbled toward her with his walker. He moved past Crystal and Whitney to hug her. "Dani and Brad brought me. I'm so sorry to see this."

"Melissa's dad said most restaurant fires start in the kitchen," said Whitney.

"He's right," said Melissa, wondering if she'd forgotten to do anything before leaving last night. The thought of her being at fault caused her legs to wobble.

Ross grabbed hold and held on tight with one hand. As if he could read her mind, he said, "It's not your fault. No matter what they find. Understand?"

Dirk made his way toward them. "Melissa! I just heard and came as quickly as I could. Are you and your family alright?"

Ross moved away so Dirk could approach her. "We're fine.

No one was hurt, but it looks like our restaurant is gone." She wiped the tears off her face with the sleeve of her shirt.

Dirk wrapped his arms around her. "I'm so sorry. If I can do anything to help, please let me know."

"Thanks, but this is one of those times when there's nothing anyone can do." She gazed at what was left of the burning building and wondered how anything could be destroyed so quickly.

"When did the fire start?" Dirk asked.

In a daze, Melissa looked at her parents standing together, a crowd of sympathizers surrounding them. "I don't know."

She moved toward her parents.

They held out their arms to her. She rushed to them, and the three of them huddled together while the firemen sprayed the embers and continued to spray the two closest buildings.

Later that morning, Melissa sat with her parents and the new, young Fire Chief, Scott Kane. The Chief was a heavy-set man who'd come with excellent references. Though his work entailed mostly small home and woodland fires, he knew about the possible causes of restaurant fires.

"It started in the kitchen," he explained. "Most probably from some faulty equipment. Can you think of what might have contributed to the cause of the fire?"

Melissa glanced at her parents. "I wonder if it could be the gas grill. We used it often last night."

"Or the deep fat fryer," said her mother. "I saw a lot of French fries and fried fish going out."

"Either of those seems likely," said Scott. "Have you been in touch with your insurance agency?"

Melissa's father nodded. "Yes. I met with him last month, and he encouraged me to raise my insurance coverage. I almost didn't."

"It's expensive, but thank God, we have it," said Melissa's mother.

"Looking over the remains, I suggest we scrape the area clean before it becomes dangerous to anyone. In the meantime, we'll fence it off. After things have cooled off, you can look for anything you might want to save. But from what I've seen, it won't be much. I'm sorry."

"Susan and I have been talking about retirement, but we hadn't expected it to happen this soon," said Melissa's father. "We'll have to think long and hard about rebuilding."

Scott emitted a sympathetic grunt. "It's such a shame to lose you. Having Fins here was a huge benefit to the town. It was a favorite of mine and everyone else's."

Melissa's father turned to her. "Well, we have a very talented chef in my daughter. We'll have to see what she thinks."

Melissa remained silent. Her emotions were so mixed. She'd complained about working such long hours, shouldn't she feel a sense of freedom? But seeing the pain on her parents' faces, she felt deep sorrow. And guilt set in. Had she or one of her staff caused the fire? She was on duty. She might have missed something.

Scott stood. "You'll have plenty of time to think things over. We'll get back to you with whatever news we have."

While her father led Scott to the door, Melissa turned to her mother. "Do you think I forgot to do something, check something?"

Her mother clasped her hand. "I was there at the restaurant too. It's not your fault or mine. You follow a routine every night. We all do."

Until they found the actual cause of the fire, Melissa knew her emotions would be in turmoil.

CHAPTER FIFTEEN

AFTER MELISSA RETURNED HOME, SHE COULDN'T WAIT TO take off her clothes and throw them in the washing machine to get rid of the acrid smoke smell from the fire. After doing that, Melissa stepped into the shower, shaken to realize her whole life had changed. The future she'd envisioned had been as burned to ashes as the restaurant.

Melissa was now free to leave town, work elsewhere, and do something as different as she'd once thought she'd wanted. But after having so many friends return to Lilac Lake, she knew she wanted to stay. But it would take months, perhaps a year to rebuild. Would she and her parents want the same kind of restaurant if they moved forward? Or something simpler?

Beneath the double sprays of water in the shower, she scrubbed her hair, hoping to return it to the flowery aroma it usually had. The warmth of the water caressed her body, and she suddenly felt so weak she couldn't stand without holding onto the grab bar on the wall of tile.

Still weak, she emerged from the shower and wrapped a towel around herself. She hadn't eaten since last night, and she'd been too upset to eat this morning. Afraid of fainting, she stumbled into the kitchen to get some food.

The doorbell rang.

Melissa crept to the door and looked through the front door's peephole. *Crystal.*

She opened the door and stepped back. "Hi. Come on in. What brings you here?"

"This," said Crystal, holding up a plate of food. "I figured you were too busy, too upset to eat much, and I brought you some of my orange chocolate chip cupcakes. They're a pick-me-up when you need something to get you going."

"Oh, Crystal, you're a lifesaver! Excuse my appearance. I just got out of the shower. Can I get you coffee, tea, water, anything?"

"No, thanks. I won't keep you. I need to get back to the café. You understand how that is." Crystal set the plate down on the kitchen counter and turned to give her a quick embrace. "I remember how kind you were to me growing up, and I'm delighted to help you in any way I can."

Tears stung Melissa's eyes. "You don't know how much that means to me."

Crystal gave her a sweet smile. "Just slide the plate in the microwave for a few minutes to heat them. See you later."

After Crystal left, Melissa put on a robe, heated the treat, and sat down to eat it. The close-knit community was one reason she didn't want to leave town.

She finished her snack and, restless, wandered outside. Ross had canceled his physical rehab appointment, so she had nothing to do. Hoping to escape the trauma that still filled her, she walked over to her garden. Getting her hands in the soil and pulling weeds was just what she needed. It would give her a sense of accomplishment.

She went to her garage and pulled out her gardening tools. Anything to keep busy. But as she worked, thoughts continued to occupy her mind. She and her parents had found their safe was intact. Therefore, they didn't lose important information or money they hadn't yet deposited as they did every morning. But had her father canceled all their food orders? What other things needed to be done?

The reality of how life would be going forward hit her once

again. Staring up into the sky, clear now after the storm, she wondered if the fire was a sign that she should move on to something new. It was both exciting and devastating to think that. Cooking was part of who she was.

"Hey, there! How are you doing?"

Melissa whipped around to find Ross approaching her slowly with a cane.

She got up off her knees and faced him. "I'm trying to keep active as we wait for news of how the fire started. I pray it had nothing to do with human error because I was manning the kitchen last night."

"That's why I'm here. Your mother asked me to check on you. She knows we're friends and neighbors. She understands you think the fire might be your fault, but neither of us wants you to dwell on it. Accidents and fires happen."

"Let's go sit on the porch. It'll be more comfortable for you there." Melissa helped him across the grass and up onto the screened-in porch.

He took a seat on the couch, and she sat in a chair nearby. "Can I get you a glass of iced tea or lemonade?" she asked.

"Lemonade will be perfect," he said. "Thanks."

Happy to have something to do, she got up, went into the kitchen, and soon returned to the porch with the lemonade.

Ross accepted the drink from her and said, "I told your mother at the fire scene I'd help in any way I can. That's why she called me."

"Thanks, I appreciate it."

"She and your father are not doing well," said Ross. "Otherwise, I'm sure she'd be here herself. She told me they might take a long break after this."

"They're thinking of retiring but won't make a move until they're sure about what I want." She sighed. "I don't know what that is. I feel as if the world around me has vanished. The only thing keeping me grounded right now are friends like you."

"At least you have that," said Ross. "Everyone is rallying around the idea of your running the next restaurant, but it's because, selfishly, we'll all miss Fins."

"Believe me, I know. But that can't be a reason for me to make a life choice." She heard her note of despair and became silent.

"I've had to go through an unexpected life change, too, so I know how you feel," Ross said. "For now, I suggest you forget it. Just bide your time."

"You're right. I've got to stop worrying about it. Answers will come in time." She studied him. "How did I ever find such a friend as you?"

Ross shrugged, though his cheeks colored. "Good friends help whenever or however they can."

"Well, I appreciate you," she said. "I'll be very happy to take you to your rehab center. It'll give me something to do while I try to recover and will be only a small measure of my thanks."

"I enjoy your company, but the sessions won't last too long. Margo says I'm doing very well."

"She'll be sad to see them end, I'm sure. She enjoys your sessions."

"She's excellent at her job. That's all that matters to me," said Ross.

Melissa was impressed that Ross wasn't the kind of man who would take advantage of a beautiful young woman helping him to recover. Some professional athletes seemed to fall into that trap.

She and Ross talked about what the fire might mean for other restaurants in the area.

"Maybe Crystal will keep the Lilac Lake Café open for dinner now," Melissa said.

"You could help her if you want to keep busy."

Melissa let out a long sigh. "So many things to think about. For now, I will take your suggestion and just chill out. Nothing must be decided yet."

Ross got to his feet. "I've got to get back to my house. I'm working on some ideas for the sports center. Mike wants me to meet with him in Florida as soon as I can to look at a center down there. But it'll be a few weeks before I can even consider it."

"How would you get there?" she asked.

"I'm not sure," he said. "The trip depends on my dad and how he's feeling."

"If I can help, you know I will," she said.

Ross gave her a little salute. "Thanks. See you later."

Melissa watched as Ross made his way to his house next door. When she'd built her house, she'd had no idea what good friends they would become.

That evening, she went to visit her parents. Ross had told her that they were not doing well with having their lives shattered. Her mother, usually so strong, was weepy about the future.

Her dad was quiet as he grilled steaks for dinner. But when they sat down, he said, "We need to make a list of items lost for the insurance people. We haven't lost much in food because we buy fresh things and keep little as a backup. I went down to see the restaurant this afternoon. Our big freezer was destroyed, and there wasn't anything salvageable. I talked to one of our restaurant suppliers, and he said we shouldn't even try to rescue heavily damaged equipment, food items, or anything affected by the fire."

"That will add to the cost of rebuilding," her mother said. "After twenty-five years in the business, we've collected many useful utensils, special appliances, and even things like unique seasonings that will be hard to replace. The thought is overwhelming."

"We can start new," her father said. "Maybe make Fins even better than it was."

"I want whatever is best for you, Melissa," her mother said. "I thought you were set for life, knowing you'd eventually own a restaurant as successful as ours."

"While it's a wonderful gesture, it leaves me trapped in a sense," she said. "I'm trying to decide on my personal life right now. I like living here in Lilac Lake, but maybe it's not meant to be. I still don't have a special person in my life."

"What about Ross?" her mother said. "You couldn't find a better man."

"It takes two people to make a relationship, remember? We're friends. Great friends. But that's as far as it's going to go. As you said, he's a decent man, but he's not interested in me."

Her mother emitted a long sigh, and Melissa was taken back through the years to the days of high school when she was the same dateless person she was now. Unable to handle her mother's disappointment, she got up from the dinner table.

"I'm sorry, but I'm not feeling well. It's all too much to think about. I'm going home."

Her mother gave her a sad look. "We love you, Melissa."

Recalling how her mother had always said that on dateless high school nights, Melissa wanted to weep.

She kept herself together as she drove her car to her home. But when she pulled into the driveway and saw one lonely light on in her empty house, she let the tears she'd held back roll down her cheeks.

CHAPTER SIXTEEN

AFTER A RESTLESS NIGHT DURING WHICH SHE FOUGHT feeling insecure and helpless, she got up, determined to have a better day. She was delighted to have the opportunity to drive Ross to his rehab clinic. The task would fill the morning.

Melissa showered and dressed, leaving her long auburn hair down to dry. Working in the kitchen, she wore it either in a bun, tied back in a ponytail, or woven into a pigtail. Her mother had told her that her hair and her eyes were her best features. Now, staring into a mirror, Melissa realized she wasn't as ugly as her mother sometimes made her feel, even though she had her father's strong nose and chin. She brushed away hurts from the past and left.

In the kitchen, she fixed a cup of coffee and carried it out to the screened-in porch. It was going to be a scorcher of a day. Cicadas were already making their high-pitched noises as if knowing it would be too hot to do much later.

Melissa loved her house and enjoyed the independence it gave her. Gazing out at the tall pines and hardwood trees lining the woods behind her lot, she looked for the telltale red of a cardinal, her favorite bird. She listened, and though she didn't see it, she heard its distinctive cry. Gratefulness for all she had filled her, pushing aside darker emotions. Somehow, she'd get through this next phase of her life.

By the time she picked up Ross for the trip to Concord, Melissa was in a better frame of mind. Considering all that could've happened with the fire, she and her parents were lucky. No one had gotten hurt.

Ross was equally upbeat as he got into the car. "Another beautiful hot day. Thanks for the ride."

"You're welcome. I'm delighted to have something to do. After I drop you off, I'll visit one of my favorite cooking stores to see what's new. I'm not sure what I want to do in the future, but I might as well check it out."

"Seems like you're missing the restaurant," said Ross.

"Yes and no," she answered truthfully. "I just need to keep busy. No matter what, I'm going to have some free time on my hands while things get sorted out relating to the fire."

After a moment, Ross said, "I talked to my dad last night. He's not doing as well as I'd hoped. I intend to drive to New Jersey as soon as I can. I talked to my doctor, who said I must wait for at least four more weeks before considering such a trip, and I'd need someone to accompany me. Something about not sitting for too long and the risk of blood clots. Is there any way you'd consider helping me drive there? I know how you feel about us being just friends. We'd make that clear to everyone. I know you're hoping to get together with Dirk."

She turned and smiled at him. "Friends ... and good neighbors. I don't even have to think about it. Of course, I'll do it. We'd drive down there and back?"

"Well, we might have to spend a night there, maybe two. But I'd get a nearby hotel room for you, and, if necessary, one for me. I've hired live-in help for Dad, so I'm not sure what the space allocations are like at home. He's still living in the house I grew up in, and we didn't have much room. But my brothers and I can't convince my father to move."

"What about the trip to Florida that you told me about?" she asked. "Would I help you get there too?"

"That's up to you and how well I've recovered. We could continue to drive to Florida, spend some time there while I looked at what Mike wanted me to see, and I could fly you home, or you could drive back with me. It depends on how much time you want away from the mess in Lilac Lake."

"Could we make a lot of stops on the way? See things I've read about but haven't seen?" she asked, becoming excited about the idea.

He shrugged and said, "Why not? We've both got the time."

"Okay," said Melissa. "We'll call it a neighborly road trip. We seem to be compatible, but we'd have to set up some rules."

He raised an eyebrow. "And what would they be?"

"I'll work on them while you do your exercises," Melissa said, grinning.

He laughed. "Okay. I might have a few of my own."

With the change in her plans, Melissa gave up the idea of visiting one of her favorite cooking stores and sat in the waiting room of the rehab center, thinking about the road trip. She didn't feel the least bit awkward about traveling with Ross. As they'd agreed, they were just neighbors making the journey together. Nothing was sexy about it. But when the time came, she wanted Dirk to know that's all it was. She liked him and still thought they'd make a couple as two of the remaining unattached young people in town.

She quickly went through her wardrobe in her mind and was satisfied that she had everything she'd need for the trip. She'd never been one to overpack because she wasn't that fussy about what she wore. Good, classic things were all she needed. Nothing fancy.

She was still thinking about the "rules of the road" when Ross appeared. Margo tailed him.

"I'm through with these sessions," said Ross. "But I have to exercise at home."

Margo spoke up. "He's doing exceptionally well. It's always

a pleasure to work with an athlete. They work so hard at it." She gave Melissa a curious look. "I hear you two are going on a road trip together in a few weeks."

Melissa held up a hand. "I'm happy to get away from town after my family's restaurant has burned down."

"Oh, yes. I heard about it on the news," said Margo. "Any idea about what started it?"

"They're certain it began in the kitchen. We don't know exactly how yet," said Melissa, feeling a pang of sorrow work through her. She'd loved the restaurant.

"It was such a classy place, with good food and a beautiful location. Did the fire ruin everything?" asked Margo.

Melissa thought of the pile of burnt lumber and the dreams her parents had had and felt a sting of tears. "Yes, it is a total loss."

"Ready to go?" Ross asked, and Melissa was grateful for the diversion.

"Sure. We have a list to talk about."

"Or two," said Ross, grinning.

The drive home was filled with conversation. Melissa and Ross easily agreed on a couple of things right away. Number one, the driver got to choose the music. Number two, the driver would agree whenever one of them needed to stop for whatever reason. "Getting to New Jersey will be an easy drive with few stops, I suppose," said Ross. "But if you want to do any sightseeing on the way to Florida or back, we'd better talk about it and devise a plan."

"Agreed," said Melissa. "As I've told you, running a restaurant meant little time for vacations or days just ambling around the country. We did the basic things, but I've never been to Savannah, for instance, or one of the coastal islands. That sort of thing."

"Like you, there's a lot I haven't seen. Little places, scenic locations. We can start a list of those and see how convenient it would be to get to them." Ross smiled. "I wasn't looking forward to the drive, but now I think it's going to be better than I thought."

The next four weeks seemed to drag or fly by, depending on the day.

Plans regarding Fins were slower to materialize than she'd thought they'd be. She tried to keep her parents' spirits up, but she could see that the trauma of it was affecting them negatively. Her mother, especially, missed her role at the restaurant, meeting and greeting people.

One of the things that helped Melissa was the new routine that she and Ross developed. She continued to rise and jog in the morning whenever possible and often met Ross when he was out walking with a cane. Afterward, they usually had coffee at her house. Occasionally, they went exploring on Ross's new golf cart, checking out new construction in the neighborhood.

On rainy or very hot days, she would offer to drive Ross to the café for coffee, anything to keep him from going crazy in his house. It helped their friendship grow.

In all this time, Dirk didn't call and seldom went to Jake's. Melissa told herself it was because of his increased responsibilities at the dental office. But she couldn't help wondering what went wrong between them.

More than that, she realized how lost she was without her identity as a working chef and told herself she didn't need any man to make her happy. What she needed was to figure out where her career was going next.

CHAPTER SEVENTEEN

AT THE END OF FOUR WEEKS, MELISSA DROVE ROSS TO the doctor's office.

She was as anxious for this appointment as Ross because it would determine when they could take their road trip.

"It'll be an escape for both of us. But I'm worried about your father's condition," she said.

"Last night, my dad told me on the phone that he's doing fine, that I'm not to worry. But that's why I'm concerned. He's tough as nails. He had to be raising four boys. But even though he'll fight his cancer as hard as he can, there's only one winner in a battle like this."

Melissa squeezed his hand. "I dread the day I have to go through anything like this with my parents. I'll be there for you."

She could feel his eyes on her as she sat behind the wheel. Finally, he said quietly, I know you will."

The appointment for Ross's doctor had been made for his suburban office in Dedham. It was much more convenient for them than having to go into Boston.

Later, as Melissa was sitting, waiting for Ross, she thought of all the culinary opportunities for her downtown. In the end, she knew she wouldn't even inquire about them because the one thing she did know about her future was her desire to stay in Lilac Lake.

Movement at the exit window caught Melissa's attention. She looked up to see Ross giving her a thumbs-up sign. The smile on his face lit his blue eyes, and her lips curved.

She waited anxiously for him to give her the details.

After he completed the paperwork and paid, he walked over to her, and they headed out the door.

"Okay, what did he say?" she asked.

"First of all, I'm a star patient. He's very pleased with my progress and said I was an excellent patient and could do well independently. But he's very glad you're going on the trip with me. He warned me about sitting too long in one position. So, we'll have to stop more often than we ordinarily would so we both can stretch our legs."

"That's easy enough. When do you want to leave?" she asked.

"Is tomorrow too early for you?"

Melissa shook her head. "It sounds perfect to me."

The next morning, she stood at the end of her driveway, her suitcase and duffle at her feet. Ross was to pick her up at ten o'clock. Because his father had late mornings and then took an early afternoon nap, they hoped to arrive in New Jersey by the time he awoke. Ross drove his silver BMW to her, got out, and they stowed her luggage in the trunk.

"I've got water and snacks for us," Melissa said.

"Thanks. I'll start driving but will stop and have you take over. We'll see how the leg does."

"Deal," she said, sliding into the passenger seat. She was pleased his car was so comfortable. She'd never driven or ridden in a car for so many days at a time. This trip would be one to remember, with interesting stops along the way. She'd revised the list of the places they might want to see, even though she knew it would be impossible to visit all of them.

Ross glanced up at the sky. "It looks like a great day to drive. The storm has chased away some of the heat, and the roads are clear."

"I'm looking forward to meeting your father," she said. "I wish it were under happier circumstances."

"Me, too," said Ross, his solemn expression revealing the depth of his love for his father.

The sounds of country music filled the car as they headed into town on their way to the highway. Ross surprised her by taking a small detour to drive past the remnants of the restaurant. Now that the fire department had completed its investigation, a bulldozer was removing the debris from the site. Her parents were standing by, watching.

Melissa gave them a wave, and Ross drove on. She was relieved to leave town to avoid dealing with the demise of the restaurant she and her parents had loved. In time, she'd have to make some decisions about her life going forward, but having this reprieve was a blessing.

They drove to Interstate 95, and Melissa asked for a stop. "I can take over the driving if you wish."

"Maybe you'd better," said Ross, getting out of the car and rubbing his leg. "Then, when we get closer to my parents' house, I'll take over."

"Okay," said Melissa. "I'll be right back. I need to use the facilities."

When she returned to the car, she slid behind the wheel and checked the dashboard to see how it was set up. Though there were differences in layout, the details were pretty much the same as her Lexus. Her parents had always insisted she have what they considered a safe car to drive, and she'd come to like the conveniences of the luxury cars they'd handed down to her.

"Thanks for taking over," said Ross as they pulled out of the gas station.

"Good neighbors, remember?" she said, and they both smiled.

Melissa played light classical music as she drove. It had taken years to find music for the kitchen that pleased all the staff. Though it wasn't the favorite of many, it was pleasant enough for everyone to work with.

Ross leaned back against the passenger seat and closed his eyes.

When they saw signs for the New Jersey Turnpike, Ross said, "Please pull into the next stop. I'll take over driving from there."

She did as he asked and pulled into a gas station. While he filled the car with gas, she freshened up inside.

When she returned to the car, a surprising tension filled the air.

"Are you nervous about seeing your dad?" she asked him gently.

Looking glum, Ross said, "Each time I see or talk to him, I realize he's getting worse. Truthfully, I dread seeing him. My brothers tell me each day is different and that some days are better than others. I hope this is one of his good ones."

"I'm sure, no matter what, he'll be thrilled to see you," she said, giving his forearm a little pat.

"Even though he tells me to go on about my business, he's always glad to see me."

"Tell me about your neighborhood," she said, trying to keep his mind occupied.

"It's a typical middle-class one, with modest houses, many kids, and happy memories. We kids played together since we were young. Our parents were all friends, and though many of them moved away to nicer neighborhoods, they all kept in touch. They were fantastic when my mom died."

"What a wonderful way to grow up," said Melissa. "Though our town was friendly and we kids all knew one another, we lived in different neighborhoods, making it a little harder to get together. And then, my parents were always working, so I couldn't have kids over very often. Still, Lilac Lake is very special."

"Yes," said Ross. "I like it."

Moments later, Ross pulled in front of a tan clapboard split-level home with neatly trimmed landscaping. As Ross had described, the neighborhood was family-friendly, with kids playing outside and bicycles, carriages, and strollers in front of some of the houses.

Ross pulled into the driveway behind a white SUV and parked the car. "Here we go," he said. "I think my brother, Dewey, must be here. I'm pretty sure that's his car. He works in IT, and he and his wife have four kids." He got out of the car, and they went up the sidewalk leading to the front porch.

A pleasant-faced, heavy-set woman wearing black slacks and a white blouse greeted them at the door. "Welcome. Happy to see you, Ross."

"Mrs. Barnard, how are you?" Ross said and turned to Melissa. "This is a friend of mine, Melissa Hendrickson. Melissa, Mrs. Barnard is Dad's nurse."

"A pleasure to meet you, Melissa. Please come in. Your father has been waiting for you, Ross."

Melissa followed them inside to the living room, where an older man sat in a brown leather reclining chair. Beside him, holding his hand, was a man who looked a lot like Ross. His eyes were as bright a blue as Ross's, and his boyish grin the same. He stood and, smiling at her, he embraced Ross. "Hey, Bro! Great to see you. How long are you here for?"

Ross glanced at his father. "I'm not sure. Hey, Dad, Dewey, meet Melissa Hendrickson. She's my next-door neighbor and is doing me a favor by helping me drive here following my knee surgery."

"Glad to meet you," Dewey said, holding his hand. "So nice of you to drive down with Ross."

"I'm happy to do it. It keeps me busy while trying to cope after a family tragedy. Our restaurant burned down," said Melissa. She shook Dewey's hand and knelt by his father's chair to say hello to him.

She returned his father's smile and studied him. His cheeks were sunken, and though his body looked frail, his blue eyes were full of life as he gazed at her. "How lucky to have a neighbor like you," he said, giving her a wink.

Melissa's heart went out to him. There was no doubt as to where Ross got his charm.

"Sit, sit," said Mrs. Barnard. "Can I get anything to drink or eat?" She gazed at Melissa.

"I'd like a glass of water," Melissa said. "Thank you."

"I'll have the same," said Ross, leaning down to hug his father. He and Dewey brought two more chairs over, and they all sat beside him. "How's it going, Dad?"

"It's going," said his father. "It's wonderful to see you. Everyone is being so kind."

"Including Lanie Southerland next door. She's living with her parents since her divorce," said Dewey, giving Ross an impish grin. "She's been asking about you."

Ross looked disgusted. "She tried to call me a couple of times, but I didn't return them."

Dewey turned to Melissa. "You're the woman he ran into on the ball field?"

Melissa nodded. "I still feel bad about it."

"Don't worry. Ross is strong, and things like that happen all the time," said Dewey.

"To you more than me," teased Ross, and both men laughed.

"I'll leave you guys alone," said Dewey. He gave his father

a loving pat on the shoulder. "Call me anytime. It won't take me long to get here."

"I appreciate that, son," said Ross's father.

Melissa was touched by the tenderness between Ross's father and his children. All three of them were easy with affection—no pretending to be so strong you couldn't handle a hug.

Melissa moved to a nearby couch and talked with Mrs. Barnard to give Ross some time alone with his father.

"How long have you been working here?" Melissa asked her.

"For about four months now," Mrs. Barnard said. "But I've known the family for a long time. I was a nurse for Mrs. Roberts when she became ill. Such a lovely woman."

Melissa gazed around the room. The fireplace mantel held several family photos. To the right of it, a bookcase was filled with trophies and more pictures of Ross and his brothers. In the center was a photograph of a beautiful woman with Ross's features. Recalling her lonely childhood, Melissa hoped she'd have many children of her own and form a family as strong as this.

"Tell me more about your family restaurant," said Mrs. Barnard, and Melissa described it and their situation.

"Then this is a very good time to be away," said Mrs. Barnard. At the sound of a doorbell, she got up and went to answer it.

She returned, followed by a pretty woman with dark hair and brown eyes who looked about Melissa's age. Seeing her broad smile and the bounce in her steps, Melissa sensed this woman must have been a cheerleader in earlier days. A very cute one.

"There you are! Hi, Ross!" said the woman, moving toward him with open arms.

Ross stood and allowed her to embrace him. "Hi, Lanie."

"When you didn't return my phone calls, I checked with your dad and learned about the knee surgery."

"Yeah, it's the same knee I injured in college. Remember?"

"Oh, yes. And then, you had that awful accident ending your career," Lanie said, drawing closer and gazing up at him.

Ross stepped back and turned to Melissa. "This is the 'girl' next door, Lanie Southerland. Lanie, meet Melissa Hendrickson, my neighbor and friend from Lilac Lake."

Lanie's dark eyes surveyed Melissa before she held out her hand. "Hi. Just a friend and neighbor, huh?"

Melissa glanced at Ross. "That's right."

Ross came over to her and put a hand on Melissa's shoulder. "And an excellent chef."

"Chef? Really? But you're so thin," said Lanie.

Melissa laughed. "After working with food day in and day out, you learn not to taste everything."

"My kids are two and four. I'm still working off the baby fat," said Lanie, chuckling.

"How are you doing on your own?" Ross asked Lanie.

"It's hard. I never should've married Rick. Lesson learned. Now I'm hoping to find a reliable man who likes children. My kids are the best."

"A boy and girl, right?"

"Yes, in fact, the boy is named after you. Samuel Ross. I insisted on it. We used to be so special together." Lanie turned to Melissa. "Growing up, we were best friends. I should've never let someone else come between us."

Ross's pained expression was notable. He shuffled his feet from side to side but didn't say anything.

Lanie walked over and kissed Ross's father on the cheek. "How are you doing today? Mom said she's sending over some of your favorite cookies."

"Thanks," said Ross's father.

"Well, I'd better go. My mother is watching the kids, and I don't like to leave her too long." Lanie turned to Ross, rose up on her toes, and kissed him. "Maybe we can talk later."

"Maybe. Right now, I'm here to visit Dad," Ross said quietly.

Lanie studied Melissa. "Pleasure to meet you."

After Lanie left, Melissa excused herself to use the bathroom. Ross and Lanie had some history, and she needed to gather her thoughts. Seeing Lanie, how cute she was, how comfortable she was with Ross and his family, she wondered if they'd get back together like Lanie obviously hoped.

When she returned to the living room, Ross's father had fallen asleep. Ross sat next to him, holding his hand.

Her eyes smarted with tears. It was such a tender scene.

Ross looked up as she came closer. "Let's get you settled in the hotel. I talked to Mrs. Barnard and think I should stay there. It'll be much easier for them both and give Dad some privacy."

"Okay. I'm willing to do whatever it takes," she said. "What about dinner? Do you want to share a meal with him? I'm happy to be alone if that's what you want."

"No," said Ross. "Mrs. Barnard has prepared a chicken casserole, something my father likes. I want you to be there with us so Dad can get to know you. It isn't everyone who has such a good friend."

"Like you and Lanie used to be?" she asked.

He chuckled. "No, nothing like that."

CHAPTER EIGHTEEN

ROSS DROVE THEM TO A CHAIN HOTEL NEARBY, AND Melissa got checked into her room, grateful to have the opportunity to freshen up before returning to his father's house for a simple meal with him.

After meeting some of his family and seeing the neighborhood Ross grew up in, Melissa had a better idea about Ross's childhood, and she thought it was no wonder he was one of baseball's favorites. His story was one of a typical kid loving the sport and growing up to become a professional.

She lay on the bed and waited for Ross to call her to tell her he was ready. So far, the trip with him had been pleasant, without any need to talk constantly. She liked that about him and hoped it would continue for the next several days.

The chiming of her cell phone awoke her. It took her a moment to realize where she was. She sat up. "Hello?"

"Are you ready to go back to Dad's house?" Ross asked her. "I've talked to my brothers and the two who haven't met you, Jack and Dennis. They may drop by to say hello to Dad and to meet you."

"That's fine with me. I enjoyed meeting Dewey."

"Good. I'll meet you in the lobby, and we'll go from there," Ross said, ending the call.

Melissa grabbed her purse and left the room.

Downstairs, she discovered Ross had already retrieved the car and had pulled it up to the front entrance for her.

She got in the car, and they took off.

Ross took a side trip past the local high school to point out the field where he'd spent many hours as a kid. "Bill Carter, the high school baseball coach, spent a lot of time with me and a couple of my friends, helping each of us. He's gone now, but I'll always be grateful to him," said Ross.

They continued for a few blocks to Ross's father's house. A gray Mercedes was in the driveway.

"Looks like Jack is here," said Ross. "He's the oldest of my brothers, named John after my father, and is a successful lawyer in the state. He and his second wife have two kids. Both girls."

"So, you have lots of nieces and nephews," said Melissa, thinking how lucky he was.

Ross grinned. "Yeah, it can get pretty wild when we all get together, which isn't often lately. But for years, when my mother was alive, and she and Dad were both healthy, Sunday dinners were a must."

"A true family event," said Melissa, getting out of the car.

Ross led her inside, and a tall, well-built man with sandy hair gray at the temples walked over to them.

"Hey, little bro." The two men clapped each other on the back, and then Ross introduced Melissa to him.

"Pleased to meet you," she said, noting the remarkable resemblance between the two men.

"It's my pleasure," Jack said. "I understand my brother and you are neighbors in New Hampshire. It's a very pretty part of the country. My family and I ski at Waterville Valley."

"It's beautiful there," said Melissa, aware of how Jack was politely assessing her and thinking he must be a formidable foe in the courtroom.

"Would you like to say hello to my dad?" Jack asked. "Do you mind giving me a moment with Ross?"

"Certainly," she said, leaving the front entry to go into the living room to see Ross's father.

He smiled at her when she approached him. "Well, I get to talk to a pretty lady while two of my sons collaborate, huh?"

She grinned. "I don't know what they're up to, but I'm happy to have some time to talk to you. How are you feeling? Is there anything I can get you? Do for you?"

"Please sit," he said, indicating the chair beside him. He studied her for a moment. "The only thing I have to ask of you is that you keep an eye on my son. He trusts and cares about you. He's had a heartbreak or two in the past, but I think he finally has met the right woman."

"Oh, but ..."

Ross's father held up a hand to stop her. "I know the two of you think you're both simply friends and neighbors, but I see it's more than that."

Stunned that Ross's father seemed so sure, Melissa was relieved to see Ross and Jack walking into the room. Saved from having to respond to him, she got to her feet.

"Go ahead and sit," Ross said to her. He stood on the other side of his father, leaned down, and gave him another hug. "Mrs. Barnard has agreed to a picnic supper right here. Sound okay to you?"

Ross's father flashed a smile. "Anything to spend time with you and your girl."

Melissa witnessed how Ross's eyes rounded and knew he was as surprised as she'd been by the idea of them being together. But she understood his father might want to see Ross settled before dying. "I'm going to help set up a table in here," Ross said. "Mrs. Barnard will dish up the food, and we can eat here in the living room at the card table."

"I'm staying too," said Jack. "Jenn and the girls have a party to go to."

"It's always delightful to have my boys around. And a beautiful woman is always a plus." Ross's father smiled at her. "You remind me of my wife, Betty. A true partner."

Melissa didn't know what to say and was grateful when Jack piped up, "He compares any woman to Mom."

"And rightly so," said Ross's father.

Sensing Melissa's discomfort, Ross said, "I'm hungry. Let's eat." He left to go to the kitchen.

Jack winked at her, and then the conversation turned to his daughters, who were now teens.

Halfway through dinner, Ross's father fell asleep after eating almost nothing. Melissa exchanged worried glances with Ross and Jack. Their father had put forth an effort to become part of the group, but it was obvious that he was too ill to continue.

Not long after the meal ended, Jack announced he was going home.

Ross and Melissa walked him to the door and said goodbye.

Ross turned to her. "I'll say goodbye to my father, and we can return to the hotel. It'll be an early start tomorrow if you want to get down south to do some sightseeing."

"Okay, I'll say goodbye too," said Melissa.

She walked over and took hold of his father's hand. "Goodbye, Mr. Roberts. I'm so happy I met you. I'll do as you asked."

"Thank you," he said, patting their clasped hands and studying her with his blue eyes.

She felt the sting of tears and turned away as Ross took her place beside his father.

Wanting to give them privacy, she walked into the kitchen to thank Mrs. Barnard for her hospitality.

"Perhaps we'll meet again," said Mrs. Barnard. "I don't like to say much, but though John has put on a positive front for you, he's growing weaker every day." She let out a sad sigh. "Such a decent man."

"I know they're grateful for your help. I'll go outside to wait for Ross. I want him to take whatever time he needs with his father."

She left the kitchen, went outside to the front entry, and sat on the narrow bench there.

Children were playing kickball on the quiet street, and Melissa could feel herself being taken back to Ross's childhood.

She looked up as Lanie walked toward her.

"Hi," Lanie said. "Is Ross inside?"

"Yes. He's saying goodbye to his father," Melissa said. "I'm giving him some privacy."

Lanie studied her and twisted her hands. "So, are you and Ross a thing? I didn't know he was dating again."

"Ross and I are just friends, like we said," Melissa said and stopped. She didn't owe anyone an explanation. And besides, she was confused, especially after what his father had said. From the beginning, Ross had been very clear about his willingness to help her with Dirk, so she didn't understand why people would think they were a couple.

"Hi, Lanie." He turned to Melissa. "Ready to go?"

Melissa could see how upset Ross was and jumped to her feet. "Sure, let's go. Nice to see you, Lanie."

"Anything I can do?" Lanie asked Ross.

"There's nothing anyone can do," he replied softly. There was such sadness in his voice that a lump formed in Melissa's throat.

She followed Ross and, without saying a word, climbed into the car feeling as helpless as she ever had.

As Ross drove to the hotel, he stared straight ahead, visibly disturbed.

He pulled into the parking lot near their guest room's entrance and turned off the engine, leaving silence behind.

Melissa reached out and touched Ross's arm. "I'm sorry. Anything I can do for you?"

Ross leaned his brow against the steering wheel. "I offered to stay another night, but Dad said I should continue my trip to Florida. He likes you and thinks it's great that we're traveling together. After you and Jack left the room, he seemed to collapse into himself, and I know the end is near." Ross's shoulders began shaking.

Melissa unbuckled her seatbelt and wrapped her arms around him.

He turned into her shoulder, careful to keep his face hidden.

Melissa rubbed his back in comforting circles and wished she could take away his pain. She'd seen how close Ross was to his father and knew his distress was real.

"I'm glad I got to meet your father," she said. "He's such a wonderful man, beloved by all his sons."

Ross quieted and looked up at her. "He's the best. Jack pulled me aside to tell me he's taken care of all the details from now on. Mrs. Barnard will stay through to the end and beyond as they get the house ready to sell. My father insisted that these things be worked out while he was still alive."

Melissa knew now why Ross's father had been so outspoken about Ross and her being more than friends. She thought it was sweet that he wanted to see Ross happily situated like his brothers. Not that she was going to mention this to Ross. She was still trying to come to terms with the idea of being with Ross.

Ross swiped at his face almost angrily. "Sorry to break down like that. Let's go inside, and if you don't mind using one of the mini bars in our rooms, I'm ready for a nightcap."

"Why don't you come to my room," she said. "I've got a small balcony where we can sit."

Her room, a standard suite, had a living area separate from the bedroom. Melissa set down her purse and went to the mini bar.

"What would you like?" she asked Ross as he headed for the balcony.

"A cold beer, thanks."

Melissa pulled out two cans and carried them to the balcony, where Ross had seated himself in one of the two chairs.

She handed him his beer and sat in the chair next to his. "Do you want to talk about it or just sit quietly?"

"I want to have this time to think things over," he said. "Thanks for being so understanding."

"Of course." Melissa sipped her beer and looked out over the landscaped space. She, herself, was shaken by all that was happening to Ross and his family and considered herself lucky she hadn't had to face health issues with her parents.

She got Ross another beer and said, "Are you hungry?"

A smile crossed his face. "Starving. Like you, I didn't eat much for dinner."

"There's a pizza place down the road. Why don't we order some?" said Melissa. "What do you like?"

He gave her a sheepish smile. "I like Hawaiian pizza, with bacon instead of ham, if you can get it." He raised his hand. "I know, I know. It's as far from authentic as possible but impossible to resist."

"I have to admit I've never tried it," said Melissa, grinning. "But maybe now is the time. I like experimenting with food. I'll place a call and have it delivered."

"Thanks," Ross said.

Later, after scarfing down the pizza and sharing beer, Melissa stood. "It's late. I'm going to bed."

"I need to get to bed, too," said Ross. "Do you mind if I stay in your room on the couch? I don't want to be alone tonight. My father and I had a serious talk, and I know I won't sleep well."

"It's not a problem for you to stay. I understand." Melissa walked over to him, leaned down, and kissed him on the cheek.

He pulled her into his lap and wrapped his arms around her. "Thanks for being here for me." He studied her face and then lowered his lips to hers.

Melissa felt as if her body had been melted by a streak of lightning so strong that she could hardly breathe. Sensations rolled through her as strong as thunder, settling into her most sensitive area. She clung to him.

When they finally pulled apart, Ross looked as shocked as she felt. "Sorry, I shouldn't have done that."

Uncertain how to respond, Melissa pulled herself to her feet. "Stay as long as you like," she said to Ross and hurried away, shaken to her core.

Later, lying in bed alone, Melissa tossed and turned, reliving that kiss. When she could stand it no longer, she got up and tiptoed to see if he was still there.

The couch was empty, and he was nowhere to be found.

CHAPTER NINETEEN

THE NEXT MORNING, MELISSA GOT UP, TOOK A SHOWER, and dressed, wanting to see how Ross had done overnight.

She buzzed his room and got no answer. Then she called his cell. "Hi. How are you?" she asked.

"Fine. Come on down to the breakfast area. I'm here."

Glad he was feeling better, Melissa went downstairs to join him. When she walked into the breakfast area and scanned the room, she stopped in surprise.

Ross was sitting at a table with Lanie.

He saw her and waved her over. "You remember Lanie, don't you?"

"Yes, I do. Hi, Lanie." She gave Ross a questioning look.

"I asked Lanie to join me."

"We've been friends forever," said Lanie, laying a hand on Ross's forearm and smiling at him.

Though Melissa's insides froze, she forced herself to curve her lips.

Lanie got to her feet and enclosed Ross in a warm embrace. "I'll see you later. Have a safe trip." She turned to Melissa. "You, too."

"Thanks," Melissa muttered, so unsettled she could barely speak.

After Lanie left, Ross said, "As soon as you finish breakfast, we should get on our way. I'm suggesting we stay on Interstate 95. We might be able to make it to Richmond or farther. I know you want to explore the coast south from there."

"All right. After that pizza last night, I don't need much for breakfast," said Melissa.

"I'll go get my luggage, fill the car at the gas station next door, and meet you out front. Is that okay?" he asked.

"Yes. I promise not to take long."

"No worries," Ross said. "We've got all the time we need to get to my appointment in Florida. The rest of the schedule is up to you."

After Ross left the dining area, Melissa poured herself a cup of strong coffee, still confused. *Ross had called Lanie?*

Ross picked her up at the front entrance, stowed her luggage in the trunk of his car, and got behind the wheel.

"Before we go, there's a call I must make. Bear with me."

He punched in a number, and the computer screen in his car lit, telling them he was connected. "Hello, Mrs. Barnard. May I speak to my father?"

"Of course. Let me put him on," she replied.

"Hello," came his father's voice, sounding weak.

"Dad, before Melissa and I take off for Florida, I need to know if you want us to stay here an extra day. We're happy to do so."

"No, son. You both have promises to keep. That's more important to me right now. Thanks for the offer. I love you."

"I love you, too, Dad." At the click ending the call, Ross turned to her. "I had to be sure."

"No problem. I'm here to help you however I can," Melissa said.

"Thanks for your help last night. Seeing Dad in his condition has brought it all home—his illness, Mom's death, life's questions."

He pulled out of the hotel's parking lot, and after weaving through streets, they were back on the Interstate highway.

They'd driven in silence for a while when Ross turned to

her. "What do you think Dad meant? That we both had promises to keep?"

"I'm not sure," said Melissa, unwilling to tell him that his father had asked her to look after Ross, and that he thought she and Ross should be together.

What was Ross's promise to his father?

Melissa and Ross alternated driving as they headed south. For part of the trip, Ross stretched out on the car's back seat to rest his leg. Melissa was happy that he trusted her so much.

That night, they pulled up to a motel beyond Richmond, relieved the trip, so far, was an easy one, even if Melissa couldn't stop seeing the passing scenery blur in her mind.

Melissa and Ross checked into their rooms, and then Ross knocked on her door. "There's a restaurant nearby that advertises delicious traditional Southern food. "Want to give it a try?"

"Sure, anything to take my mind off the drive. We made good time, but I need a complete break." She gathered her purse and headed out the door with him.

Lulu's was an upscale bar and restaurant. The dark paneled walls were offset by the white linen-covered tables. Fresh flowers in crystal vases sat in the middle of the tables and accompanied the crystal water goblets, sparkling silverware, and crisp black napkins.

"What a lucky find," said Melissa. She could already smell the aroma of butter, olive oil, garlic, and spices. She loved discovering new food and always took careful mental notes of any recipes she wanted to remember.

"This is my treat," said Ross after they were seated. "I know how independent you are and how you wanted to keep expenses separate, but I owe you big time. This has been a difficult trip for me, and you've helped to make it easier."

"I'm delighted I could be of help," said Melissa. "And now you have Lanie to help you. What's the story between the two of you?"

"We were best friends growing up. My brothers were much older than I was, and having a friend next door was cool until a certain age. Then, later, in high school, we dated. I thought we'd marry one day, but Lanie met Blake Worley. He was the older high school kid who seemed to have everything—rich parents, a sports car that was the envy of every male in the school, and an unstoppable way with women. Lanie was over the moon with him."

"Did they get married?" asked Melissa.

"Yeah, right after high school. But nobody thought it would last. They were as different as night and day. After they divorced, Lanie thought she could hook up with me. But I'd already seen it wouldn't work between us either."

"I think she's hoping you'll change your mind about her," said Melissa.

Ross shrugged, obviously uncomfortable. "She called me this morning. That's when I thought it might be a good time to talk to Lanie about her and me, and I called her back.

"How long did you stay on the couch last night?" she asked. She remembered their kiss and what it had done to her and wondered if he'd felt the same connection as she.

"I got up sometime around two and made it to my room. I appreciate your letting me stay there for a while. It gave me time to settle my thoughts." He covered her hand with his and smiled his famous smile.

She gazed into his blue eyes, wishing she could see what was going on in his mind behind them.

He looked away and picked up his menu. "I know what I'm going to have. It was posted on the menu board as we came in. What about you?"

"I've glanced at the menu and want to study it more. What are you ordering?

"The Southern Fried Chicken," he answered easily. "That, and grits and greens. A real southern meal."

"Hmmm, I might try the catfish," she said. "It's something we don't have at home, and I like to try new things."

"Let's start with a glass of wine," said Ross. "Your choice."

"Okay, I suggest a pinot noir," Melissa replied as a waiter came to take their orders.

Later, sipping their wine, Ross lifted his glass. "Here's to friends. All of them. I realize how lucky we are to have so many in Lilac Lake."

"Hear, hear. I'll toast that," said Melissa, tapping her glass against his.

After they'd each swallowed, Ross cleared his throat. "About last night..."

He gazed at her with a questioning look.

Melissa set down her wine glass. "I'm happy it happened. It's helped me to rethink things."

"Such as?" Ross's blue eyes bored into her, demanding an honest answer.

Melissa sighed and looked away. "I realize Dirk and I aren't a couple. We never had the same spark I felt with you." She was embarrassed to say more, but she knew what real passion was after kissing Ross. She'd never been kissed like that before.

Ross reached across the table and clasped her hand. "I want to get to know you better as more than a friend."

"Me, too," she said, loving the feel of his fingers wrapped around hers. Being away from Lilac Lake would give them the perfect opportunity to explore their new feelings.

CHAPTER TWENTY

THEIR DINNERS CAME, AND ROSS AND MELISSA concentrated on their meals briefly. Melissa was sure the catfish she ordered must have tasted delicious, but with her pulse racing, it was as tasteless as cardboard. All she could think of was what might happen after they left the restaurant.

When at last they stood outside, Ross turned to her. "Ready to go back to the hotel?"

Melissa nodded, suddenly shy.

On the way, Ross filled the car with small talk, and Melissa wondered if he was as nervous as she was.

He pulled into the parking lot and brought the car to a stop. "Why don't you come to my room? There's a baseball game on television. We could relax and watch it together."

"Okay. I'll freshen up and meet you there."

After washing her face and recombing her hair into her normal ponytail, Melissa left her room wondering how the evening would go. She'd had such high hopes for a relationship with Dirk, but now she realized they'd both been trying too hard.

Ross greeted her at the door to his room with a smile. "Come on in. The Yankees are ahead by two."

"They're not playing the Red Sox, are they? You know I'd have to root for them."

He laughed. "No. They're playing the Braves." He led her over to the couch and sat down. Wearing shorts and a T-shirt, he looked as relaxed as any guy watching a favorite game.

She sat beside him and accepted the bottle of water he handed her. She knew something about baseball, but sitting next to Ross, listening to his take on the situation, she was learning much more about the game.

At one point, a Yankee player hit a home run. Cheering, Melissa turned to Ross, and in their excitement, they embraced. As he stared at her, Melissa felt the world turn silent. Then his lips were on hers, and behind her closed eyelids, colors erupted like fireworks.

When they finally pulled apart, they were both breathing hard.

"I've wanted to kiss you for a long time," said Ross, cupping her head in his hands. His blue eyes drew her in, and she sighed as his lips met hers again.

He tugged her down on the couch, and they lay there, side by side. Melissa was surprised by how well they fit together. She snuggled closer, enjoying the feeling of Ross protecting her. From what, she didn't care. In his arms, she felt as if she'd found the man she'd been searching for all along.

Facing the television, they continued to lie together, watching the action. With a score of seven to two in the eighth inning, the game was pretty much over. Not that Melissa cared about the numbers. She could only think of being this close to Ross.

When the game ended, Ross rolled to his side and faced her. "I know we've been together a lot in the last few weeks, but I never got the chance to say how beautiful you are."

She gazed into his eyes. "I thought you weren't interested in me, and that's why you offered to help me with Dirk."

"At first, that might've been true. But as I got to know you better as a friend and neighbor, my feelings changed, and I didn't know how to tell you. Besides, I didn't think you were interested in me."

She put her arms around his neck and drew him closer so she could kiss him.

He responded by pressing his torso against hers, and she knew he was as aroused as she.

She reveled in the knowledge that she'd made him feel this way and realized the mutual attraction they shared. Her body loosened and filled with a fire she had never experienced.

When kissing and caressing weren't enough, they moved to the bedroom, where Ross demonstrated just how fit he was.

The next morning, Melissa awoke and lay in bed next to Ross. She was grateful to him for alleviating any awkwardness between them, making their lovemaking one joyful discovery after another.

She turned to find Ross smiling at her. "Come here," he said gruffly, and she went into his arms, eager to demonstrate how much she'd learned from him.

Sometime later, Melissa got up and hurried to her room to get ready for the day. They planned to drive to Charleston to spend the night. She'd always wanted to see Charleston and was pleased when Ross easily agreed.

The drive to Charleston seemed to pass in no time while Melissa and Ross talked more about their childhood and their dreams and hopes for the future. The more they talked, the more Melissa was convinced, as Ross's father had suggested, that she and Ross were made for one another.

Melissa looked up information on Charleston. Her excitement grew after reading about the cobblestone streets, horse-drawn carriages, and pastel antebellum houses in the French Quarter and Battery districts. She couldn't wait to walk the streets and taste the food.

"Look up hotels. Let's get one where the action is," said Ross. "Then I won't have to walk so far."

Her heart pounded. "One room or two?" She waited for his answer, needing him to affirm that their time together was right.

He glanced at her from behind the wheel. "I say one. How about you?"

"For sure," she said happily, smiling at him.

He grinned and reached for her hand.

A few hours later, they made their way through the streets of Charleston to a four-star hotel between the waterfront and French Quarter. Called an Art Hotel, The Vendue advertised over 200 pieces of art throughout the hotel. That, the food, and the rooftop bar had made it an easy choice.

A bellman led them to their room, where sparkling white walls brightened the dark wooden floor. Red accents inside the room complemented the red on the guest room door. Melissa stared at the king-size bed and felt heat rise to her cheeks, remembering the lovemaking she'd shared with Ross.

Ross caught her attention and winked at her as if knowing what she was thinking.

She forced herself to listen to what the bellman said about amenities and was more than ready for him to leave.

"If you don't mind, I'm going to rest a bit before going out," said Ross. "My leg is hurting."

"Of course, I don't mind. They have an old-fashioned tub. Do you want to soak your leg?"

"Only if you join me," he said and laughed at her surprised expression. "I'll just lie here on the bed for a bit, and then we can look around."

"There's enough to see in this hotel to have us exploring for hours," said Melissa. "While you rest, I'll read up on Charleston."

He gave her a sexy look, waved her over, and laughed when she said, "Or maybe not."

They lay together atop the bed, cuddled close. Ross closed his eyes, and as Melissa kept an eye on him, his breathing slowed until he was sound asleep. It was sometimes easy for her to forget that not long ago, he'd had major surgery.

Quietly, to avoid disturbing him, she got up and decided to look around the hotel by herself.

Melissa was captivated by the artwork as she went from space to space. She loved the bright, bold colors of many of the works. But she especially loved paintings done by FRED. She inquired about them at the front desk and was handed a pamphlet on him and his work.

She eagerly read: "Born in Southern Belgium and a world traveler most of his life, he took Charleston's art scene by storm. His Charleston cityscapes are not seen with a traditional eye. The sky is generally dark, the trees assembled color masses."

The more she read, the more convinced she became that she wanted one of his paintings for her house. A painting of his would add to the décor and give her a loving memory of the time she spent with Ross.

When she returned to the room, Ross looked up at her and grinned. "Do some exploring?"

"Yes, wait until I show you what I want to buy for my house. It's unique."

He stood and pulled her to him. "You're pretty unique yourself."

She smiled and met his lips, wondering why they'd hidden their feelings for so long. It felt so right to be together. She'd been naïve to think she could just wish for a relationship to happen. She now knew one had to be formed with two hearts, not one.

"Let's look around and then enjoy a drink on the rooftop," he said.

"Okay. We're both tired. Why don't we eat dinner early? Tomorrow, we'll go to the waterfront and explore other areas of the city. I want to go to the City Market, for sure."

The driving, the emotional meeting with his father, and all their lovemaking were beginning to slow them down.

Up on the rooftop, Melissa drew a deep breath of satisfaction. The view was everything the hotel had promised. Gazing down at the old brick and stucco buildings in an array of colors and then beyond to the waterfront, Melissa knew she'd always love this city.

She gazed at the man beside her and leaned against his shoulder. Life had taken on a special meaning, and she had him to thank for that. She was happy they'd discovered one another away from Lilac Lake, where old expectations might bind her. Being with Ross opened her to possibilities she'd never contemplated.

Ross smiled at her. "You're looking a little smug."

"Definitely," she replied, chuckling. "I'm just thinking how lucky it is that we found one another after thinking neither of us was interested in a romantic relationship."

He leaned down to kiss her.

Their cocktails came, and they sat at their table. Melissa had ordered a Planters Punch to keep with tradition and enjoyed the taste of rum, orange, and pineapple juices, along with other ingredients of her red drink.

The evening air swirled around them. It was, Melissa thought, a perfect evening.

Later, they discovered a restaurant downtown that served high-end, low-country meals. Pleased to be accepted for an early dinner, Melissa gazed at her She-Crab soup. Creamy, with lots of crab meat, the soup was topped with orange roe, designating it was made specifically with female crabs.

Melissa tasted a spoonful, closed her eyes, and savored the taste.

"That good, huh?" teased Ross.

She laughed. "You can take the chef out of the kitchen, but you can't keep her away from yummy food."

"It's an experience to share meals with you. You enjoy them so much," he said, grinning.

"It's fun to discover new tastes," she said, thinking of how she might fix something similar for Fins. Then, she felt a pang of regret that those days might be over.

After they finished their crab soup, they sipped a crisp white wine and waited for their next course.

Melissa couldn't resist ordering shellfish over grits as her main course. Sauteed shrimp and sea scallops were served over white grits with a lobster butter sauce.

Ross had ordered Parmesan-crusted snapper with a citrus beurre blanc sauce.

When it was served, Melissa studied both of their dishes. "I'm glad we don't have to confess to Emmett Chambers what we are about to eat. I'm sure it wouldn't pass his idea of what every doctor hopes his patients eat."

Ross laughed. "Married to Crystal, he already knows what delicious food is. I don't think even he would pass up a meal like this."

Still smiling, Melissa took a forkful of food and let out a moan of pleasure. "M-m-m, as wonderful as I thought it might be."

Ross chewed a piece of fish. "Delicious."

Melissa was delighted that Ross was an adventuresome eater. Her life revolved around food and would continue to do so whether or not she worked in a restaurant. Thinking of that now, she knew she wasn't ready to commit to a new family enterprise.

Too full for either of them to order dessert, Ross asked for the check, and after paying, they left to walk back to their hotel.

With Ross's fingers entwined in hers, Melissa thought it seemed natural for them to hold hands. They couldn't seem to get enough of one another. Even with a healing leg hindering some movement, Ross made sure she was satisfied. She'd never felt so treasured.

When they got to the hotel, there was no talk of an after-dinner drink on the rooftop. They went directly to their room.

As Melissa unzipped the dress she wore, she hesitated. She'd always been uncertain about her body, which seemed so tall, so strong, so angular.

Ross came up behind her and nuzzled her neck. "Need any help?"

She turned to him, and when he drew her closer, she opened her lips to his kiss.

When they pulled apart, he helped her out of her dress. Overcome with shyness, she stood before him in her panties and nothing else.

"I know you don't believe it, but you're beautiful, Melissa."

Her eyes filled. She'd spent her life thinking she'd never meet the beauty standards her mother had set for her.

Ross kissed her and led her to bed, where he made her feel as beautiful as she'd always wanted to be.

CHAPTER TWENTY-ONE

THE CHIMING OF HER PHONE PULLED MELISSA FROM sleep. She groaned and reached for her cell phone on the bedside table, wondering who would be calling at such an early hour. She checked caller ID and sat up—her *mother*.

"Hello, Mom? What's up?" she said, startled.

"It's your father. He's had a heart attack and is in the hospital in Portsmouth. It's serious. I think you should come home."

Melissa heard the fear in her mother's voice and said, "We're in Charleston, but I'll see what flights I can get and be there as soon as I can." She paused. "Daddy is going to be all right, isn't he?"

"I certainly hope so, but I'd be lying if I told you I'm not worried about him. He's in surgery now to clear some arteries."

"Okay. I'll let you know what flight I'll be on," said Melissa, brushing tears from her cheeks. After seeing Ross's pain over his father dying and the support he had from his family, she realized that as an only child, she was her mother's sole family support.

"What is it?" Ross asked, sitting up beside her.

Melissa explained the situation to him, and he immediately started researching airports and flights.

A short while later, Ross said, "I've found a flight that leaves from Columbia late morning to Boston. It'll take us approximately two hours to get to the airport. Why don't you let me call to see if we can get on that flight? If we can, I'll arrange for a driver in Boston."

"We? You'd do that for me?" asked Melissa, still shaken by the call.

"Sure. You've been here for me, dealing with my father," said Ross. "It's my turn to help you."

Melissa threw herself into his arms. "Oh, Ross. Thank you! I'm so worried. I don't think I could get through this without you."

A few hours later, Melissa and Ross boarded a plane for Boston. Ross left his car in long-term parking, hoping they could continue their trip at some point.

Sitting together, Melissa was grateful for Ross's solid presence beside her. She'd always prided herself on being self-contained, but now she could hardly keep her emotions in check. The thought of losing her father was devastating. They were more than father and daughter; they were a working team. She prayed he'd survive.

Ross reached over and clasped her hand. Against her cold fingers, his own felt hot.

She stared out the plane window and gazed down at the scene below. Rolling hills and houses seemed miniature. She couldn't help wondering if her father's heart attack meant the end of Fins or any restaurant that might follow. She still hadn't made up her mind about returning to the life of owning a restaurant.

"Are you okay?" Ross asked gently, and Melissa realized her cheeks were wet with tears.

She took a tissue from her purse and wiped her face. It was best to get the tears over with now so she could be strong for her mother.

When they arrived in Boston, they went to the limousine Ross had waiting for them.

Less than two hours later, they were taking the elevator to the cardiology unit at the Portsmouth Hospital. The Heart & Vascular Institute was known for providing excellent care and a reputation for meeting national standards for speedy handling of heart attack patients.

When Melissa's mother saw them enter the waiting area, she burst into tears.

Melissa hurried to her. "Is Dad ... okay?"

"Yes, but he's lucky we got him here in time. He's resting now. They found two blocked arteries. As part of the recovery, he will have to participate in a heart-healthy program through the Center for Rehabilitation and Wellness. After cooking delicious meals for all those years, it will be hard for him to change his lifestyle."

"May I go to him?" Melissa asked. She needed to see for herself that he was okay.

Her mother walked her to her father's room and left.

Melissa stood at the doorway, stunned to see her father lying in bed, hooked up to a monitor. He looked ... well ... old ... and smaller than she'd always thought of him. Her breath catching, she went over to him and said, "Dad? It's me. Melissa. I'm here."

He opened his eyes and smiled at her, bringing a sob from her throat. "Oh, Daddy! I thought we might lose you."

"Not me," he said with some of his old spark. "I've got a lot more living to do."

"I'm so relieved," she said, hugging him.

He looked up at her. "I think I scared your mother."

"You scared both of us," Melissa said. "Luckily, Ross helped me get back home to you."

"He's a good man," said her father as his eyes drooped.

Melissa kissed him and left the room, clasping her hands with thanks.

When Melissa returned to the waiting area, she found her mother and Ross in a deep discussion. Her mother looked up at her and smiled.

"I was just thanking Ross for all he did to make sure you got here as quickly as you did. Your presence is such a comfort."

Melissa glanced at Ross, wondering what he might have told her.

He stood and wrapped an arm around her shoulders. "Your mother asked about us, and I said we were seeing where our relationship might take us."

"Good," said Melissa. She didn't want to hide her feelings for Ross. She'd never felt a connection like this before and wanted to enjoy it in front of everyone.

"Tonight, let's talk about some logistics going forward, and then you and Ross can continue your trip," said her mother. "At this point, there's nothing you can do physically for either your father or me. The emotional support is important, and you both have shown us that." Melissa wasn't surprised by her mother's matter-of-fact way of speaking. She'd been as much a business partner in the restaurant as her father. She was the one who kept it going to allow her husband to cook.

"Thanks, Mom. Our trip thus far has been difficult. Ross's father is dying of cancer."

"Oh, I'm so sorry to hear that, Ross," said her mother. "What can I do to help?"

"At this point, there's nothing we can do but keep in touch. I plan to go back and pick up my car in Columbia and continue to Florida with assurances that people will call me when it's time to return to New Jersey to say goodbye."

"And I'm going with him," said Melissa, taking hold of his arm.

Ross smiled at her. "Thanks." He turned to Melissa's mother. "My family loved meeting Melissa. My father, especially."

Her mother studied them. "I see."

Observing her mother's inspection, Melissa was grateful when Ross pulled her to him. She'd felt unattractive for so long that it was thrilling to have Ross's attention. He'd even told her she was beautiful.

"Ross has been wonderful to me," said Melissa.

"I'm happy to see you together," her mother said, beaming at them. No doubt everyone in town would soon know Melissa was dating Ross, but she didn't care.

Later, Ross and Melissa left the hospital to get checked into a hotel.

Melissa was happy to have some time alone with him. She knew it was only a matter of time before he got a call from a family member to come home.

"Are you sure you don't want to stay with your father?"

"I feel comfortable Dad is on the road to recovery, and I don't want you to be alone."

"For selfish reasons, I'm glad you'll be with me."

"Me, too," she said. "But, Ross, I'm pretty sure my mother will decide no more restaurant business for either of them."

"How do you feel about that?" he asked her.

"I know this might sound crazy, but I wondered if there was a spot for a small restaurant at the sports center you're building with Mike. I'm not sure I'd want to do more than that."

"That might be terrific. We left some space on our drawings for something like that. We can talk it over with Mike in

Florida," Ross said. "Crystal has offered to supervise a snack bar with high school students running it, but I think it makes more sense to have you in charge of a bigger operation than that.

"It's just something to think about. I'm not sure what I want," said Melissa. Maybe her new life was finally coming together.

Later, when a discussion of the future came up at dinner with her mother, Melissa wasn't surprised when her mother announced that they definitely wouldn't be rebuilding the restaurant.

"Those 24/7 days of working are over," her mother said. "Your father and I have agreed his heart attack was a wake-up call. With the insurance money from the fire and the sale of the land, we should be comfortable enough to retire." She kept a steady gaze on Melissa. "Does that ruin your plans? We always thought you'd take over the restaurant one day."

Melissa was quiet, thinking about how best to put it without hurting her mother's feelings. "In many ways, it's a relief for me. Now, I'm free to make plans of my own."

"Yes, that's true. I'm grateful we agree on this." Her mother reached across the table and squeezed her hand. "You've been a wonderful daughter and a terrific help to us with the restaurant. I want you to know that."

Melissa blinked hard, too emotional to speak. Compliments from her mother were rare.

Ross waved a waiter over to them. "I think we're ready to order now."

Melissa felt as content as a cream-fed cat after a main course of baked scrod and fresh vegetables. Tomorrow, after seeing her father again, she and Ross would head to the airport for a flight south on what was sure to continue to be an emotional journey.

CHAPTER TWENTY-TWO

THAT NIGHT, AS MELISSA LAY WITH ROSS IN BED, SHE turned to him. "At least now, I know I won't be working at a family restaurant in Lilac Lake."

"How do you feel about that?" asked Ross.

Melissa had been thinking a lot about all the recent changes and answered truthfully, "I feel free. It's going to take me a while to get used to it, but I want to be able to move forward in life in my own way."

"We're both at a crossroads," Ross said. "My business is expanding. I like the idea that I can get away from the cold in a New Hampshire winter to go to my business in Florida and, vice versa, leave Florida in summer."

"That's ideal," said Melissa. She said nothing more because she didn't know if this conversation would lead to thoughts of a future together. She waited, but Ross didn't mention it. He cupped her face in his broad hands and kissed her.

Melissa melted against him.

The next morning, after a hearty breakfast of bacon and eggs at a nearby restaurant, Melissa and Ross returned to the hospital.

He was sitting in a chair when they got to her father's room.

"How are you doing, Dad?" Melissa asked and went to him. "It's great to see you out of bed."

Her mother stood by. "He's going to take it easy and then get to work on his rehab program."

Melissa saw the look of resignation on her father's face and held in a chuckle. Her mother was determined to see that her father had the best care. That made it much easier to leave them.

"Nice of you to come, Ross," said her father.

"Of course. I want to support Melissa just as she's supported me," Ross said.

She smiled at him, and he put an arm around her shoulder.

"Ah," said her father, and Melissa was relieved when he didn't say anything more. The smile of approval he gave them spoke volumes.

Melissa and Ross chatted with her parents, and after giving them an itinerary for their trip, Melissa announced it was time to head to the airport.

Ross shook her father's hand and said goodbye to her mother.

Melissa gave them each a lingering hug. "I'll check in regularly."

"Thank you, darling," said her mother. "The worst is behind us."

Melissa left her father's hospital room feeling more settled than she had in years. She still had decisions to make about her future. The longer she stayed away from the kitchen and her family's business, the more intrigued she became with new possibilities.

Back in Columbia at the airport, Ross retrieved his car. Before taking off, he called his father's house to check on his status.

After he ended the conversation, Ross turned to her. "Mrs. Barnard said Dad's sleeping, but things are pretty much the same. She'll tell him I called."

Melissa squeezed his hand. "I know how hard this is for

you. What do you want to do?"

"I think we'd better keep going. We'll stop at some of the places you want to see on our way back. Is that all right?"

"It's fine. I know your meeting with Mike is important."

"We'll meet him in Jacksonville, look at some baseball camps there, and then join him at a year-round training center outside of town. If things go well, we might be able to squeeze in a trip to St. Augustine. I know you wanted to see it."

"Whatever works. I know you have a lot on your mind," she said. Neither of them could forget what the future held for his father.

Melissa sat quietly in the car while Ross drove them out of the Columbia area. He'd said it wouldn't be a long drive to their meeting, perhaps three hours or so, depending on traffic. They'd switch off driving and meet Mike in the late afternoon.

She glanced at Ross. He seemed to be lost in thought as he drove with ease. So many emotional things had happened to them in the last few days that she understood his pensiveness. She decided to open her Kindle to pass the time.

Melissa was deeply engrossed in her book when Ross spoke. "You mentioned you might want to do something simple with food at the tennis and baseball sports center Mike and I are working on. Do you mean that?"

She set down her reader and thought for a moment. Is that how she wanted her life to be in the future? Doing something right, even for a small food venue, wasn't simple. And because she was known as an excellent chef, she couldn't ever do anything halfway.

"I'm not sure what I want to do going forward," said Melissa. "But I do know I want to continue my professional life in some capacity."

"Okay, we'll tell Mike we might locate a small food

operation there," said Ross. "It could be something as simple as having mothers of the players selling hot dogs or something like that. But we'll leave room for something bigger if you want it."

"Just leave it open-ended until more thought has gone into it," she suggested.

"Mike has a new idea about expanding our center to include a year-round baseball practice area. The tennis center will, of course, be open year-round regardless."

"Do you have the land to expand?" she asked.

Ross smiled at her. "Yes, we do. We can even build a separate building for the baseball camp idea Mike has in mind."

"Speaking of land, I'm wondering what my parents are going to do with the land on which the restaurant stood," she said.

"I'm betting another restaurant will want to buy it and rebuild something. It's the perfect spot, and Fins will be truly missed. There's already a built-up demand for one there. Is that something you want to do?"

"No. That's one thing I do know. I want a life outside of the restaurant business, which is 24/7, no matter what you plan."

Ross glanced at her. "There's a lot to think about for each of us."

She smiled at him.

They arrived at the Bob Williams Baseball Camp at 4 PM. It was a hot, muggy afternoon, and the Florida humidity attacked Melissa like a grumpy, fluffy cat. She stood with Ross outside a caged area and watched several high school boys go through batting practice with machines that kept baseballs coming at them.

Mike came up to them. "Hi, Ross, Melissa. Glad to see you

finally made it." He turned to her. "Thanks for helping Ross get here."

She smiled. "This has been a rough week, but we've helped each other."

Ross placed an arm around her and pulled her close. "Melissa has been great." At Mike's questioning look, Ross continued, "My father is hanging on, but Melissa's father had a heart attack. We went back to New Hampshire to see him, and then we came here."

"I'm sorry. Is your dad going to be okay?" Mike asked her.

"Yes, but any thought of reviving Fins is gone forever," said Melissa. "That's fine with me."

"And me," said Ross, turning to Mike. "Melissa is staying in Lilac Lake regardless of what happens. She might even help us out at the sports center."

"Whoa! I've not committed to doing that," said Melissa, chuckling.

"Right. It's just an option, and we're keeping our options open," said Ross, grinning at her.

"I wanted to meet you here," said Mike, "because Bob Williams has a unique building with enough room for indoor training for batting, pitching, and even a small track for running sprints. Because of the weather in New Hampshire, let's add that to our sports center. We've got the room." He gave Ross an impish grin. "It means we might have to raise more money, but I think it'll pay off. And quickly. I've got a contact with the Boston Red Sox, and you have one with the Yankees."

Melissa could see the excitement on Ross's face as Mike continued to speak. "Lilac Lake makes a fantastic retreat in the winter. Signed players might not be allowed to ski, but they and their families can enjoy a winter wonderland. We might be able to work something out with the inn."

"I'm liking that idea," said Ross. "Let's you and I meet with Bob, go over his construction plans, and do some cost analyses before we make any decisions."

"I've set up a meeting with Bob tomorrow morning. And I've made hotel reservations for the two of you right on the beach," said Mike.

"We only need one room," said Ross.

Mike's eyes widened. "Oh, no problem."

Melissa was happy she was standing in the hot sun so no one would notice how her cheeks got even redder.

CHAPTER TWENTY-THREE

THE HOTEL WAS RIGHT ON JACKSONVILLE BEACH AND boasted an exercise center, restaurant, bar, shop, and other amenities. Best of all, for Melissa, a brick sidewalk led to a wooden boardwalk onto the nearby white, sandy beach.

After she and Ross settled in their room, Melissa said, "I want to go for a walk on the beach. Want to come with me?"

"A little later. I'm meeting with Mike to develop a game plan for tomorrow's meeting. We need to review the cost estimates to construct a year-round baseball training center. It's important to me to work it out because I know you want to stay in Lilac Lake, and so do I."

She gazed at him.

Ross came over to her and drew her into his arms. "I don't want to do anything to mess up this, whatever it is, between us."

He lowered his lips to hers, and she felt herself dissolve in his arms. She'd waited for so long to have a man kiss her like this that she didn't want to mess it up either.

Melissa changed into the turquoise bikini. After covering her limbs and face with suntan lotion, she put on a cover-up, said goodbye to Ross, and left for the beach carrying a hat and her phone.

After she reached the edge of the beach, she slipped off her sandals, wiggled her toes in the white sand, and sighed with pleasure. She gazed out at the water rolling into the beach in a continual pattern and drew a deep breath of the salty air. She'd been to a beach before but not often, electing instead to stay and work by her favorite lake in New Hampshire.

Melissa put on her hat, tucked her phone into a pocket, and strolled down to meet the water. Their heads bobbing, sanderlings, sandpipers, and other small birds scurried along the water's lacy edge, looking for food.

Above, seagulls and terns wheeled in the wind, crying mournfully as they circled.

A peace came over Melissa as she strolled along the hard-packed sand at the edge of the breaking and receding waves. She lifted her face to the blue sky and whispered thanks that her father would be okay. She felt so lucky compared to Ross, who was facing his father's death.

As she walked, she thought of Ross, the man, not the neighbor, and liked what she'd seen so far. It was obvious that he loved his family, and they loved him. He was unlike most of the other men she'd dated. Being away from Lilac Lake, she understood better why she'd been drawn to Dirk and how loneliness had played a part. They both deserved better than that.

Now, Ross's attention, his kisses, and the excitement she'd never felt with another man all played a part in helping her to believe their relationship was real. Though she'd thought she knew Ross, she now realized he was so much more.

A round, red ball hit her ankle, and a little brown-haired boy shuffled up to her.

She stooped and picked up the ball. "Are you looking for this?" she asked, handing it to him.

The boy's mother, just two steps behind, prompted, "Say thank you, Tim."

"Thank you," the boy said, smiling at her, and Melissa resisted an urge to sweep him up in her arms. Melissa stopped in surprise. Where in the world had that thought come from? She liked children, but she'd never fallen for one so quickly.

Was that female hormones talking?

Melissa stopped and stared out at the moving waves racing to shore and retreating in a pattern as old as time. She had always been so practical and independent that she wondered if she should slow down her relationship with Ross. Sometimes he was all she thought of. Still, she was learning how to share love, and the intimate, supportive conversations after making love benefited them both. Especially now with family trauma going on.

She felt the sun's heat and removed her light cover-up, allowing the sun to embrace her body. The tension of the last few days eased. She stepped into the cool water, watching as the sand at her feet was pulled away by the receding waves before shifting again.

The rhythmic pattern was calming, and she reminded herself to let things unfold naturally and enjoy her time with Ross.

She heard a man call her name and turned to find Mike walking toward her. "Hi! Ross told me I'd find you here. He's on his way. He needed to call his family first."

"Isn't this delightful?" she said and twirled in a circle.

He grinned. "It's beautiful." He studied her. "I had no idea you and Ross were dating. From what Ross has said, it seems pretty serious."

"We're just starting to date," Melissa said. "But he makes me very happy, and I think we're both hoping it'll last."

"Are you okay with him going into business with me, traveling back and forth to Florida from Lilac Lake?"

His steady gaze unnerved her. "I know it's what he wants," she replied, "and I understand."

"What about you? What are you going to do now that the restaurant is gone? Do you want to set up something at the sports center?"

"I'm not sure," she said.

"I think there's room for a real restaurant on the property. We've got a lot of land."

"I don't want to own and run a restaurant," Melissa said. "That's one thing I know for certain. I want to find something that allows me to cook on occasion. I'm trying to come up with some ideas and will let you know when I do." She looked up and saw Ross making his way toward them, and she was relieved. The truth was, she couldn't imagine what the future held for her. There were too many things left unsettled with her life in Lilac Lake.

"Hey, you two, how about going back and having something cool to drink and some food? I haven't eaten much today." Ross approached her and put an arm around her as if to make clear to Mike that they were a couple.

The three of them walked together to the Beach Bar and settled in chairs at the bar. The men ordered beers, and she ordered a margarita before looking at the menu.

"I've been here for a couple of days and highly recommend the grouper sandwich," said Mike. "They do a tasty one."

"That's perfect for me," said Melissa, and Ross quickly agreed.

They ordered their food, and Melissa settled back, feeling very relaxed. She turned to Ross. "How are things at home?"

"Holding steady at the moment, but I'd like to head back right after the business meeting tomorrow morning. Is that okay with you? I promise you another trip to St. Augustine and some of the islands we missed on our way down. We can stop in Savannah on our way home."

"Okay," said Melissa. They could visit St. Augustine another time. She knew how anxious Ross was to see his father again.

"If our sports center goes through, you'll have plenty of

opportunities to come to Florida and travel along the east coast," said Mike, trying to be helpful.

After dinner, Ross was ready to retire. Melissa noted his limp and realized he'd overdone it. His new knee was protesting.

"No problem. Let's go upstairs. I'm happy to sit and watch the sunset from our balcony and have a decent night's sleep. The bed looks comfortable." At Ross's fake leer, Melissa laughed.

"You know what I mean."

Ross took hold of her hand, lifted it to his lips, and kissed it. "You're gorgeous."

A flush of pleasure surged inside Melissa. This was something new. She'd never been called gorgeous.

"Okay, you two, I'll leave you. Ross, I'll meet you for breakfast at eight o'clock. Okay?"

"Sure," said Ross. "We can review the numbers once more before meeting with Bob and his financial guy."

Mike left, and Ross took her arm. "Sorry to be such a slug."

"No apologies necessary," said Melissa. "It's been a crazy week, and you're still healing. Let's go up to our room."

They took the elevator to their room. It was decorated with a beach theme, with white walls, white furniture, and turquoise and yellow accents everywhere.

"Oh, look, the sun is setting," she said. "Let's go on the balcony to watch it."

Outside, they sat in chairs facing the water. Though they were facing east, the sky above them reflected the setting sun's colors, creating an abstract painting of reds, oranges, and yellows.

"This is such a beautiful place," said Melissa. "As we drove south, I realized each state has its own beauty."

Ross reached for her hand and squeezed it. "I'll take another trip with you, here in the States or Europe. Places we can discover together. That's one reason I like your idea of not owning a restaurant."

"Yes," Melissa agreed, even as she realized how unsettled her future was.

After the colors faded and dusk quickly turned dark, Ross stood. "Guess we'd better get to bed."

Melissa followed him inside. "You go ahead and use the bathroom. I'll follow."

Alone, Melissa called her mother. "Hi, I'm just checking in. How are things going? How's Dad?"

"It's a bit of a struggle," her mother admitted. "After being so scared, the reality of life from now on is a little hard to accept for a man who's used to being busy and eating anything he likes. But we'll work on it together, even though your father's usual pleasant humor is gone. The doctor said it's not unusual for some patients to be depressed by all the changes. But eventually, your father will make peace with the changes, and he'll definitely feel better."

"I'm glad. You're terrific support for him," she said.

"Thanks. How are things going with you and Ross?" her mother asked.

"Wonderful. Being with Ross is different from any relationship I've ever had." She wasn't about to tell her mother about the exciting lovemaking she and Ross shared. "He makes me feel beautiful."

"It's wise that you're taking your time with this new relationship," said her mother. "I'm sorry your father isn't here to talk to you. He's meeting with the people from the rehab center. He should be available later."

"Okay, I'll talk to you both later," said Melissa.

Melissa ended the call, wishing she wasn't worried about a

future relationship with Ross. Thinking about it, she decided the real issue was she didn't know about her future, and until that was settled, she couldn't think of life with him. She'd worked too hard to succeed in her field to give it up.

Ross walked toward her wearing just his undershorts, and Melissa's lips curved. Seeing him smiling at her, she felt her spirits lift, and she told herself that she'd been foolish to worry when he made her happier than anyone else ever had.

Later, after making love, she snuggled against his broad chest and sighed with pleasure. It was this, more than the worries she conjured up, that mattered.

CHAPTER TWENTY-FOUR

THE NEXT MORNING, SHE AND ROSS ORDERED ROOM service. While they waited for their food, they lay in bed and discussed the sports center in Lilac Lake. The more they talked about it, the more certain Melissa became that she didn't want to have any part of a food operation there. The sports center was Ross's creative enterprise. She needed one of her own.

"Are you sure you don't want to set up a restaurant, snack bar, or something there?" Ross asked.

"I need to do something different. I'm still trying to come up with a couple of ideas that will satisfy me."

Ross gave her a steady look. "I understand how you must feel. After suddenly having baseball taken away from me, it took me a long time to discover what I wanted to do with my life. Having the opportunity to help kids with the sports center is important to me. I want you to feel the same about whatever you choose."

His statement touched her heart and soul. Melissa threw her arms around him. "Ross, I love ... the way you ..." She stopped. Ross hadn't told her he loved her. She shouldn't be the first to say it, should she?

He hugged her close, and just before his lips met hers, a knock on the door was followed by a voice saying, "Room Service."

Melissa rose from the bed, slipped on the terry robe the hotel had provided, and walked to the door while Ross went into the bathroom to dress.

The staff member gave Melissa a cheery smile as he wheeled the service cart inside the room. "It looks like it's going to be another beautiful day."

Melissa glanced at the drapes still drawn over the sliding glass door to the balcony and felt her cheeks grow hot at the knowing look he gave her. But he was right. She and Ross had been too busy making love to bother with the drapes.

"I've got everything you've ordered for breakfast here. Is there anything else you need?" the man asked.

"I think this will be fine. Thank you." She signed the check and waited until he was gone before calling Ross.

She walked over to the sliding door, drew the drapes, and said, "Let's eat outside. It's so beautiful."

They took their meals out to the balcony. The warm air caressed Melissa's skin as they ate, and the smell of the salt air increased her appetite. That, and last night's exercise with Ross. She thought of a future life with him, living part-time in New Hampshire and Florida. Could they make that work?

Ross's cell phone rang. He set down his fork and picked it up. "Hello? Hi, Jack. What's going on?" Ross listened and said, "Okay, right after I meet with Mike and Bob, we'll head north. Are you sure I don't need to fly there right away?"

Melissa watched sorrow mask Ross's face, and her heart went out to him. She placed a hand on his shoulder as he talked with his brother.

After he clicked off the call, Ross turned to her. "Jack said we need to head north right after my meeting this morning. He promised me we have time before the end, but he knew I'd want to see Dad before things got worse." He held her hand. "I'm sorry. I know this trip hasn't been at all what we'd hoped."

"No apologies are necessary," said Melissa. "I know how hard this is for you."

Ross leaned over and kissed her. "I'm glad you're here."

Melissa walked around the baseball camp while Ross met with Mike and Bob. Seeing children of all ages working at different skill levels, she couldn't help wondering about children of her own. She wanted them but knew she wasn't ready to start a family. Sometimes, she felt like she was two different people—a woman who wanted to be a mother and a wife and a career person who wanted to focus on her job.

Ross approached her as she stood by a fence watching a few boys go after balls batted at their feet.

"Pretty interesting, huh?" he said.

"This camp is a clever way to teach kids skills and give them the opportunity to improve." She smiled. "Practice makes perfect."

He beamed at her. "I think we've come up with some great plans for Lilac Lake, which will affect the entire Northeast."

Mike came over to them. "Have a safe trip north. I'll take care of what we discussed, Ross. Good luck with your father."

The men exchanged bro hugs.

"Thanks for being such a big help to Ross," said Mike, giving her a grateful smile.

"My pleasure," said Melissa.

She got into the car and waited for Ross to ease behind the wheel. It would be a long drive ahead, but it would be worth it. She knew how worried he was about getting home to see his father.

They made it as far as Philadelphia before stopping for a few hours of sleep and then went to Ross's father's house. They wanted to be somewhat rested before facing the hard days ahead.

Inside their room, Ross was asleep the minute his head touched the pillow. Melissa lay awake beside him, trying to erase the images of scenery flashing by that filled her mind. Finally, she closed her eyes.

What seemed moments later, she was awakened by Ross moving around the room.

"Time to get up?" she asked.

"Yes. Hurry. Jack has texted me to say things are going downhill. I want to be on our way as soon as possible."

Relieved she'd taken a shower the night before, Melissa quickly dressed. "We can eat on the road."

Downstairs, they grabbed cups of coffee and a sweet roll to take with them and left the hotel.

As they approached the car, Melissa said, "Do you want me to drive?"

"No, thanks. I need something to keep me busy, and it won't take us long," Ross said. "We've all dreaded this time for months, and now that's it here ..." he stopped speaking.

"I understand," said Melissa, touching his arm. She and Ross had started as neighbors and friends. Their relationship was now so much more.

Melissa could sense his escalating tension as they got closer to Ross's boyhood home.

When they pulled in front of the house, the driveway was full of cars.

"All my brothers are here," said Ross quietly. "C'mon. Let's go inside." Outside the car, Melissa took hold of Ross's cold fingers, and they went to the front door together.

A pretty woman with short, curly dark hair and bright blue eyes greeted them. "Go right to your father's room," she told Ross before turning to Melissa. "Hi, I'm Addie, Dewey's wife. You've met him."

"Yes," Melissa said. "It's a pleasure to meet you, though I wish it were under different circumstances."

"Me, too. My father-in-law is a prince of a man—gentle, sweet, and encouraging. He's been more a father to me than my own." Addie pulled a tissue from her pants pocket and dabbed at her eyes.

Melissa hugged her.

When Addie pulled back, she smiled. "His father has spoken about you too. As Dewey said, Ross hit a home run with you."

Addie's easy acceptance of her brought tears to Melissa's eyes as she followed her inside. Two other women sat in the living room, talking quietly. They looked up and smiled when Melissa entered the room.

Addie introduced her to Jack's wife, Jenn, and Dennis's wife, Lisa. The difference between the two women was striking. Jenn looked like the wife of a very successful lawyer, with her striking features, expensive clothes, and blond hair pulled back into a classic bun. Lisa, married to a farmer, wore jeans and a knit top and had let her brown hair flow down to her shoulders. Though pretty, she made little effort with makeup. But all three women seemed friendly and supportive of one another as they faced their family's sadness.

"I understand you and Ross have driven here from Florida. Jack told me that Ross met you in New Hampshire, where he's built a new house," said Jenn.

"We're next-door neighbors. But living in our small town means everyone knows everyone else, so we were bound to meet anyway."

"What's this I hear about you being a chef?" asked Addie. "I bet you have some recipes to share."

Melissa smiled. "Mine are a little complicated. But I do have a way of streamlining them for home cooking."

"I heard there was a fire at your family's restaurant," said Jenn.

"Yes, it was destroyed. My family isn't going to reopen it, so I'm at loose ends trying to figure out what I want to do next," said Melissa.

"Well, you won't have to worry about that if you marry Ross," said Lisa. "The Roberts men like large families. I'm still working on baby number four."

The women all chuckled. Melissa joined in. But secretly, she was uneasy. She and Ross had talked about many things, but not marriage per se and not about children. She couldn't imagine handling four children.

Mrs. Barnard stepped out of the bedroom. "I'm sorry to say that John is gone. If you'd like to see him privately, you can take turns. The boys are saying goodbye now."

Jenn, the wife of the oldest, stood. "I'll be first if you don't mind."

As she left, Ross and his brothers walked into the living room. Observing Ross's face, Melissa stood and went to him.

"I'm so sorry," she said as they embraced. "He was such a sweet man."

"The best," said Ross, holding her tightly. He lifted her face and smiled even as tears filled his eyes. "He told everyone I hit a home run with you."

Melissa's vision blurred.

"Come sit with me out back," Ross said. "I need to get some fresh air."

She followed him to a ground-level deck and sat in one of the chairs next to his. "I know your father's death was expected, but that doesn't make it any easier. What can I do?"

"Just be here for me. I always feel better when you're around." He smiled at her. "You're such a good friend ... no, much more than that. Ah, I don't know what I'm saying."

Melissa squeezed his hand. "Look at the sky. It's filled with white, puffy clouds forming different shapes. I think it's an interesting way to remember things about your father. You were lucky, Ross, to grow up in a family like yours."

"Both of my parents were incredible people. I hope to be that for any children of mine."

Melissa froze, wondering what might be coming next, but Lisa walked out on the deck, followed by a man who looked a lot like Ross. "Melissa, you haven't met my husband, Dennis."

Melissa stood and shook hands with him. "I understand you have a farm."

He grinned. "It's what I've always wanted. As a kid, Ross played baseball, and I grew vegetables. It's all worked out well."

"Yes, and now I get to help other kids learn to play ball," said Ross.

"I remember how it was, all the practices and games," said Dennis. "It sure made you a star player. My two boys might be taking after you."

"Our daughter is athletic, too," said Lisa. "It runs in the family."

"Did you know Dad was a fantastic player back in the day?" Ross said. "That's why he gave me so much time. He wanted me to do what he hadn't been able to do for himself. I always felt like I owed him for any success I had."

"It was his joy to do that," said Dennis, clapping a hand on Ross's shoulder. "We're all going to miss him."

When Ross glanced at Melissa, she saw a sheen of tears in his blue eyes.

She smiled at him, and he returned a shaky one.

A few minutes later, the rest of the family joined them on the deck.

"I'm taking care of the legal end of things," Jack

announced. "Jenn and Addie are taking care of the details of a memorial service for Dad, and Dennis and Lisa will do the flowers for the service. That leaves you, Ross, to speak at the service. Will you do it?"

"When is it?" Ross asked.

Jenn spoke up. "Addie and I thought we'd have the service a week from today to give us time to take care of any unexpected issues."

"Okay," said Ross. He glanced at Melissa. "That gives me time to get home and get ready."

"I hope you'll both return," said Jenn, giving Melissa a sweet smile.

Ross glanced at Melissa, and she nodded.

"We'll fly next time," said Ross.

"I can pick you up at the airport," said Dennis.

"Or I can arrange a limo and make it easy on everyone," said Ross.

Melissa listened to them with fascination. There didn't seem to be any arguments about anything. She guessed the family had been trained to talk as a group from a young age.

"The reading of the will can take place anytime," said Jack. "We know what to expect. If any of you women want something from the house before it's sold, you can speak up. As we'd all agreed earlier, the house will be put on the market as soon as it's cleared out. The family cottage will remain as it is, with the four of us owning it equally."

Melissa tuned out the conversation and thought of her own circumstances. What had once seemed a complication with the destroyed restaurant was now much simpler. Melissa knew her parents intended to use the insurance money from the fire and the land sale for their retirement. They'd talked of keeping their house in Lilac Lake and going to Florida or Arizona for at least part of the year. She dreaded the time when they grew older, and she'd have to face an issue like this.

Movement around her brought Melissa's attention back to the present. "You two are welcome to stay at our house tonight," said Jenn. "I understand you want to leave first thing in the morning."

Melissa turned to Ross.

"That would be great, Jenn," said Ross. "Is that okay with you, Melissa?"

"Yes," she answered, suddenly anxious to be back in her own space. The last several days had been intense, and she needed to unwind and think.

While Ross talked with his siblings, Melissa excused herself to take a walk. That, she hoped, would help alleviate some of her stress.

As Melissa left the house, Lanie Southerland walked out of the house next door and waved. Melissa had no choice but to wait as Lanie approached.

"Has it happened?" Lanie asked her.

Melissa nodded, and Lanie's eyes teared up. "John Roberts was such a special person. Everyone loved him." She turned to go. "I have to go to Ross. I know how heartbroken he must be."

Melissa waited until Lanie left, then went to the sidewalk for a walk through the neighborhood. As she observed the houses on the street, she saw that it was a neighborhood of older residents and young families. It was like Lilac Lake with people of all ages and backgrounds.

People were friendly, waving as she walked by.

After circling several blocks, Melissa returned to the Roberts' house, feeling more settled.

When she walked inside, Ross excused himself from talking with Lanie and walked over to greet her. "Have a nice walk?"

"Yes, thank you. It felt good. I'm not used to doing so much sitting."

Lanie joined them. "Ross has invited me to his house. I hope to see you later this summer."

Melissa glanced at Ross.

"Lanie is thinking of making a change and wants to look at Lilac Lake to see if that's someplace she'd like to live," said Ross. "I told her it's a town where it's easy to meet other people."

"But with you there, why would I want to do that?" Lanie said, beaming at him as she leaned against his body.

Ross's cheeks flushed, and he eased away from her. "There are several unattached men in town for you to meet. I'm dating Melissa."

"Oh," said Lanie, glancing from him to Melissa. "I thought Melissa was another of your women."

Ross looked embarrassed.

Melissa's mind spun. She hadn't known Ross for long. Had she misread their relationship?

CHAPTER TWENTY-FIVE

ROSS DROVE MELISSA TO JACK'S HOUSE, A NEWLY constructed, two-story contemporary home on Wayside Place in Montclair. Inside, Jenn showed Melissa to a lovely guest suite on the second floor. "I know you won't be staying here long, but hopefully, being here will give you a decent night's rest," Jenn said.

"It's beautiful," said Melissa. "Where are the girls?"

"Brace yourself," teased Jenn. "The two of them will be here soon. Their school runs late. They adore Uncle Ross, so I know they'll come right home. Nan is driving now, and Kate will soon be. It's a mother's nightmare worrying about them, but as Jack tells me, I must let them go."

"I can only imagine," said Melissa.

Jenn studied her. "How long have you known Ross? You just started dating?"

"Ross has been in town for almost two years," Melissa said. "We got to know each other as neighbors and are now together."

"Really? I've never seen Ross like this. And though we've met other women he's dated, I don't think he'd have you here now if he didn't consider your relationship to be serious."

"Lanie said he's had lots of women," Melissa said, still conflicted.

Jenn shook her head. "Lanie will never get over losing Ross, even though it was her choice. The truth is, Ross has dated a lot but never seriously. And as for Lanie, they're friends and will never be more than that. The fact that Ross is even nice to her shows what a kind person he is."

Melissa wanted to hear more about Ross, but he walked into the room and effectively ended the conversation.

"Jack said to come down to the kitchen. The bar is open, and we all need to toast Dad," said Ross.

Melissa followed Ross downstairs and entered a stunning kitchen. She liked the layout, the indoor grill, and the entertainment area attached to the kitchen, which held white cabinets and all the latest equipment.

Jack, a tall, handsome man, always seemed in charge. He motioned for them to gather around as he opened a bottle of champagne. He then poured the bubbling white wine into each tulip glass and handed them out.

He raised his glass and said, "I promised Dad we'd celebrate his life with a toast after he was gone. He didn't want to be remembered as he was at the end of his life but as the father we all loved and honored. So, here's to Dad!"

"Hear! Hear!" said Ross, and Melissa whispered, "To you, John."

Jenn caught her eye and smiled as if she understood that Melissa was too shy to say it aloud.

The arrival of Nan and Kate ended what might have become maudlin talk.

"There you are," said Jenn. "Uncle Ross is here with a special friend, Melissa Hendrickson. We're just toasting Grandpa John's life as he asked us to do."

Nan was a stunning sixteen-year-old with blue eyes like her father. She went to him. "I'm sorry, Dad. I loved Grandpa John so much."

Kate clung to her mother, her shoulders shaking as she cried softly. "I hate cancer."

"We all do," said Ross.

Kate turned to him. "It's all so sad."

Ross rubbed Kate's back. Shorter than her sister and with blond hair, she looked more like her mother.

Nan came over to Ross, and he opened his arms to her. When they pulled apart, Nan turned to her mother. "Can Kate and I toast Grandpa too?"

Jenn exchanged a glance with Jack. "Yes, just this once. We want to remember the good times with Grandpa John and celebrate that we knew him."

"I want you girls to meet Melissa Hendrickson," said Ross.

"Your special friend," said Nan, holding out a hand to her.

A bit awed by the teen's composure, Melissa shook her hand and then did the same with Kate, who greeted her with a friendly smile.

"It's very nice to meet you. Uncle Ross hasn't brought a girlfriend around for a long time," said Kate. She stopped talking when her mother cleared her throat in warning.

Once again, everyone lifted their glasses, and Jack said, "Here's to Grandpa John, Dad, the husband to our dear mother and grandmother. He was a fine man."

Everyone clicked glasses and then swallowed the wine.

Kate coughed from the bubbles and burst out laughing. "That's delicious."

"Grandpa would've been happy with beer, but this is a very sweet gesture," said Jenn, giving Jack a nod of approval.

Though she didn't have much experience with gatherings like this, Melissa liked the openness of this family.

After the toast, Jack said, "I've ordered food from China Dragon."

"Yay!" said Kate, clapping her hands. "We haven't had that in a long time."

"Not with all those calories," said Nan, giving her sister a reproving look.

"Let's use this time to celebrate without worrying about

other things," Jenn said quietly, and the girls grew silent.

Melissa had heard many horrible stories about teenagers but was impressed by the girls' behavior.

While they waited for dinner to be delivered, the girls went to their rooms, and Melissa settled on the outdoor porch with the other adults. The screened-in porch was as stunning as the rest of the house, with an outdoor kitchen, fireplace, and comfortable seating. The landscaped backyard was lush and held a small fountain that tumbled water into a koi pond.

"This is lovely," Melissa said, "I have a big backyard, but it's mostly a vegetable and herb garden."

"Which is appropriate for you," said Ross, smiling at her before turning to Jenn. "Melissa is a fantastic chef. At the restaurant her family owned, the food was always served fresh and delicious. Unfortunately, the restaurant burned down."

"What will you do now that the restaurant is gone?" Jack asked her.

"I'm still trying to figure that out," said Melissa. "I spent years learning about food and earning a reputation as an excellent chef. I don't want to walk away from that."

Jack shrugged. "That's understandable. But aren't you helping Ross with his project?"

"I'm encouraging him and trying to help in any way I can, but I need to do things for myself," Melissa said.

Ross caught her attention and winked. He knew she needed her independence.

Their dinner arrived, and Melissa became lost in choosing what she wanted for her meal. She took small servings of everything so she could go back for more. Jack had ordered enough food for a crowd double their size.

They sat at a long, pine table in the kitchen dining area. Melissa took a bite of the House Special Chicken, closed her eyes, and savored the taste of chicken strips and fresh vegetables in a spicy sauce.

"Delicious, huh?" said Ross, grinning at her.

She opened her eyes and let out a soft laugh. "A fantastic blend of tastes. It's wonderful to have authentic food like this."

"One thing about living in this area is that we're exposed to many different foods," said Jenn. "You'll have to visit for a foodie weekend."

"I'd like that," said Melissa, realizing how pleasant it was to be included in the family.

"You two can stay here when you return for Dad's service," said Jack.

"Of course," said Jenn with a warmth that touched Melissa. Was this what it would be like to be a permanent part of Ross's family?

After dinner, Jenn told the girls, "Go ahead and spend some time with your father and Uncle Ross. Melissa and I will do the dishes. It'll be nice for the four of you to spend some time talking about Grandpa John."

"I'm going to write a poem about him," said Nan.

"That would be lovely, sweetheart," said Jenn. "We all have so many things to remember about him."

"What about Grandma Betty? Do you think they're together again?" asked Kate.

Jenn smiled. "I'd like to think so."

The girls left the room with the men, leaving Melissa with Jenn.

"What was Ross's mother like?" Melissa asked her.

Jenn stared into space and turned to her. "Betty was not your average wife and mother. She was gentle but tough and could wrestle life with four active boys. She attended everyone's sports games, encouraged Dennis with his love of plants, and commanded the boys' respect. She was quite an athlete herself. She was built a lot like you."

"She sounds like an outstanding mother," Melissa said.

"All the Roberts men adored her. John, most of all. She was very kind to me. I'm Jack's second wife, and I was eager for her to see I wouldn't hurt him like his first wife did." Jenn said quietly, "His first wife was a troubled woman. Thank goodness they had no children. That's all I'll say about her."

"And Betty supported you," said Melissa, wishing she'd known Ross's mother. She and John had raised four wonderful men.

"You're different from anyone else Ross has ever dated," said Jenn. "You're unlike some who were after Ross's money and status."

Melissa straightened. "I don't need either. I have my own."

Jenn's eyes widened, and then she burst out laughing. "Yes! That's what I'm talking about. You're different, all right, and I love it. I think we could become real friends. And Lisa and Addie are easy to get to know. You'll like them."

Melissa took it all in, both excited and nervous about the idea.

Ross walked into the kitchen, glanced from Melissa to Jenn, and said, "What's going on?"

Melissa shrugged. "I'm just learning about your family."

"You've done a fabulous job finding Melissa," said Jenn.

Ross beamed at them both.

Later, lying in bed with Ross, Melissa said, "I'm happy I got to meet your father. Jenn tells me your mother was a wonderful woman."

"The best," said Ross. "I've been lucky my whole life. Growing up, I had great parents and some super opportunities. I'd wish the same for any children I might have."

Melissa didn't say anything, just let that thought settle.

CHAPTER TWENTY-SIX

THE NEXT MORNING, MELISSA AWOKE TO AN EMPTY BED. She checked the time, saw that it was still early, rose quietly, put on some clothes, and went down to the kitchen, intending to get a cup of coffee.

When she walked into the room, Jenn and Ross looked up at her and smiled.

"Am I interrupting anything?" she asked them.

Ross shrugged. "I'm just getting advice from my sister-in-law. I didn't disturb you getting out of bed, did I?"

"No," said Melissa. "I know you want to get off to an early start and sensed it was time to get up."

"Help yourself to a cup of coffee," said Jenn, indicating a Keurig machine on the counter. "It's easiest for everyone to pick what they want and make it themselves."

"Perfect," said Melissa. She chose a decaf blend and joined Jenn and Ross at the kitchen bar after fixing it.

"I'll make flight reservations for both of us to return," Ross told her. "I told Jenn we wouldn't stay long—just two days. Anything else can be handled from a distance. Does that sound okay with you?"

"Yes," Melissa said. "I'll be here for you, however long."

"You're so easy to get along with," said Jenn. "Is this how you always are?"

Melissa grinned. "In the kitchen, I demand a lot of myself and everyone else. But I try to be fair, making sure everyone is doing what they're supposed to do. It's a lot like leading an orchestra."

"I admire you for having such an interesting career," said Jenn. She glanced at Ross. "And I'm pleased you are considering having some project of your own. Two strong people need their separate things. You know?"

Ross settled his gaze on Melissa.

"Hang on, everybody," said Jenn. "The world has awakened, and the girls will blow through here like a tornado on their way to school."

"If you don't mind, I'm going to take my coffee back to the bedroom while I get ready to leave," said Melissa.

"By all means, go ahead," said Jenn.

"I'll be up in a while," said Ross. "I want to spend some time, however brief, with my nieces."

Melissa gave him a little wave and left the room, eager for a quick shower before dressing for the day.

Melissa had just finished brushing her hair when Ross knocked on the bathroom door.

"Come on in," she said, and he opened the door wearing only his boxers.

"I need to grab a quick shower. Okay?"

She studied him, admiring his strong body, remembering what it had been like to make love with him, and forced herself to focus. "Sure. I'm leaving."

He caught hold of her arm and drew her to him. "'Morning." His lips met hers, and she thought about how right it was to start the day like this.

Aware of his response, she moved away. "I'll finish packing and be ready anytime you are."

"Thanks." Ross stripped off his shorts and entered the oversized shower.

Melissa marveled at the ease between them. She'd seen naked men before, of course. But she'd never shared a relationship like the one she had with Ross. He was so natural, so loving, and sexy with her.

Later, on the road, Melissa thought about Jenn's telling them that two strong people need their own interests. Sometimes, it took someone else's words to make sense of things. A thought had been playing in her mind, and now, she wanted to act on it.

She gazed out the car window, content to keep it her secret.

Ross asked if she would drive. "I want to review some numbers so I can discuss them with Mike tonight. He's going to stay at my house."

She took over the driving, happy to have something to focus on.

Back in Lilac Lake, Ross dropped her off at her house. "I'll call you later, okay? I don't know how long Mike will stay with me, but I want to see you."

Melissa nodded and waved before she rolled her suitcase to her front door. Inside her house, she placed a phone call.

Later, she drove to the Lilac Lake Café and waited for Crystal to finish closing the restaurant for the day. She and Crystal were friendly, but she didn't share a close relationship with her because of their constant restaurant work. But Melissa wasn't going to let that stop her from moving forward.

Crystal closed out the cash register for the day and walked over to Melissa. "Hey, girl. How are things going with you? I hear you and Ross are together now. Guess it took a road trip to make you both see you're perfect for one another."

Melissa smiled and looked away, fighting tears.

Crystal took hold of her hand. "What's wrong?"

Melissa let out a shaky breath, relieved to be able to talk

about her doubts and her fears. "Ross is wonderful. But I'm not sure it will work out now that we're back home. All of my previous relationships have ended quickly. I'm afraid this will too."

"Let's take this step by step," said Crystal. "You and Ross are or have been sleeping together. Right?"

Melissa nodded.

"You've always been good neighbors, and that isn't going to change, right?"

Melissa shook her head.

"Has Ross shown you how much he cares about you?" Crystal asked.

Melissa caught her lip. "Yes."

"Okay, then. You're pushing things a bit during a tense several days for both of you," said Crystal sweetly, putting her arm around Melissa. "What's going on with you? Why do you think your relationship with Ross won't last?"

Melissa hesitated.

"You can speak freely. I promise I won't discuss it with anyone else."

Melissa closed her eyes and drew a deep breath. When she opened them, Crystal's look of concern encouraged her to be honest. "As my mother says, I tend to ruin things. If someone gets too close, I push them away before they can hurt me." Melissa forced herself to go on. "Growing up, I was always being compared to other girls by my mother and coming up short. In some ways, I can't believe Ross is truly interested in me. I can't help wondering if what we've shared is just a nice ... interlude ... for him."

"I'm not as wise as Genie Wittner, but I know what she'd say because I understand what it's like to grow up feeling you aren't equal to others. She'd tell you the same thing she told me—you are your own person, warts and all, and you owe it to yourself to be true to who you are inside, not what other people want you to be. And you need to allow others the same opportunity."

Melissa kept quiet. Gazing at Crystal, she was thrilled she'd had the nerve to approach her. Crystal was a lovely, sensitive woman. "Ross is a good man. Give him and yourself a chance," said Crystal. "You're looking for problems that don't exist. You're an attractive, accomplished woman. Any man would be lucky to have you. Stop short-changing yourself."

"Thanks," said Melissa. "I've never told anyone else what I've just said to you."

"Just give it time. It'll all work out the way it's meant to be. Another of Genie Wittner's sayings," said Crystal.

"Thanks for listening to me," said Melissa. "It means a lot. I wanted to talk to you about an idea I have." She straightened in her chair, more in control. "I can't simply walk away from a career that I love. My parents and I have no desire to rebuild the restaurant or to run a restaurant full-time. But I thought there might be a way I could still do some professional cooking. What would you say to my using the café once a month to put on a gourmet dinner? You have the perfect setup."

Crystal's eyes lit with excitement. "So, you'd use the restaurant, dress it up a bit, work in the kitchen, and put on a gourmet dinner?"

"Exactly," said Melissa. "I'm also thinking about doing some catering. I don't want to work full-time. I just want to do enough to keep my hand in while I have time to do something other than work and pursue other interests."

"What are you thinking? Who would you get to help you?" asked Crystal.

"I'm still working on those details. I thought I'd talk to some of my staff from Fins," Melissa said.

"What about me? I'd love to cook with you. I'm thinking of selling the café and love the idea of cooking gourmet dinners from time to time."

"Maybe you could make gourmet dinners part of the sales deal," said Melissa excitedly. A sudden thought struck her. "I know someone who might be interested in buying the café. A friend from culinary school and her fiancé. I stayed in her apartment in Boston when Ross had surgery on his knee."

"Really? I haven't even put together figures, but have your friend come to Lilac Lake to see the operation, and we can all talk about it."

Heart pounding with enthusiasm, Melissa left the café and headed for her car, which she'd parked at the restaurant.

She walked along the street, enjoying the opportunity to exercise. She saw Dirk walking with an attractive woman and waved. He led the woman across the street. "Hi, Melissa. I'm glad to see you, and I want to introduce you to my ex-girlfriend, Samantha Waters. We're together again. Sam, this is Melissa Hendrickson, a friend and wonderful chef in town."

Melissa chuckled and shook hands with Samantha. "An ex-chef since the family restaurant burned down. But I'm coming up with lots of ideas for future events. I'll let you know all about it when the time comes."

"Guess you and Ross are back in town for a while," said Dirk.

"Yes, for a few days only. His father's funeral is this weekend, so we're flying back to New Jersey for it," she said. "It's a pleasure to meet you, Samantha. I'm sure I'll be seeing you around town. Welcome to Lilac Lake."

As Melissa continued on her way, she burst out laughing. Like Genie Wittner told Crystal, "Just wait, and things will work out."

CHAPTER TWENTY-SEVEN

WHEN MELISSA GOT HOME, SHE CALLED NETTIE Mancini, her friend from school. When she was in Boston with Ross's hospitalization, it had been wonderful to reconnect. Melissa felt Nettie and her fiancé, Jason Rockwell, might be open to something new. Nettie had mentioned in a recent text that commercial leasing rates were skyrocketing in Boston, particularly in the North End.

Nettie gave her a cheerful hello and said, "How are things going with your family and the restaurant issue?"

"That's why I'm calling," said Melissa. "My father had a heart attack, and though he's recovering, there's no way my mother and he want to go back to running a restaurant. They're going to sell what remains of it, including the liquor license and land."

"I'm happy to hear he's alright, but there's no way Jason and I could afford to buy the restaurant," said Nettie.

"I have a different offer for you. My friend, Crystal Owens, is selling her very successful breakfast and lunch café, and she and I have come up with an idea that could include you. Is there any way you and Jason can come to Lilac Lake to talk to us? It's best if you see the situation before seriously discussing it."

"Let me ask Jason. Moving and owning a café would be a big change for us. I'm not sure he'll want to do it, though he's become discouraged about keeping the restaurant profitable here in the city. As I mentioned to you, rental rates are skyrocketing. You know how low the profit margin is in the restaurant business."

"Indeed, I do. Please think about the concept. It would be great to have you in town. I'm sure you'd both love it here."

"I admit the idea is very tempting," said Nettie. "The pace in the city is sometimes overwhelming. The idea of listening to birds sing or watching them swim in a lake sounds pretty darn tempting. But Melissa, I'm pretty sure our siblings won't be willing to leave Boston. So, we'd have to find staff there."

"Call me back as soon as you and Jason have had time to discuss it. You're welcome to stay at my house."

"How's that hunky neighbor of yours?" asked Nettie.

Melissa felt a smile cross her face. "We're more than neighbors. I don't know how long it will last, but as my friend Crystal said, 'Things will work out how they're meant to be.' Keeping that in mind, I'm letting things evolve on their own."

"A wise plan," said Nettie. "I'll let you know if or when we want to come to Lilac Lake. Thanks for thinking of us."

Melissa ended the call and did a little dance. The thought of having Nettie involved in her plan was thrilling. No matter what the future might bring, she loved having time for herself and being able to keep a hand in professional cooking.

She'd just poured herself a glass of mint lemonade when Ross appeared at the sliding glass door of her kitchen.

Glad to see him, she went to greet him.

Grinning, he kissed her. Then, he handed her a bottle of chilled white wine. "Nice to be back home, huh?"

"Yes. Come in. I want to tell you about my day." She glanced around. "Where's Mike?"

"He went to Jake's to meet with some of the gang. I think there's someone he's interested in. He said something about a new teacher in town."

"Speaking of new people in town, Dirk introduced me to his ex-girlfriend, whom he is now dating again. Her name is

Samantha Waters, and she seemed nice."

Ross gave her a steady look. "So that relationship is definitely behind you?"

Melissa smiled. "It was never going to work."

"Good," he said, kissing her again.

Melissa's body grew heated as his lips told her how much he liked her. But thoughts of feeling unworthy and of her screwing up the situation appeared in her mind, and she pulled away.

"How about something to drink?" she asked. "I'm making something simple for dinner, but I'm willing to share."

"That would be great," he said. "I don't know about you, but nothing tastes better than your home-cooked meals."

"I want to tell you about an idea that Crystal and I are working on," said Melissa. She led him into the kitchen and got him a beer from the refrigerator.

They went out to the porch, took seats on the couch, and faced one another.

"What's going on?" he asked.

Melissa told him about Crystal possibly selling the café, her friends from Boston hopefully visiting, and her idea of monthly gourmet meals. "There's a lot to think about, but this is something worth working toward. It could be so much fun."

"If the café doesn't work out, maybe you could use the Sports Center in some way for those dinners."

"We need a commercial kitchen," Melissa said. "That's why the café is so perfect. But, as I said, there's a lot to work out. The thing is, I don't have to give up cooking altogether. That's important to me if I ever want to get back into it. If the café doesn't work, I suppose I could apply for work at the Inn."

"I thought you wanted to take time before jumping back into something," said Ross.

"I do. But I don't like the idea of not doing anything

creative for myself," she replied. "I'm waiting to see how things unfold."

Ross was quiet but nodded thoughtfully.

Their conversation moved to the sports center and some of the ideas Ross and Mike were working on. It was good to be able to talk about it. One thing was certain: she wasn't about to bring up a future between them without knowing exactly what Ross had in mind.

Having had the discussion with Crystal, Melissa felt a new sense of peace.

When Melissa moved indoors to put together a simple summer salad with tomatoes, sweet peppers, cucumbers, and fresh herbs, Ross followed her.

While she was fixing it, Ross's cell rang.

He took the call, and after ending it, he turned to her. "That was Jenn calling to say all the arrangements for Dad's memorial service have been made. I'm going to give a short speech along with my three brothers. They decided they all wanted to say a few words about him. I'm relieved because that takes a lot of pressure off me."

"It's very sweet of them. You have a wonderful family."

He came over to her and pulled her into his embrace. "They think *you're* wonderful. I do, too."

Melissa smiled with pleasure but didn't know how to respond. She finally said, "Do you want me to add sliced chicken to your salad? I can do that and add some other things to make the salad heartier."

"That would be good," he said, squeezing her before releasing her. "I'll open the bottle of wine whenever you're ready."

He watched as she prepared the salad with sure, smooth movements.

"It's fascinating to watch you work," he said. "You make it look so easy."

"It's like anything else, it just takes practice. But I like preparing food. I always have."

He studied her. "What are we going to do?"

"About what?" she asked.

"About us. Things are chaotic with my dad's death, but I'd like to keep seeing you, being with you."

"Me, too," she said.

"How about my spending the night? Mike might be staying at my house, but he's on his own. I don't want anyone to interfere with what we have."

Melissa was dying to ask him what they had, but she remained quiet.

He came around the island and wrapped his arms around her. "Put down the knife," he whispered in her ear.

She placed it on the counter and turned to him, her heart pounding. His lips met hers, and she filled with desire. He'd taught her how to make love with him, how to please him and herself. Now, all she could think of was how she wanted more than his kiss. When he took her hand and led her away, she followed eagerly. It had been a couple of days since they'd made love, and she was more than ready.

Later, they lay together in her bed, sated and happy.

Ross turned to her. "I'm thankful you're my neighbor. It makes being with you easy."

Melissa bristled. Did he think she was easy?

Ross seemed to sense her distress and cupped her face with his hands. "I like being able to be with you. That's what I meant. After all the years of being single and turned off by the idea of someone after my money, you're worth the wait."

Satisfied, she raised her face to meet his lips.

CHAPTER TWENTY-EIGHT

MELISSA WAS IN THE KITCHEN GETTING HER MORNING coffee when her cell rang. *Nettie.* Her pulse sprinted. "Hello?"

"Hi, Melissa. Great news, I think. Jason and I are willing to come to take a look at Lilac Lake. Neither of us is about to jump ship easily, but we're excited to think of other possibilities. That's all I'll say. How about we come in two weeks? There's a quiet period after school starts. We can come then for the first few days of that week."

"Wonderful! That will give me time after returning from New Jersey with Ross to give my full attention to the idea. In the meantime, Crystal and I will think about what we need to discuss. Oh, Nettie! Maybe this will work."

Nettie chuckled. "I'm liking the idea more and more. The dinner restaurant service night after night is a real grind."

"Tell me about it," said Melissa, relieved she wouldn't have to be part of that now or maybe ever.

"I'll talk to you later," said Nettie. "I'm looking up information about Lilac Lake and the entire area online."

"Smart idea," said Melissa. "No matter what you might read, it's even better when you see it for yourself."

As soon as she ended the call, Melissa phoned Crystal. "Let's meet. I've got some encouraging news."

"Okay, come by the café mid-afternoon. I should be able to talk then."

After ending the call, Melissa decided to visit her parents. Her father was home from the hospital, and though he reportedly was grumpy from his change in diet and the need to exercise, her mother promised her that he was fine.

She drove to their house in an older, quiet part of town. Houses there tended to be large and on good-sized lots.

As she pulled up in front of the gray clapboard colonial, Melissa remembered her days as a child living there. Often, her parents were gone, working at the restaurant, and she'd been alone with her babysitter, an older woman named Mrs. Williams, or Willy, as Melissa had called her.

Gazing at the house, Melissa thought of Ross and wondered if he, like his brothers, wanted a large family. She wasn't sure about having a lot of kids, but she knew she wanted at least two. As an only child, she'd often wished for a sibling to talk to to help her navigate life with a mother who both approved and disapproved of her, making life difficult and creating insecurity in her. It was hard not measuring up in appearance and behavior but winning accolades for her help in the kitchen.

Melissa decided to say as little as possible about her relationship with Ross, do as Crystal suggested, and wait and see how it evolved. She cared about Ross in a way she'd never experienced.

Melissas shook her head at herself. She might as well admit the truth. She loved Ross, loved the way he made her feel, loved that he was a friend as well as a lover. But until she knew he felt the same way about her, saying nothing was her best protection.

She got out of the car and went to the front door.

Her mother greeted her, looking frazzled.

"Mom? Is everything all right?" Melissa asked.

"We're still trying to get into our new routine while working with our lawyer and real estate advisor to try and sell the remains of our restaurant. The sooner we get it sold, the better it will be. Your father is already having second thoughts about leaving the business even though he promised me he would."

Her mother looked so fragile, so Melissa reached out and hugged her. "Even though it's inevitable, change can be hard. I've got some news to share."

They walked into the huge kitchen at the back of the house to find her father sitting at the kitchen table.

"Hi, Dad," said Melissa. "It looks like another beautiful day. I swear I smell a hint of fall in the air."

Her father smiled hello and went back to the papers he was reading.

"What's this?" Melissa asked after kissing him on the cheek. "Do you have a buyer already?"

Her father made a face. "Looks like it might happen. The people who run Fresh Restaurant outside of town are considering buying it. Though I wouldn't say I like the thought of selling, their concept of fresh, farm-to-table food is appealing. And, they're excited about adding fresh fish to their menu."

"I think they'd do well in town," said Melissa.

"They'd be getting a hell of a bargain," grumped her father. "All those years of building our reputation certainly helps them. Right now, it's caught up in many legal and financial issues, but your mother is delighted everyone wants to make it work."

"Except you?" Melissa asked, giving him a knowing look.

He gave her a sheepish grin. "I know it's the right thing to do. I'm just not ready."

"Dad, you've been talking about retiring for the past three years. It's time." Seeing him looking as frail as her mother brought tears to her eyes. After going through the pain of Ross losing his father, seeing them this way scared her.

"What can I do to help?" she asked as her mother placed a hand on her father's shoulder.

"It's all going to work out," her mother said calmly. "Now tell us what's going on with you."

"Let me grab a cup of coffee, and I'll fill you in." She poured herself a cup of the drip coffee she loved and sat at the kitchen table. "I've come up with an idea to explore."

She told them about Crystal possibly selling the café, that Nettie and Jason were visiting, and about her idea for scheduled gourmet dinners at the café. "I want to keep my hand in cooking, but I don't want to commit to a full-time job until I've had a chance for some time to myself."

"What about Ross?" her mother asked.

"We'll see how that plays out. The most important thing is for me to figure out my next move. I need a creative outlet, and cooking does that for me," Melissa replied, unwilling to say more.

"He's a fine man. You could have an outstanding future with him," her mother said with a note of warning.

Melissa took a deep breath so she wouldn't snap back at her. "I'm just taking it day by day."

"How's he holding up with his father's death?" her mother asked, her words gentle now.

"It's hard, but he has a wonderful family who are supportive of one another," said Melissa. "That helps. We're flying to New Jersey on Friday. His father's service is going to be on Saturday."

"It's nice that you can support him," said her mother.

"These gourmet dinners would be once a month?" asked her father. "What if the demand is for more?"

"That's something we'd need to think about," said Melissa. "Crystal is very excited to do a different kind of cooking. We're both at a point where we want some time to ourselves."

"I feel bad that you've worked so hard at our restaurant," said her mother. "But that's the business."

"Yes, we all know that, which is why coming together might work for Crystal and me," said Melissa. "Besides, you know I loved working in the kitchen with Dad."

"It was a privilege to have you there," said her father, getting a little emotional.

Melissa exchanged glances with her mother.

Her mother checked her watch. "It's time to go to the rehab center, Fran."

"Not that again," her father grumped.

"I'll leave you to it," said Melissa, taking the opportunity to leave. Since the fire at the restaurant, things had been very different for all of them.

Melissa stood with Crystal in the Café's kitchen, inspecting all its features.

"What suggestions do you have for making it better for the type of cooking you want to do?" Crystal asked.

Together, they made a list of additional items that could be added.

"And remember the table linens, silver, dishes, and glasses for the dinners," said Melissa. "If we're going to do it, we should make it upscale, don't you think?"

"Yes," said Crystal.

They walked into the main room and studied it.

Crystal indicated the area with a sweep of her hand. "Fortunately, the room will lend itself to making it more upscale, and the outdoor dining area is perfect except for those winter evenings that will make it impossible without heaters and firepits."

"A lot will depend on what Nettie and Jason think and if they're willing to make a major change in their lives," said Melissa. "If they don't, maybe you and I can work something out."

"I'm not giving up my independence by marrying Emmett," said Crystal. "But I want more time with him. He's very busy as the new doctor in town, but we want to enjoy things together."

"I understand completely. I don't feel I have to be married to live life well, but I want a loving relationship." Melissa looked at Crystal.

Crystal clapped a hand on Melissa's shoulder. "Well said. And, God help me; I'm tired of having to get up at the crack of dawn to open the café for breakfast."

"I understand," Melissa said. The few early mornings she'd had making love with Ross was a wonderful way to start the day. "When are you and Emmett going to get married?"

"I don't know. His father is a U.S. Senator, so his parents want a big wedding. But with his mother's ongoing recovery from alcohol addiction, we'd rather have a small, private affair. I was even thinking of an outdoor wedding on the grounds of Emmett's house. It's lovely by the river."

"Oh, that sounds perfect," gushed Melissa.

"Why don't you and Emmett plan to come to my house for dinner tomorrow? I'd love to have you. Ross and I will leave for New Jersey the next day, but I want the four of us to get together sooner rather than later."

Crystal smiled. "I'm sure we can work it out. Let me check with Emmett, and I'll get back to you. Thanks for the invitation."

"Just let me know. It won't be a gourmet meal, just something summery and easy." Melissa left the café full of excitement, thinking of not only working with Crystal but also forming a real friendship with her.

Later, she walked over to Ross's house.

Mike answered the door.

"Is Ross here?" she asked.

"Sure, come in. We're working in the den. We're stoked about adding the indoor baseball facility. I think it's going to work."

"I heard you might be interested in someone in town," said Melissa, unable to resist teasing him.

"Yeah, well, I'm not sure who I'm interested in right now. I'm used to playing the field, or in my case, playing the court."

Melissa laughed at Mike's tennis joke. He was a likable guy, someone Ross trusted. That meant a lot to her.

Ross looked up from his computer when Melissa walked into the room. "Hi. How'd your meeting with Crystal go?"

"Good. I've invited Crystal and Emmett for dinner tomorrow night. I hope you're free."

"If he isn't, I am," kidded Mike. "Anything for your cooking."

"Okay, you're invited too," said Melissa, pleased.

"Better make a lot of food. Mike's a big eater," teased Ross. "And yes, I'll be there. Do you want to go out to dinner with me tonight?"

"Can we go to Fresh? I haven't been there in a while, and I want to check them out," said Melissa.

"I'll call and make reservations. Mike, you're on your own," said Ross.

"I've already made plans," said Mike. "That's the thing about staying here with you. We don't have to worry about one another."

The guys laughed, and Melissa joined in, liking their easy companionship. Being business partners with someone meant you had to get along and think alike. She wondered how that would work between Crystal, Nettie, Jason, and her.

CHAPTER TWENTY-NINE

MELISSA HAD ALWAYS LIKED FRESH — THE THEME, THE food. Now, as she entered the restaurant with Ross, she took a closer look. Was it the proper kind of restaurant to take over the space for Fins? Though her parents wanted to sell their restaurant, they had enough stake in it to want any replacement to be as refined and successful as they had been. It was an ego thing, but it mattered.

They were led to a table by a window overlooking part of the herb garden — a touch Melissa liked.

The table chinaware had a botanical look to it, which Melissa also liked. It added to the white and dark green color scheme of the interior, whose white wainscoting met dark green walls.

Ross ordered a bottle of sparkling rosé wine and then chatted with Melissa about the choices on the menu. She quickly decided on a lemony Zucchini Ribbon Salad and Tequila Lime Grilled Shrimp. Ross went with shrimp gazpacho and a steak served in the Fajita style.

The restaurant wasn't as fancy as Fins, but it was tastefully decorated, with excellent food and service. Melissa thought the addition of more seafood would fit in well. Or maybe they were thinking of two locations, with the one in town being more like Fins. Either way, Melissa thought it might work. The place was busy with happy, satisfied customers and a small line waiting outside.

"What do you think?" asked Ross. "Do you think it will work in town?"

"Yes. My parents are lucky to have found someone like the owner of this restaurant as a potential buyer."

She looked up as a middle-aged man in a white chef's coat approached the table. "Hi, Melissa Hendrickson. Someone told me you were eating here."

Melissa smiled and introduced the chef to Ross. "I couldn't wait to come after talking to my parents about your interest in buying them out."

"And?" he asked, his eyes searching hers.

"I like the idea a lot. You'd offer seafood choices?"

"Yes. People in the area have always loved Fins and the fresh seafood there. We'd want to build on that."

Melissa smiled with satisfaction. "I hope it works out."

"Thanks. I appreciate hearing that from you. And remember, we'd love to have you work for us. "Once cooking is in your blood, it's always there. A job is yours whenever you want it."

"Thanks," she said, even though she knew she wouldn't want to work in a replica of her family's business.

Their meal came, and Melissa enjoyed each bite she sampled.

As they ate, Ross said to her, "What will happen if your idea about gourmet meals doesn't happen?"

"I may do some catering work," Melissa said. "Something on my own but not full-time. I'd like to do some traveling."

"Maybe we can travel together," said Ross, waiting for her response.

"That would be fabulous." She knew he wanted to be with her and enjoyed her company, but he never talked about a real future with her. It bothered her. She was certain she loved him. And she enjoyed their lovemaking. But she didn't want to be left with nothing if it didn't work out.

After dinner, Ross said, "Want to watch a baseball game

with me? The Yankees are playing, and I want to keep an eye on them."

"Sure. You can teach me more about the game. I know most of the rules, but watching with a pro is always helpful."

He laughed. "I *was* a pro."

He paid the bill, and they left the restaurant.

"Uh, oh, it looks like it's going to rain any minute," said Melissa. "The weatherman said it would happen later."

Ross grabbed her hand. "Let's make a run for it. That lightning looks fierce. You go ahead. I'll follow as fast as I can."

As thunder boomed overhead, they dashed for the car.

Ross closed the passenger door after her and hustled around the car to the other side.

The rain hit the car's surface in a steady, pounding stream.

Ross slid behind the wheel laughing. "God! I'm soaked."

"We'd better get you home. We don't want you to be sick for this weekend."

He leaned over and kissed her. "I'm fine. It'll take more than this to bring me down."

But as they approached their neighborhood, he drove right into his garage and got out. "Help yourself to whatever you want to drink, and I'll meet you in the media room. I'm going to get out of these clothes." He gave her a sexy grin. "Or better yet, come with me."

She laughed. "I'll wait for you there."

Melissa went into the kitchen, fixed herself a glass of ice water, and went to the media room. While waiting for Ross, she wondered what they'd do about their houses if they ever decided to live together. She loved her kitchen. He loved his media room. Somehow, they'd have to make it work. If only ...

Ross came into the room and took a seat on the couch beside her. He smelled of the citrus aftershave lotion she loved—clean, fresh, and appealing. When he leaned toward her and kissed her, she responded with enthusiasm. He always made her feel so alive.

He turned on the game, and they sat back to watch. It became a different game as every time the Yankees got a hit, Ross kissed her. They laughed and then grew grim as the Yankees got behind. At the end of the game, with a Yankee loss, Melissa sighed unhappily.

"Wow, you really got into it," said Ross. "You're such an old softie."

"That big screen makes it seem even more real," she said as he lowered his lips to hers.

"Come with me. I'll make you feel better," he said, giving her a sexy smile that she couldn't resist. He knew exactly what she needed.

The next morning, still in Ross's bed, Melissa stirred when he sat beside her and handed her a cup of coffee. " 'Morning, Sleepyhead."

She sat up, not caring that the sheet had slipped down, and sipped the coffee. "Is this something you do for damsels you rescue from unhappy baseball games?" she teased.

He grinned and then grew serious. "There's only one damsel, and I've heard delivering coffee in bed is not a bad idea for someone you care about."

Disappointment washed through her. He'd had an opportunity to say he loved her, but he hadn't. A voice in her head said, "Relax," and she sighed. She was growing in confidence but had moments of insecurity like this.

"Hey, what's up?" Ross asked softly, gazing into her eyes.

"Nothing," she said, shaking off her concern. "Thanks for the coffee. It was sweet of you to do it."

He gave her a little salute. "Mike's hoping you'll cook up some breakfast."

"Ah, an ulterior motive," she said.

"Not from me," Ross said. "I just wanted to help you start the day. Last night was ... well, superb."

As he left the room, she took another sip of coffee and then got out of bed.

A few minutes later, freshly showered, Melissa appeared in the kitchen.

Mike looked up at her and grinned. "Hungry?"

"No, but I hear you might be," said Melissa. "I'll be happy to fix breakfast."

"You're the best," said Mike. "Ross is a lucky man."

Ross gave him a little punch on the arm. "You're sounding like a male chauvinist pig."

Mike gave her a sheepish grin. "Sorry about that."

"No worries, as long as you leave a clean plate," she said, shaking a finger at him and making him laugh.

Later, sitting at the breakfast table with the men, listening to them talk about the sports center, Melissa thought about the possibilities of gourmet dinners, a catering service, something to keep her busy. She was sure Crystal wouldn't want to sell the café to see it become a different kind of restaurant. It was a cherished spot for breakfast and lunch for every local.

Thinking of preparing food, she got to her feet.

"I've got to take off if I'm going to have company for dinner tonight. We'll start with drinks at six. It will be an early evening because Crystal has to get up early, and Ross and I are leaving for New Jersey."

Ross stood and kissed her. "If you need any help with anything, I'm here."

"I'll remember that," she said, smiling into his mesmerizing blue eyes.

That evening, promptly at six, Crystal arrived at her door with Emmett. Shortly after that, Ross and Mike showed up.

As Melissa fixed a plate of appetizers in the kitchen, she listened to everyone greet one another. She didn't know Emmett that well but loved the idea of the wealthy son giving up any idea of following in his father's political footsteps to become a local doctor. With her humble background and ultimate success, Crystal was the perfect match for him.

"Remember those smaller Fourth of July celebrations?" she asked Melissa now.

Melissa nodded. "The most fun were the crazy canoe races."

"You were good at them," said Crystal. She turned to Emmett. "Melissa was always the best at sports."

"Another reason for Ross to love her," said Mike.

Melissa felt heat rise in her cheeks and looked at Ross, who winked at her.

"With a father in politics, holidays like that were big deals for my family," said Emmett. "I much prefer the celebrations here in Lilac Lake."

"Spoken like a true resident," said Crystal, kissing him quickly.

They moved out to the porch for drinks, and Melissa quietly studied the interaction between Emmett and Ross. It was important to her that they get along. Even though it might be on a part-time basis, she and Crystal might be working closely together.

For dinner, Melissa served cold poached salmon with a lemon and caper sauce, fresh green beans in a cold salad with a balsamic vinegar and spice dressing, a green leafy salad, and toasted garlic bread. The secret to the bean salad's deliciousness was setting the beans still warm from parboiling into the marinade dressing.

Melissa had designed her dining area as part of the kitchen, allowing her to communicate with her guests while working there. She loved being able to use it.

As the meal ended, Mike sat back. "Delicious. Thank you, Melissa." He turned to Crystal. "You said you brought lemon tarts?"

Crystal grinned and exchanged amused glances with Melissa. "I brought extra. Melissa told me you're a big eater."

"True, but I don't often get a chance to dine like this," said Mike returning Crystal's smile.

Crystal stood to help Melissa clear the table. "I'll get the desserts."

Melissa was pleased that Crystal easily stepped in to help. The dinner had been about seeing how everyone would react to one another, and so far, it had been a success.

After everyone had gone, Melissa sat in the dark on her porch, listening to the nighttime activities of the creatures around her. She heard an owl hooting, and in the outside light from a house a couple of doors away, she saw a bat sweep down for something to eat. She liked living at the edge of the woods, feeling close to nature.

She thought of the weekend ahead with Ross's family and stood to go inside. The trip was bound to be difficult, and she wanted to support him.

After getting ready for bed, she lay under the covers and hugged the pillow, feeling lonely. She'd gotten used to having him beside her and wondered if he felt the same way.

CHAPTER THIRTY

THE NEXT DAY, MELISSA WAITED AT THE END OF HER driveway with two small carry-on bags. Ross had hired a limousine to pick her up. The morning was cooler than it had been, an early harbinger, perhaps, for fall. Autumn in New Hampshire was glorious, with a leafy rainbow of colors brightening any scene. But she wasn't ready for the future. Not until she knew more about her plans.

Pushing her concerns aside, she focused on Ross's needs. She knew him well enough to know this would be a tough weekend for him. On the baseball diamond, he'd been a man in control, full of fun and talent. But she'd learned he was a much quieter man, a thoughtful one who loved his family.

The limousine driver pulled up and hurried out of the car to open the passenger door for her and to take her bags.

She slid into the backseat and faced Ross.

"Morning," he said and leaned forward to kiss her.

"Hi," she replied, sounding a little breathy after the way his lips had lingered on hers. "Thank you for making all the arrangements. We're staying with Jenn, right?"

"Yes, she called to make sure we would. She likes you, Melissa."

She leaned against the leather seat, "I like her and your entire family. They're all very easy to be with."

He lifted her hand into his and squeezed it. "Thanks for coming with me."

"I'm happy to do this for you," she said sincerely, loving being able to support him.

"I'm glad I got the chance to get to know Crystal and Emmett better at dinner last night," said Ross. "I see how well you and Crystal could work together. You complement one another."

"I hope it'll work out. If not, something else will come along," she responded, remembering her new outlook on life at Crystal's suggestion.

He studied her. "I understand. You can't let anyone stand in your way. As you have made clear, your career is who you are or who you were meant to be."

"Yes, and I want other things, too," she hastened to say.

But his back was turned to her, and he was looking out the window.

The flight to New Jersey was smooth and easy, but seeing Ross grow tense with the memorial service looming was difficult.

Ross had hired another limousine to take them from the airport in Newark to Jenn's house in Montclair. As the driver made his way through traffic, she realized how practical it was to have a driver.

Jenn greeted both of them with open arms, turning from Ross to Melissa. "It's such a pleasure to see you again, Melissa, though I wish it were under different circumstances."

"Thanks. It's nice of you to have us stay with you," she responded.

Jenn walked them inside and into the kitchen. Moments later, Jack showed up. "Sorry. I was on a call." He gave his brother a bro-hug and turned to Melissa. "How's the chef?"

She laughed. "Good, thanks, and you?"

"Busy as usual, but it's that time of year for me." He spoke to Ross. "After the service, there will be a small meeting for us to go over Dad's will. Nothing unexpected, but necessary, just the same. I think we have a buyer for the house."

"Really?" said Ross. "That was quick."

"It's a friend of Lanie's. She's ready to be on her own again and loves the neighborhood and the idea of living close to her family, who will help with her kids," said Jack. "I figure all of us will be willing to make it a fair deal, but we'll vote on it. It hasn't been submitted to a real estate agent yet, but it's nothing I can't handle."

"That'll make it easy," said Ross agreeably.

"The service tomorrow is going to be lovely. Addie is terrific about organizing, but then raising her and Dewey's four kids, she's had to be on top of things," said Jenn.

"We've planned a reception right at the church so all the neighbors can easily attend. Heaven knows what we'll do with all the food they've dropped by at the house. We'll freeze some and give what we can to the church's pantry."

"You guys hungry?" asked Jack. "We can order some of Ross's favorite pizza for lunch."

Ross grinned. "I could go for Enzo's pepperoni pizza."

"Coming up," said Jack.

"Tonight, I thought we'd have Jack grill some steaks," said Jenn. She glanced at Melissa. "I'm not promising a gourmet meal for our chef, but I do make a tasty greenleaf salad and lemon-garlic potatoes to accompany the steak."

Melissa waved away her concern. "No problem. I'm a foodie who'll enjoy anything you cook."

"I hope you brought your swimming suit," said Jack. "The pool is all ready for us."

"I did." Melissa hadn't paid much attention to the pool when she'd visited for a quick overnight, but Ross had told her to be sure to pack one.

Jack ordered pizza, and soon after, they sat outside by the pool, eating some of the best pizza Melissa had ever had.

"Okay, time to relax," said Jack, standing. "I'm going to change."

"We won't be far behind you," said Jenn.

Melissa helped Jenn clean up from lunch and went to the room she shared with Ross to change. He'd already put on his swim trunks. Seeing him standing there, observing his broad shoulders and trim waist, the scars on both legs, she couldn't resist smiling.

He saw her and walked over. "Hey, mermaid," he said, wrapping an arm around her.

She nestled against his chest and gazed up at him.

He lowered his lips to hers, and she felt her body melt.

Ross pulled away and said, "Guess I'd better go cool off. I hear the girls. They must be home early from school."

Downstairs, Nan and Kate were in the kitchen eating slices of pizza.

"Hello," said Melissa, feeling self-conscious in her bikini. She wasn't as thin as the teenagers before her.

"You look terrific," said Nan.

"I hear you're good at sports," said Kate. "Is that how you stay in shape? I'm thinking of going out for track, but I'm not certain."

"Girls? Are you finishing up here?" asked Jenn, coming into the room. "Hurry and get changed." Jenn gazed at Melissa. "I wish I had your figure. But being on the short side, I will never be as tall or thin as I'd like."

"You're lovely," said Melissa sincerely. Jenn was beautiful.

When the two of them stepped outside, both men stopped splashing each other like the brothers they were and stared.

"Wow!" Jack said. "You two are hot. Really hot."

"Thanks, honey," said Jenn, walking to the steps at the shallow end of the pool and dipping a toe in the water.

Nervous and unsure of what to do, Melissa found a place to sit on the pool's edge and lowered herself onto the pool deck.

Ross swam up to her. "I thought mermaids loved to swim."

"I have to get used to the water first," she said.

He gently tugged on her leg, and she slipped into the water beside him. Facing him, it seemed natural for them to kiss.

When they pulled apart, Jenn caught Melissa's attention and gave her a subtle thumbs-up sign. At Melissa's soft giggle, Ross said, "What's going on between you two?"

Jenn spoke up. "I'm just letting her know I think you two are perfect together."

Melissa started to say something, held back, and then blurted, "Me too."

That night as she lay in bed with Ross, he faced her. "So, you think we're perfect together, huh?"

"Yes, I do," she answered boldly for her.

"Good. Because I know a game about a sea captain and a mermaid," he said, making her laugh as he drew her close.

CHAPTER THIRTY-ONE

THE NEXT MORNING, ALL PLAYFULNESS WAS SET ASIDE AS the family prepared for a day that Ross's father had wanted to be a celebration of life, not a day of mourning. But how could they not mourn a man they'd all loved dearly? Melissa understood. In her one short meeting with Ross's father, he'd made her feel welcomed and aware of his kindness and love of life.

Ross had dressed in a dark suit that did nothing to hide his broad shoulders and athletic body. He pulled at the starched collar of his white shirt and gave Melissa a look of resignation. "It's a lot easier to play on a baseball field with thousands of people watching than speaking in front of my friends and family."

"I'll be sitting in front. Just look at me," said Melissa. "You'll do fine."

"But words will never be enough to show my love for my father and all he did for me," said Ross.

"Any speech you give, no matter how long or short, will mean a lot to everyone. Just say what's in your heart."

"I've made a few notes, but you're right. I'll just talk about what an amazing man my father was," said Ross.

Melissa squeezed his cold fingers before getting into the limousine that would take them to the neighborhood church. His father had asked to be cremated, which eliminated a full funeral and burial service. Something they all were grateful for.

Later, listening to Ross speak in front of the congregation, Melissa and others fought tears. His tribute to his father was touching with his sincerity, his simple message of thanks and love.

Ross cleared his throat. "Dad, I hope one day to be a father as awesome as you were to me. Having you show me how might be one of the greatest gifts of all." Ross glanced at Melissa and away before ending his talk.

Each of Ross's three brothers took a turn eulogizing their father, ending with Jack. As the oldest, he then invited everyone who joined them to attend the reception in the social hall next to the church.

Melissa and Ross followed the rest of the family out of the church and stood in a receiving line to thank people for coming. Jenn stood next to her and seemed to know everyone who passed through. Melissa, who'd grown up an only child in a small town, was overwhelmed by the people who greeted her as if they knew her. Then, she reminded herself living in Lilac Lake was the same, with everyone in the neighborhood knowing everyone else.

After the receiving line dissipated, Melissa and the family members went to the social hall where Addie was overseeing the reception she and Jenn had planned.

Because it was shortly after noon, a buffet table held an array of tea sandwiches, green salads, pasta salads, and meat and cheese platters, along with cakes, cookies, and other sweets that ladies in the church's social circle had prepared.

"Nice," murmured Ross. "I understand Dad's male friends had their own party at Mickey's neighborhood bar a couple of nights ago. That would be more natural. But I know how much the church meant to Dad, especially after my mother died, so he'd appreciate this too."

Addie came over to them. "Please eat. As usual, we have more food than we need. The church will take care of any leftovers by delivering them to those who might enjoy them."

Melissa dutifully filled a plate with food, although her emotions had dulled her appetite. She couldn't stop thinking of Ross's sweet tribute to his father, how his family pulled together, and how lucky she was that her dad was recovering. She wasn't ready for the death of her parents. But she knew she, like Ross, would have to deal with that one day.

Lanie came up to her as Melissa was eating and took a seat beside her. "I'm not sure what is going on between you and Ross, but I plan to win him back. We'd always planned to marry."

"And what happened?" Melissa asked, shocked by Lanie's boldness.

"I made a big mistake, and now I'm going to correct it," Lanie said.

They studied Ross, who was standing across the room and talking to a man Melissa didn't know.

Ross looked their way and waved Melissa over.

Lanie got up with Melissa and went with her to Ross's side.

Ross seemed startled to see Lanie but said, "Dave, I want you to meet my friend, Melissa Hendrickson, and I think you already know Lanie Southerland, my next-door neighbor." He turned to Melissa. "This is my college coach, Dave Titus."

"Hello," said Melissa. "You must be so proud of Ross."

"Indeed, I am. I hear you live in Lilac Lake. A friend just bought a house there. It sounds like a great place to live," said Dave.

"It's very easy small-town living with lots of things to do for all sorts of sports, especially with the new sports center Ross and a friend are creating," said Melissa.

"I'm thinking of moving there," said Lanie. "Ross has

invited me to stay with him for a while."

Melissa glanced at Ross, but he didn't seem surprised by her words. Feeling unsettled, Melissa hardly heard the conversation between Dave, Lanie, and Ross. *Did Ross know that Lanie intended to get him back?*

Jenn came over to them. "Anyone want coffee and dessert? There's plenty."

Melissa used that excuse to leave and go outside for a quiet moment. She couldn't allow her insecurity to mar her relationship with Ross. She'd thought she and Ross had something special. Wait! They *did* have something special.

Feeling more secure, Melissa returned to the reception and helped Addie, Jenn, and the ladies from the church clean up. It was good to keep busy, though she tried to keep herself from observing how Lanie clung to Ross's arm.

Addie came over to her. "I see Lanie's at it again. She's determined to snag Ross now that she's divorced the loser she married. But don't worry. Ross knows better."

When the clean-up was done, the women joined the men who were outside talking in groups. Melissa went over to Ross, who was standing with Jack and Lanie.

"Things all done inside?" Ross asked her.

Melissa nodded. "Lots of food leftover, but the church will handle that."

"We've been talking about Lanie's friend who wants to buy Dad's house. Jack's going to handle the sale, so none of us will have to worry about it."

"That makes it simple and easy," said Melissa, pleased for them.

"Let's go back to my house," said Jack. "I think a swim in the pool would be perfect."

"Me, too?" asked Lanie.

Jack hesitated and then shrugged. "Sure, I guess. You're welcome to drop in."

"It's easiest if I come with you," said Lanie. "Stay right here. I'll hurry home, get my suit, and be right back."

"Don't take too long," said Jack. "It's getting hot."

"What's Lanie up to?" said Jenn, joining them.

"She's coming to the house for a swim," said Jack. "I couldn't say no to her."

"Why not? It'll be a nuisance taking her home, and she is NOT staying overnight," said Jenn, annoyed. She turned to Melissa. "Some men don't get it."

"Don't get what?" Jack asked.

"Lanie is trying to win back Ross. For God's sake, it's so obvious."

"Not gonna happen," said Ross firmly.

"Then you'd better make that clear to her," said Jenn. "C'mon, Melissa. Let's get in the limo. It's air-conditioned."

Melissa left the two brothers talking and climbed into the car with Jenn and her daughters. Soon, Jack joined them. "Ross said he'd take care of it."

Melissa remained quiet while Jenn and Jack rehashed the situation. She was pleased she hadn't said anything about it. This was between Ross and Lanie.

Several minutes later, Ross climbed into the limousine. "That's settled. I've told Lanie before that I wasn't interested, but now, I think she believes me." Ross glanced at Jenn and turned to Melissa. "I'm sorry for any misunderstanding."

"I'm happy you resolved the matter," said Melissa. "I know how much Lanie wanted you back."

"What she and I had ended years ago. It's time for her to accept it." Melissa felt her entire body relax. She would feel more secure if only Ross said those three magic words to her. But they'd only been together for a short time.

###

Back at Jack and Jenn's house, Melissa was changing into her bikini when Ross walked into the room.

"Hey, beautiful," he murmured, wrapping his arms around her. "I hope you weren't bothered by all that business with Lanie."

"No, I trust you to be honest with me," she said.

"It's why I waited to see how you and Dirk were doing together before letting you know I was interested." He grinned. "I *am* interested, you know."

"Really?" She gave him a saucy smile, and he lowered his lips to hers.

They both got into their bathing suits and headed downstairs.

Jenn greeted them with glasses of iced tea for each. "Time to relax and enjoy ourselves after a grueling day. Later, we can have a light supper. I know you're getting up early to catch a flight home."

"Friends of mine are coming to Lilac Lake to talk about a business prospect, and Mondays and Tuesdays are the easiest days of the week for them to get away."

"Melissa wants to be able to offer some gourmet dinners from time to time or do some catering. Anything to keep her hand in cooking," explained Ross.

"Hey, all! Come on in! The water's great," called Jack from the pool.

Ross turned and jumped into the water.

Jenn took Melissa by the arm and led her away from the water. "What's going on with you two?"

Melissa sighed, unable to hide a note of frustration. "I'm not sure. We know we're interested in each other. That's as far as it's gone."

Jenn frowned. "I don't know why I should be anxious about

it, but Ross has had other relationships that went nowhere, and I think you and he are perfect together."

Was that what was happening here? A relationship going nowhere? Rather than fall back into her old insecurities, Melissa observed Ross and Jack horseplay in the water and remembered Crystal's advice.

Jenn put an arm around her. "Don't pay any attention to me. Jack tells me to mind my own business. I'll just stay out of it."

Melissa smiled at her, even as her thoughts spun.

Ross called to her, and Melissa approached the pool's edge. "How's the water?"

"Fantastic. Come on in," said Ross. "Jack and I won't splash you. I promise."

Melissa went to the steps at the shallow end and walked into the pool, gasping when the cool water covered her. Then she settled on a step, letting the air dry her off.

Ross sat down beside her. "I'm happy you're here. It meant a lot to have you support me as I was speaking about my father. The fact that he liked you so much made it all seem natural. You know what I mean?"

"I do, and I'm glad to be here with you."

Later, as she and Jenn made sandwiches in the kitchen, they found a lot to talk about.

"Jack and I will try to come to Lilac Lake for a visit. Maybe in the fall when all the colors are out on the trees," said Jenn.

"A leaf-peeper, huh?" said Melissa, chuckling with Jenn. She hoped that if anything tore apart her relationship with Ross, she and Jenn could somehow be friends. Jenn was like the big sister she'd always wanted.

They carried the tray of sandwiches, chips, pickles, and cookies out to the patio.

"Enjoy, everyone," said Jenn, setting her food tray on the large round table where they had gathered.

Though Melissa liked the idea of being part of this family, she understood she'd have to wait to see if or how she fit in. As Crystal had suggested recently, time would give her the answer.

CHAPTER THIRTY-TWO

BACK IN LILAC LAKE, MELISSA FELT ON FIRMER GROUND thinking of her career and what she hoped to do in the future. She met with Crystal and reviewed the pros and cons of Crystal selling the café and forming a partnership with her. They had no idea if Jason and Nettie would agree to their idea.

"Selling the café to be something other than it already is doesn't work for me," said Crystal. "I feel as if I owe it to everyone in town to keep providing them with breakfast and lunch and tea for all their support over the last several years."

"I understand and agree with you," said Melissa. "I think you can make the sale work, but if it doesn't, I have other options."

"In truth, I want to get out of the business so Emmett and I can get married and start our own family. We're both at a time in our lives when it makes sense. I never thought I'd say it, but I want a big family with Emmett."

"That's so sweet," said Melissa. Knowing Crystal's background, her eyes stung with tears. "I'm not ready for a family yet. But I am ready to settle down." She chuckled softly. "That makes it seem as if I've had many opportunities, which you and I know isn't the case. But I have the feeling that Ross is the man I've waited for all my life."

"Now you're making me all emotional," said Crystal. "I think we're both ready for a change, which is good. Right?"

"Yes, but I would've liked knowing it was coming. To have my life ripped apart by a disaster was shocking. Funny, without the restaurant, I wasn't sure who I was. I guess it's all been for good."

"Some of the best out of that disaster is us becoming friends," said Crystal. "I'm grateful for that."

"Me, too," said Melissa, feeling warm inside. "Nettie and Jason will get in town late tonight, arriving at my house around midnight. We'll meet you here tomorrow at 4 when you close the café. That will give me time to show them around town."

"Perfect," said Crystal. "Are you and Ross going to join the group at Jake's tonight?"

"I hope so. I think it'll be relaxing for Ross." Melissa hugged Crystal goodbye and left, wondering what the next few days would bring.

Melissa was outside working in her garden when Ross approached her. "Great to be back home?"

She smiled. "It's always nice. Have you caught up with Mike? Plans still in place?"

He sat beside her on the grass. "Yeah, now that Dad's service is over, I can think of other things. You've got a lot to think about, too."

"Yes. I won't know what will happen with the café until Nettie and Jason decide about buying it. When I saw Crystal earlier, she asked if we would join the gang at Jake's. I told her I hoped so. What do you say?"

Ross shrugged. "Fine by me. It'll be nice to see everyone."

"Okay, that's what we'll do," said Melissa. She fluttered her eyelashes playfully. "Want to help me with the weeding?"

He laughed at her teasing and said, "No way. I'm outta here. See you later."

That night, Melissa and Ross left for Jake's around seven

in Melissa's car. That would give them plenty of time to socialize before Jason and Nettie arrived.

Melissa looked forward to seeing everyone. It was wonderful to be included. Though it was a diverse group, everyone was congenial.

She and Ross entered Jake's to find most of their friends there, filling tables at one end of the bar.

They sat at a table with Dani and Brad Collister and Taylor and Cooper Walker. The two Gilford women looked radiant as usual. They had a way of dressing and putting themselves together that Melissa had always tried to emulate.

At the table next to them, Dirk sat with Samantha Waters, who was showing everyone the diamond she'd just received from him. Surprised, Melissa leaned over to congratulate Dirk, but he spoke before she could.

"Good to see you and Ross. Melissa, you've already met Samantha, my fiancée."

"Yes, congratulations to you both," she said.

"It's sweet when people can rekindle a romance," said Dani. She grinned at Ross. "What about you two? You're a new couple, but it seems like it might be becoming serious."

Ross's cheeks flushed. He leaned toward Dani and said softly, "We're friends..." He turned as Mike spoke to him.

Silence followed.

Melissa felt her body stiffen. It struck her then that while it had been nice knowing how much his family loved the idea of Ross and her being together for real, Ross wasn't thinking that way.

Melissa waited until the conversation turned to something else, then stood. "I'm sorry, but I'm not feeling well. I'll see everyone tomorrow."

"Are you alright? Do you want me to drive?" asked Ross with concern.

"No, thanks," she managed. "You stay. Maybe Dani and Brad can take you back home."

"Sure," said Brad. "No problem."

On the ride home, she allowed her tears to fall. She felt shredded. Whenever the idea of a future together came up, Ross backed away. How was it going to continue if he couldn't acknowledge their relationship? She wanted a man who was as committed to the idea of being together in the future as she was, a relationship with marriage in mind.

At home, she told herself to hold it together. Nettie and Jason would arrive soon, and their visit was more important than ever for securing a future for her talents. Surely, she should be able to find employment between plans for the café and the Lilac Lake Inn.

Later, when Nettie and Jason arrived, she greeted them with enthusiastic hugs and offered them drinks and a light snack. But after working all day and driving to New Hampshire, they were ready for bed, which was fine with her.

The morning sun streaking across her bed caused Melissa to open her eyes, feeling drugged from the lack of sleep.

It was still early and quiet in the house. Silently, she got out of bed, slipped on a silk robe, and went barefoot into the kitchen, taking care not to make any noise.

She made coffee and took a cup to her back deck to enjoy the morning moment. She liked to observe nature greeting the day by listening to the songs of birds and, most mornings, seeing brown bunnies hop across her lawn to where her garden was fenced in.

She watched as a bunny tried to get under the chicken wire mesh. He was persistent but made no headway. It was more or less how she felt about her relationship with Ross. No matter how much she wished for a real relationship with him, she couldn't break through to something that promised a future.

As if she'd conjured him up, Ross entered her vision. He didn't wave as he walked toward her.

She waited to see what he would do or say.

He opened the screen door and stepped inside. Pulling a chair close to her, he said quietly, "We need to talk. I realize my conversation with Dani upset you. Let me explain."

"Explain that you want to be friends with benefits?" she asked, unable to stop herself. That thought had been circling her mind.

Surprise widened his eyes. "Why would you say that? You know that's not true."

"That's what it made our relationship seem like. Let's talk another time. Nettie and Jason are here, and I'm going to be busy with them all day. I need time to think over things."

Ross let out a long sigh, then stood and moved the chair back in place. " You've got the wrong idea. I get that this isn't a good time, but we need to have an honest conversation. Let me know when you're ready. I'm not going to give up on us."

He left the porch and walked away.

As Melissa was fixing herself a second cup of coffee, Nettie appeared.

"Good morning! How did you sleep?" Melissa asked, handing her a cup of black coffee as if she knew Nettie liked it.

"Very well. That bed is so comfortable. Jason is still sleeping, but I thought that would give us some 'girl time' to talk."

"Come out to the screened-in porch with me. It's a perfect place for a morning cup of coffee and a chat with a friend. I'm so glad you're here."

"I'm looking forward to seeing the town and meeting some of your friends. Crystal sounds impressive on the phone."

"She's worked hard to have a very successful business. I both like and admire her," said Melissa, thinking how lucky she was to have gotten to know Crystal better.

Nettie took a sip of her coffee and set her cup down. "Between you and me, I think this is a perfect time to ask Jason to make a change. We have the wedding coming up, and because we've waited so long, we want to start a family soon. I think we can have a more normal life by getting away from working dinner hours. The restaurant business is tough, as you well know. And knowing our siblings will still be part of the restaurant in Boston takes a lot of pressure off of us."

"I've had so many mixed feelings about my family's restaurant being destroyed that I get it. One minute, I'm feeling free; the next, sad and at loose ends."

"What about your neighbor who isn't just a neighbor anymore? How's that going?" Nettie asked.

"It's going nowhere. His family loves the idea of the two of us together, but last night, among a group of friends, Ross made it clear he's not about to commit to anything. He tried to discuss it with me this morning, but I put him off." Melissa felt Nettie's eyes boring into her and shifted in her seat.

"You're not pushing him away, are you?" said Nettie.

"Not really. I just don't want to be friends with benefits," said Melissa. "I want a real relationship."

"Whoa! Where did that come from?" Nettie said.

Melissa shot Nettie a helpless look. "Crystal tells me to let time take care of things."

"Wise advice," said Nettie, taking hold of Melissa's hand. "Why aren't you listening to her? We've been friends for a long time. I'm here if you need me. But you know I'm going to agree with Crystal. For heaven's sake, give Ross a chance. You've only been dating for a few weeks."

"You're right," said Melissa. "I'm not used to being in this situation. I love him, and it scares me."

"Yes, I understand, but you've got to give him time to reach the same point. Isn't that what you want? For him to feel the same way you do?"

Melissa nodded, allowing Nettie's words to sink in.

"It's all going to be fine. Slow down and let the relationship develop. Now, let's talk about the town and why Justin and I should move here," said Nettie, eliminating some of the tension in the air.

Jason appeared carrying a cup of coffee. He sat in a chair next to Nettie. "Morning. What are you talking about?"

"The town," said Nettie. "I want Melissa to tell us what living in Lilac Lake is like."

Melissa sat back and drew a breath. "Lilac Lake is very special. It's small-town living for sure, but the lifestyle is one of being healthy, living each day well with lots of outdoor activities, and having time for enjoyment," she said, realizing how much she loved it.

The conversation turned to more practical matters like health care, schools, sports, and other things most people want to know about anywhere they live.

"I'm going to show you around the town, and we'll pop into the café for breakfast so you can see the operation and taste the food. Crystal doesn't know we're coming, so it'll be a surprise, which is the best way for you to make a fair judgment."

Melissa didn't say that by dropping in on a regular morning, Nettie and Jason would understand better how important the café was to the town.

CHAPTER THIRTY-THREE

WHEN THEY WERE DRESSED AND READY TO GO, MELISSA and her friends piled into her car. She began the tour by riding through her neighborhood, showing them the houses and the lake activity connected to them. Then, she pulled into the Lilac Lake Inn on her way into town.

"Come take a look at it," said Melissa, turning off the engine and getting out of the car.

The new owners, of whom Ross was one, had done a fantastic job of renovating the inn, bringing its original beauty to life with the updates.

They strolled around the grounds and went inside to look.

After speaking to the manager, they were offered a kitchen tour. It gleamed with the latest equipment. Melissa realized that if it came down to it, she could be happy cooking here. She noticed Nettie's interest.

"The Inn is a beautiful hotel," said Jason. "It helps to know it's drawing people to the area."

"Wait until you see the town with its charming storefronts, shopping, and food. And as you've already seen, the lake is another reason for bringing visitors here," said Melissa with pride.

"I want to see where your restaurant was," said Nettie. "I mentioned it to a few people in Boston, and one person I spoke to might be interested."

They drove into town and pulled up behind the cleared

land where the family seafood restaurant, Fins, had stood. It made Melissa sad to see it.

"We can park here and walk to the café," said Melissa.

They moved past the fencing that had been placed around the perimeter of the land and entered Main Street.

"That was an ideal location for a restaurant," said Jason, turning back and looking at the bare spot. He gazed down the street and pointed to the sign for the Lilac Lake Café. "That's another."

"Main Street is a treasure trove for any visitor," said Melissa. "Beyond the café is a bar called Jake's. It's where many of us gather in the evening for conversation, drinks, and food. I'll take you tonight and introduce you to some of the locals."

"Now, let's surprise Crystal," said Nettie. "I want to see the café in action."

They made their way down the street, slowing now and then so Nettie and Jason could look in some shop windows. Each store appeared alive with activity, some more than others.

"It's charming," gushed Nettie. "I love the colorful awnings and pots of flowers by each door."

"Even during the winter months, the shopkeepers try to dress up their windows with color," said Melissa.

They entered the café and paused, observing the crowd and the waitresses moving through the tables carrying trays of food. Conversations filled the air with excitement that softened the flow of music from speakers.

Melissa breathed a sigh of relief. It was a normal morning.

Crystal noticed them and hurried over, the new streak of purple hair over her brow bobbing.

"This is Nettie Mancini and Jason Rockwell, whom you've met and talked to online," said Melissa.

Crystal hesitated and then hugged them both. "I know we'll talk later, but I'm pleased to meet you in person. It's such a beautiful day; why don't you take a table outside, and I'll send a waitress right over."

Melissa led them to the last empty table on the patio and sat down, pleased by the smiles on Nettie and Jason's faces.

"This routine is the opposite from what we're used to," said Nettie, "but I think a change like this will allow us to have a more normal life, with time in the late afternoon and evenings for friends and activities."

"We'll see," said Jason, watching carefully as a waitress approached carrying menus and a pitcher of water.

"Welcome to the Lilac Lake Café," said the waitress, Dorothy, an older woman with gray-streaked hair. "How can I make your morning better?" she asked, handing out the menus and pouring water into their goblets.

"I'd like regular black coffee," said Nettie.

"Me, too," Jason said.

Melissa said, "Make that three. Thank you."

"Coming right up," responded Dorothy.

After she left, Jason said, "I like the fact that Crystal has older staff."

"Crystal's very aware that people of all ages need the opportunity to work. Dorothy is a gem. She works as a teacher during the school year and helps Crystal in the summer. You'll find the community pulls together in many ways like this."

Jason nodded thoughtfully, and Melissa and Nettie exchanged hopeful glances.

After ordering enough food for a broad sample and eating most of it, Jason put down his fork and sighed with pleasure.

Crystal appeared. "How was it?"

"That was one of the best breakfasts I've ever had," said Jason. "The omelet was fantastic, and those biscuits were like eating melted butter. Wow!"

"Recipes can come with the sale," Crystal said, making them all laugh. She grew serious. "Today was busy as usual, with everyone starting a new week. Most days are like this, with locals making up most of the customers. Would you like to see the kitchen in operation?"

"Definitely," said Nettie as all three of them rose from their seats at the table.

After observing the kitchen routine, Crystal led them upstairs to show Nettie and Jason the apartment above the café. It contained two bedrooms, a small office, and a bathroom, kitchen, and dining/living area.

"The kitchen has been updated, the carpet is new, and the walls were painted a year ago," said Crystal. "The balcony is where I keep watch on the town, especially when a parade goes by."

"If we're not in the annual Fourth of July parade, we're here watching it," said Melissa.

"My sister, Misty, is living here with me, but she's about to move into one of the river cabins in town. I'll be moving out to live with my fiancé."

"When is your wedding?" Nettie asked.

"We haven't decided. We want to elope, but I'm not sure that's possible," said Crystal. "We're working on it."

"It might be nice for us to be married here in Lilac Lake," Nettie said to Jason.

"First things first," said Jason, sliding his arm around Nettie's shoulder.

They left the café and walked back to Melissa's car. "How about a canoe ride on the lake?"

Nettie grinned and turned to Jason. "I'm game. Are you?"

"Sure. I haven't had time to do something like that in a long while."

"We brought our bathing suits as you asked," said Nettie. "We're taking your suggestion and staying until the end of the week. This can be a working vacation."

"Perfect," said Melissa. The longer they stayed in town, the more likely they'd choose to go forward with a deal. They just had to make the numbers work.

At the neighborhood dock, Melissa was relieved Ross wasn't in sight. She needed time before discussing their relationship. She was on unfamiliar ground and knew it.

She asked Jason to help her move the canoe to the water's edge. Nettie stood holding the life jackets and canvas bag containing water bottles and sunscreen.

Jason and Nettie got into the canoe, and Melissa pushed it off the shore and hopped in, rocking the boat enough to make Nettie gasp.

Sitting in the bow of the canoe, Jason helped keep it steady.

"Okay, let's make our way down the lake. We may get as far as the Lilac Lake Cottage the three Gilford girls own. They're my friends, and are the granddaughters of Mrs. Wittner, the woman who originally owned the Inn. I love that so many people our age have returned to town."

"It makes it special because you already are friends," said Nettie.

"Not to worry," said Melissa. "You two won't have any problem making friends here."

They grew silent as they glided through the water, surprising ducks paddling on the surface and coming upon Great Blue Herons feeding at the edge of the lake where reeds grew.

Being close to nature like this, Melissa felt the tension leave her body.

They paddled as far as the cottage, saw no one was there,

and headed back to the other end of the lake with Nettie paddling in the bow for the return trip.

When they reached the neighborhood dock and clubhouse, they were ready for a cool drink on Melissa's back porch.

They quickly stored the canoe and the gear and walked back to Melissa's house, where they stretched out on lounge chairs on the porch.

"This is the life," murmured Jason, accepting a cold beer from Melissa.

Nettie smiled at Melissa. Maybe this idea would work.

Later, they dressed and went to meet Crystal. This meeting would be about the nuts and bolts of a sales contract. There was room for negotiation, but the basics had to be agreed upon. For this initial phase, there would be no lawyer. It would be a different story later when Jason would also need one to sell his share of the restaurant in Boston.

Melissa dropped Nettie and Jason off at the café for their meeting and, on a whim, decided to go see Mrs. Genie Wittner. Grandmother to Whitney, Dani, and Taylor, she was a woman who was generous with financial help to people in town and was willing to share wisdom with those who asked.

Since renewing her friendship with her granddaughters, Melissa had grown closer to Mrs. Wittner, or GG, as everyone called her. She played the role of a sweet grandmother for some of the kids in town, including her, who didn't have one. For others, she was often the source of unrequested financial help just when they needed it most, almost like a Genie granting people's long-held wishes. Melissa had always thought the name Genie was appropriate.

Before she left town, Melissa stopped in Petals, the flower shop at the end of Main Street. She knew GG loved flowers and had a sweet tooth.

Judith Keim

A short while later, Melissa pulled into the parking lot at The Woodlands, the assisted living facility where GG lived. She stared at the lovely, one-story wooden structure. It was the first big project Brad and Aaron Collister had undertaken and demonstrated how clever and hard-working the half-brothers were. The whole town applauded them for it.

Inside, Melissa asked the hostess at the lobby desk if she could see Mrs. Wittner and was told to go right along.

Melissa eagerly went down the hallway and knocked on GG's door. Hearing her cheerful "Come in," Melissa stepped inside to find GG sitting on the couch with an open book. Her warm smile erased some of Melissa's nervousness.

"Well, hello, Melissa. It's so good to see you. Come sit down."

Melissa handed GG the flowers and chocolates she'd bought. GG sniffed the flowers and sighed, then grinned at seeing the candy. "Oh, my! Two treats. We'll have to open the box of candy. First, will you put my flowers in a vase for me? There are vases beneath the kitchen sink."

Delighted to be able to do something for her, Melissa found several vases stored there, chose one, and added the flowers and water to it.

After Melissa set the vase of flowers on the coffee table, GG patted the cushion next to her on the couch. "Now, tell me what brings you here. Is it that baseball player that I hear about?"

A chuckle escaped Melissa. GG's communication system was as complete as ever. "I was talking to Crystal the other day, and she mentioned how your words about time taking care of things have helped her. I wanted you to know I'm using them to help me decide about my future."

Her blue eyes sparkled, and GG said, "I see. Sometimes, we simply must leave issues to resolve on their own so they unfold how they were meant to. I don't mean we shouldn't guide our lives; our determination makes many things happen. But there is a time for faith to play a part."

Melissa drew in a deep breath and began. "Ross Roberts and I have been dating. It hasn't been that long, but we enjoy one another. His family was excited to meet me and loved the idea of us being together. I don't have much experience, so I was surprised when Dani asked him about our relationship, and he said we were just friends." Tears welled in Melissa's eyes.

GG sighed and shook her head. "With the death of his father and all the emotional turmoil that accompanies it, I would think Ross wouldn't be thinking too far ahead. As you said, it hasn't been that long."

Melissa forced herself to ask the question gnawing at her insides like some sharp-clawed beast. "Do you think I've been a fool?"

"No," said GG. "Women are planners who handle a lot of thoughts at the same time. Men think along one line at a time. Ross was probably shocked at the question, but that doesn't mean he won't ponder it now. I understand you're afraid his feelings aren't as deep as yours. I'd suggest letting things move at their own pace."

Melissa sat back against the cushion and let out a sigh of relief. She turned to GG. "How'd you get so smart?"

GG laughed. "Many years of learning after making many mistakes. Now, let's see what's in that box of chocolates."

"Like the line from Forrest Gump – *Life is like a box of chocolates*," said Melissa, smiling.

"It's pretty much true," said GG, grinning as if she had a secret. She bit into a piece of candy and held it up. "See? This is sweet with a little sprinkling of nuts. That's good enough for anyone's life."

Melissa gave GG a gentle hug. "Thank you so much for hearing me out. I've always admired you, and now I know why so many of my friends love talking to you."

Leaving The Woodlands on a high note, Melissa drove to the café to see how talks were going for Crystal, Nettie, and Jason. She hoped they were coming to some agreement but decided to let things flow, as GG had suggested.

Her phone pinged. She waited until she parked to check. Her message was from Ross: *I had to go to New Jersey to finalize some issues. I'll see you when I get back. We need to talk. Call me if you get a chance.*

Melissa replayed the message again. She was relieved she wouldn't be seeing him. She needed more time to sort her feelings.

When she walked into the café, Crystal gazed up at her with a dazzling smile. "Hi, Melissa. I believe the three of us are on the same page. We've agreed on most points. Now, we'll get the lawyers involved, finalize numbers, and take it from there."

Melissa clapped her hands. "That's a wonderful beginning."

"There's a lot to work out on our end," said Jason, "but it's doable. First, I must complete the sale of my share of the restaurant. One of our financial backers is interested in buying me out."

"We're giving ourselves time to make it work, but I think it will," said Nettie, beaming at her. "In the meantime, I want to enjoy this area. I'm even going to talk to the owners of the Inn to see if they'd be interested in hiring me."

At Melissa's questioning look, Nettie continued. "I'll have to work elsewhere until the café takes off under new ownership, especially with all the changes we want to make.

Crystal has already mentioned putting on some gourmet dinners, and that sounds intriguing."

"We won't have to think of housing, to begin with," said Jason. "That makes a huge difference."

Melissa listened to the excitement in their voices and knew she'd been right all along. Lilac Lake was a perfect place for Nettie and Jason. The town would be happy to have them.

Now, all they needed was time.

CHAPTER THIRTY-FOUR

THAT NIGHT, MELISSA TOOK NETTIE AND JASON TO Jake's, hoping to be able to introduce them to her friends.

When they walked into the bar, someone called her name, and Melissa turned to see Dani waving at her. She led Nettie and Jason to the table and introduced them to Dani and Brad, David Graham, Crystal's fiancé, Emmett, and Crystal's sister, Misty.

Mike joined them.

"Where's Ross?" asked Dani.

"He went home to New Jersey to help with family matters," said Mike.

They all sat after pulling a couple of tables together. Though Jason tended to be on the quiet side, Nettie more than made up for it with her friendliness and sense of humor. Melissa was pleased to see how easily accepted they were.

Dirk arrived with Samantha, and the evening promised to be pleasant, with much laughter, good food, and plenty to drink. Melissa looked around the group, happy to be part of it.

On the drive home, Nettie said, "What a nice group of friends, Melissa. I can't wait until we become a permanent part of the town. Right, Jason?"

"Yes. Emmett invited me to come to his house to do some fishing. His house is right next to a river. And Dirk says winter skiing is fantastic. I like the idea of a new work schedule."

"Thank you, Melissa, for thinking of us," said Nettie. "Now, if I can only get some work at the Inn."

Melissa didn't say anything. She'd hoped working at the Inn would be a possibility for her. They'd have to wait and see how it turned out.

Melissa enjoyed her time with Nettie and Jason but refused to call Ross. She knew he must be busy with family, and she was determined not to push him into a relationship she wanted more than he.

Friday morning, Nettie and Jason prepared to leave.

"Time to go back to Boston. I have a lot to take care of," said Jason. "You've been terrific about helping us and making us feel at home, Melissa."

"I'm so excited about everything," said Nettie. "Most of all, enjoying our relationship daily will be awesome again. Thanks for everything. I'll be in touch."

"I'm so happy that everything seems to be working out. I hope it continues that way," said Melissa. "It would be fabulous to have you two in town."

"We want to make it happen," said Nettie, taking hold of Jason's hand.

He smiled at her. "We'd better get going."

Nettie got into their small Honda's passenger seat, and Jason slid behind the wheel. With a final wave to her, they took off. Melissa was still standing in the driveway when she saw a limousine pull into the driveway next door. She turned and went into her house before Ross could get out of the car.

She wasn't surprised when she heard her doorbell ring a few moments later. Feeling uncertain, she went to the door.

As she suspected, Ross was standing there.

He studied her. "May I come in?"

"Sure." Her nerves played hide and seek inside her. "How was your trip home?"

"Good," he answered as he walked into her house. "We had

some details to finish. Dad's house has been sold to a friend of Lanie's. Other estate affairs were taken care of, too. Sad as it is, there's no reason to go back there except to visit my brothers and their families."

"I'm sure you're relieved you had the chance to settle everything," said Melissa.

Ross stepped forward and lifted Melissa's hand. "We need to talk. I was caught off guard by Dani. But you didn't let me explain."

"Okay." *Better get it over with*, she thought.

Ross cleared his throat. "I love being friends with you, but I want more. I've been trying to take things slow. We've both been through a lot. My dad's failing health, the accident during the baseball game, my knee replacement, and the fire that destroyed Fins. Then my father's death and your father's heart attack. Now, you're reassessing your career. So, we've both had a lot to deal with. But we've done it together. That means a lot."

She nodded. *Where was he going with this?*

"I didn't want to rush you into something you weren't ready for. I'm not Dirk, the man you believed was your perfect match." He shook his head. "I wasn't even on your radar as boyfriend material."

Melissa clapped a hand to her mouth, seeing things in a new light.

"I want to prove to you how much you mean to me. Give me a chance to show you. Let's start with a promise you'll meet me for dinner. I'll call with the details later."

He drew her to him. She wrapped her arms around him, and she heard him sigh. He tilted her face up and met her lips with his. Melissa closed her eyes and enjoyed the sexual sensations that filled her body. She loved him and loved how he made her feel.

"I've got meetings with Mike and the construction crew at Collister. You'll meet me for dinner?"

Melissa smiled. "I'd like that."

After Ross left, Melissa replayed his conversation in her mind, savoring every detail. He wanted to be more than neighbors and friends, just like she did.

She did a dance in her living room, swaying to the music she heard in her head. She felt so … alive and happy.

After spending the day cleaning up and straightening her house from her guests' stay, Melissa spent time washing her hair, making an emergency appointment at the nail salon, and buying a new dress.

Later that afternoon, Ross called to ask her to meet him at the new sports center before they had dinner.

Wearing a new sundress, Melissa headed to the edge of town.

Ross greeted her when she pulled into the parking lot. "Glad you're here. I have something special planned for dinner."

"How nice," she said, feeling a rush of energy race through her.

He took her hand. "Come with me."

Melissa and Ross walked past the construction site toward the baseball field. The sports center, expanded into something bigger now, would take longer than they'd thought to complete. But Melissa thought it would be worth it, especially with Collister Construction doing the work.

The baseball field was now ready to play on. David Graham and his father and crew from Graham Landscaping had done a magnificent job creating it and building it to exact measurements.

"Isn't this terrific?" Ross gazed at the baseball diamond

with pride. "They finished it while I was gone."

"It's beautiful," she replied. "I heard that more than one family in town is converting their house to an Airbnb to handle families who want to come for a stay in town while their children participate in one of the programs you'll be offering."

"Fantastic news." Ross kept hold of her hand and led her to a spot beneath a maple tree at the far end of the field. A wicker picnic basket sat beside a tartan plaid blanket spread on the grass.

"What's this?" said Melissa, lowering herself to the blanket.

"A special picnic. Crystal helped me with it," said Ross, sounding eager to please her.

He sat beside Melissa and drew her into his arms. "I love you, Melissa. You're everything to me."

She couldn't help the tears that escaped her eyes. Those words and being in his arms were precious to her.

He thumbed her tears away. "Don't cry. I mean every word I say. I want time together to prove how much I love you. You've been my rock during some difficult times. I realize I'm a much better, happier man with you by my side. I see a future with you. Will you promise to see where our relationship takes us?"

Half-laughing, half-crying, Melissa flung herself into his arms. She'd questioned herself and him along this journey but always came back to the same thing. She loved him deeply and would do her best to show that to him by chasing away her insecurities. "Yes, Ross Roberts. I will! I love you!"

Ross rocked her in his embrace. "This beats any home run I've ever made."

She laughed and held on tight as his lips met hers.

# # #

Thank you for reading *Love's Home Run*. If you enjoyed this book, please help other readers discover it by leaving a review on Amazon, Goodreads, BookBub, or your favorite site. It's such a nice thing to do.

Sign up for my newsletter and get a free story. I keep my newsletters short and fun with giveaways, recipes, and the latest must-have news about me and my books. Welcome! Here's the link:
https://BookHip.com/RRGJKGN

About the Author

A *USA Today* **Best-Selling Author**, Judith Keim is a hybrid author who both has a publisher and self-publishes. Ms. Keim writes heart-warming novels about women who face unexpected challenges, meet them with strength, and find love and happiness along the way. Her best-selling books are based, in part, on many of the places she's lived or visited and on the interesting people she's met, creating believable characters and realistic settings her many loyal readers love. Ms. Keim loves to hear from her readers and appreciates their enthusiasm for her stories.

Ms. Keim enjoyed her childhood and young-adult years in Elmira, New York, and now makes her home in Boise, Idaho, with her husband and their lovable miniature Dachshund, Wally, and other members of her family.

While growing up, she was drawn to the idea of writing stories from a young age. Books were always present, being read, ready to go back to the library, or about to be discovered. All in her family shared information from the books in general conversation, giving them a wealth of knowledge and vivid imaginations.

"I hope you've enjoyed this book. If you have, please help other readers discover it by leaving a review on Amazon, Goodreads, Bookbub, or the site of your choice. And please check out my other books and series:"

The Hartwell Women Series
The Beach House Hotel Series
Fat Fridays Group
The Salty Key Inn Series
The Chandler Hill Inn Series
Seashell Cottage Books
The Desert Sage Inn Series
Soul Sisters at Cedar Mountain Lodge
The Sanderling Cove Inn Series
The Lilac Lake Inn Series
The Lilac Lake Books

"ALL THE BOOKS ARE NOW AVAILABLE IN AUDIO on Audible, iTunes, Findaway, Kobo and Google Play! So fun to have these characters come alive!"

Ms. Keim can be reached at **www.judithkeim.com**

And to like her author page on Facebook and keep up with the news, go to: **http://bit.ly/2pZWDgA**

To receive notices about new books, follow her on Book Bub:

https://www.bookbub.com/authors/judith-keim

And here's a link to where you can sign up for her periodic newsletter! **http://bit.ly/2OQsb7s**

She is also on Twitter @judithkeim, LinkedIn, and Goodreads. Come say hello!

Acknowledgments

As always, I am eternally grateful to my team of editors, Peter Keim and Lynn Mapp, my book cover designer, Lou Harper, and my narrator for Audible and iTunes, Angela Dawe. They are the people who take what I've written and help turn it into the book I proudly present to you, my readers! I also wish to thank my coffee group of writers who listen and encourage me to keep on going. Thank you, Peggy Staggs, Lynn Mapp, Cate Cobb, Nikki Jean Triska, Joanne Pence, Melanie Olsen, and Megan Bryce. And to you, my fabulous readers, I thank you for your continued support and encouragement. Without you, this book would not exist. You are the wind beneath my wings.

www.ingramcontent.com/pod-product-compliance
Lightning Source LLC
Chambersburg PA
CBHW022108240626
47153CB00007B/2277

the streets in a never-ending chain of horror." Aunt Astrid cleared her throat. "At least, that's what they say. Those bits of property each belonged to a different member of the coven. They would have been the overseer of those Kly."

"Nice. Nothing more than glorified babysitters for ugly, fiery demon babies," I said, shaking my head and having another sip of coffee.

It took us into the late afternoon to get all the books back in order. Once we were all done, I saw a look of worry on Aunt Astrid's face.

"What's the matter?" I asked.

"One of my books is missing," she said. "Oh dear. It was a good-sized book with a font of information in it that could become dangerous in the wrong hands. Oh, if Cedar managed to abscond with it somehow, we could be facing this challenge again."

Then it hit me: I had taken that exact book and had been planning to take it with me so Bea wouldn't read the diabolical plans the Sect of Symmetry had had in store for her little bundle of joy.

"Nope. She doesn't have it," I said, happily trotting to the bookcase by the door. There it was, just an old, nondescript book that blended in with all the others. I brought it back and handed it to my aunt, shaking my head and telling her it was a long story.

"What do you think of the name Steve?" Bea asked out of the blue.

"For the baby?" I said. "How about Elvis?"

"Are you serious?" Bea asked.

"Yeah, Elvis is a cool name," I replied.

"I think Trevor is a nice name," Aunt Astrid piped up.

"Trevor sounds like a piece of farm equipment. 'I gotta jump on the old Trevor and get to the fields pronto or the crops ain't gonna grow.'" I sniffled and cleared my throat.

"I agree with Cath on that one," Bea replied.

"How about Rudolph?" Aunt Astrid asked as she got to her feet and smoothed out her muumuu.

Bea and I both looked at her as if she had lobsters coming out of her ears.

Just then, my eyes fell to an astrology book, and I snapped my fingers.

"How about Galileo?" I said.

The room fell silent. At first, I wasn't sure if it was because they liked my idea or if they'd been struck dumb.

"Oh, come on. It's not that bad."

"I love it," Bea replied.

"Really?" I gushed.

"I do too," Aunt Astrid replied. "Galileo Johnson. That would be lovely."

"I think it's perfect. And I think Jake will love it too," Bea said. "If it's a boy, I think we'll name him Galileo."

"Right. If it's a boy," I replied, smiling happily.

ABOUT THE AUTHOR

Harper Lin is a *USA TODAY* bestselling cozy mystery author.

When she's not reading or writing mysteries, she loves going to yoga classes, hiking, and hanging out with her family and friends.

For a complete list of her books by series, visit her website.

www.HarperLin.com